COVID ICU

OTHER BOOKS BY ANJULA EVANS

Young Adult Sci-Fi Titles:

Antares Trap

Illustrated Children's Titles:

I Kicked the Ball in Gym Class: Self-esteem & Identity

School Day Worries: The Link Between Thoughts & Anxiety

The Anti-Bullying Project

Why is Skin Color Different?

Where is My Gigi? Losing Someone You Love

What is Foster Care? Emma's Journey

The Super-Hero Survival Guide

The Super-Hero Survival Guide: Red Alert!

The Super-Hero Survival Guide: Close Encounters of the Green Kind

Illustrated Young Adult Titles:

Living with an Acquired Brain Injury

Living with an Acquired Brain Injury: Adapting to Change

COVID ICU

ANJULA EVANS

First paperback edition 2020
First hardcover edition 2020

Cover Art by Gareth Brown
garethnbrown.co.uk

Paperback ISBN 978-1-989803-12-7
Hardcover ISBN 978-1-989803-13-4

Dedicated to those who have sacrificed so much in the fight against COVID.

Alanna and Gareth, thank you for your countless hours of dedication.

Thank you to those at Mind Forward who have encouraged me to write.

TABLE OF CONTENTS

PART ONE

CHAPTER ONE

Karly

Morning, Mon., May 3, 2021

I linger in that place between sleep and awake, dreaming of the sun on my face, and laughter of the children playing in the park across the street.

Suddenly, I hear Pink's raspy voice:

"It ain't easy—growing up in World War III. Never knowing what love could be..."

I roll over with a groan, eyes closed, and reach for my alarm clock with my hand. My arm is uncoordinated since I'm woozy, and I hit the wrong switch. Pink's voice morphs into shrill pulsing. My hand gropes around until it silences the annoying beeping.

I sit up, rubbing my eyes, as everything comes flooding back to me. The nightmare we've all been living in for the last twelve months. It might not be a literal World War III, but the worldwide pandemic has completely transformed our lives. We're no longer living in a temporary global "emergency situation"; it's just the way life is now, and how we can expect it to be for a long time to come.

I slide out of bed and check my closet for an outfit for the day. I pull out a light-weight shirt and pants, suitable to wear underneath my hospital garb. Today I'm doing a 15.5 hour cross-cover shift at the hospital, so I'm aiming for comfort. I toss the outfit onto my bed and walk into the bathroom.

The hot water streams down over me, and the steam clears my sinuses. One of life's basic necessities now stands out like never before, and I'm reminded of it every day. The ability to breathe. It is no longer taken for granted by those of us who provide medical care, since we see people in respiratory distress every day. Every breath for them is a struggle. I inhale deeply then exhale as I step out of my shower and start rubbing moisturizer into my wet skin.

After my shower, I grab a breakfast bar to eat while I'm getting my things together for the day. I put on a warm jacket, comfortable shoes, and my mask, lock my apartment, and hit the elevator button with my elbow. I get out at the ground floor, and call an Uber.

We arrive at the hospital, and I clip my ID badge to my collar as I take off my seatbelt. "Thank you." I reach for the door handle.

The driver nods back at me. He speaks through his mask, his kind eyes reflected in the dash mirror. "We all appreciate what you are doing. Stay safe." I nod back and smile with my eyes. It's not the first time a stranger has thrown some encouragement my way. On some days, those words are the only thing that give me the strength to keep going.

At the entrance of the hospital, I go through the normal "screening". Security scans me, checking my temperature, heart rate, blood pressure, and level of oxygenation in my blood. I'm asked the routine questions while being scanned. "Have you had any symptoms—fever, cough, difficulty breathing, loss of taste or smell?"

"No, I'm good."

"Any contact with anyone who's been out of the country?"

"Nope. I'm in isolation at home except for essentials." Security looks at the readings, nods, acknowledging my ID badge, and lets me pass.

I walk to Diagnostics and am fast-tracked to take the mandatory test for the virus for health-care workers. The rapid virus test should come back within 10-15 minutes. I walk back outside after nodding to the security guy, and have a seat on a bench to wait. I pull out my phone, and check the latest updates on the news.

The breeze is chilly today and the metal bench feels cold through my pants, but the sun will soon start to warm up the day. A shiver runs down my spine, but it's not due to the weather. I feel nervous and excited, since I'm no longer a med student. As of today, I'm an intern, and will be taking on more responsibilities than I've carried in the past.

The last year has been intense, going through the new accelerated program. It was designed to put med students out on the front lines as quickly as possible as new doctors, where they are needed most. Given the lower risk category we are in, and the amount of new energy we bring to medical teams, we're a vital part of the strategy to help patients in their recovery from COVID-19.

I browse the usual news sites to get a glimpse of what's happening today in the world, and to check the status of the coronavirus spread. I've been placed at a hospital in the hotspot of Ontario where there have been constant outbreaks. The hospital is in the final stages of preparation to quickly expand the Intensive Care Unit. The demand for beds is rising and we're about to see a surge.

In less than ten minutes I get a call from Diagnostics, giving me the "all clear". I walk back inside, through the lobby of Credit Valley Hospital. Instead of waiting for the elevator, I automatically take the stairs. Otherwise I'll be waiting forever. Social distancing has been ingrained in me, and I'm not one to take health risks. I jog up two flights of stairs to the second floor.

"Hey, wait up!" I hear a male voice at the entrance to the stairwell, and can tell someone is rapidly taking the stairs two-by-two. I'm about to exit, but I hesitate, realizing I'm the only other person in the stairwell. The voice seems somewhat familiar. I look backwards, and see a guy on the next landing down a flight of stairs from me, hands on his knees and facing down, panting from his race up the stairs.

A quote from an old movie pops into my head. *"Who is that masked man, anyway?"*

"Give me a minute," he pants. "I ran all the way from Diagnostics." I wait as he pauses to catch his breath. After about twenty seconds, he raises his head. "Whew! That was quite the workout." Then he stands up, flips open his mask so I can see his face, and looks up at me with a lop-sided grin. My eyes widen as I inhale sharply. I recognize him from med school.

"Clay?" My heart rate starts accelerating. *He's only the most drool-worthy bachelor, sought out by women left and right.*

He loops his mask back over one ear. "Yup, that's me—and you're Karly." He flashes a big smile that reaches his beautiful blue eyes, as he reaffixes his mask. I stand stunned, floored that he even knows my name. *And how does he even recognize me with my mask on?*

I try to make my voice sound casual, even though my heart rate is elevated. "Uh, that's right. Sooo...what are you doing here, Clay?" I'm curious, but also feeling a bit anxious at the same time. Visitation of patients is disallowed, since we're on the cusp of the third wave of the virus, so he wouldn't be at the hospital to visit a patient. I start to get an inkling of why he's there. The same reason I'm here. I wonder what department he's been assigned to.

"I'm an intern here. I'm assuming that's why you're here as well?" I can't break away from those mesmerizing eyes.

Suddenly, I realize I'm just standing there, looking like a dork. I manage a weak laugh. "Oh right, me. My placement is here, too."

"You're in the ICU?" Clay gestures to the doorknob my gloved hand is resting on. The sign on the door lists the Intensive Care Unit as one of the destinations.

"Yes. Staffing is really low and we're about to enter the third wave of the pandemic, so I applied to be placed at a local hospital. What about you?"

"Same here—ICU. Looks like we both decided to fight this thing where it's causing the most critical devastation." I detect the seriousness in Clay's voice, and can see that his eyes are now reflecting determination.

I feel a bit stunned that both Clay and I are in the same hospital, in the same department. *How did this happen?* Clay covers the last flight of stairs two-by-two. I am in the middle of opening the heavy door, when Clay easily reaches over my shoulder and pushes it open the rest of the way. "After you." He holds the door for me.

"Thank you." My heart flutters a bit, then settles. *I'm surprised he even knows who I am or even recognized me. We never really talked when we were in school together.* Inside I'm shaking my head in disbelief. *But really now. He knows who I am?*

As he holds the door for me, I can smell his fresh, clean, masculine scent. I inhale the wonderful aroma before stepping through the door. His heady scent causes my mind to spin and land elsewhere.

I remember the first day of classes, three years ago, when I saw Clay for the first time at the St. George Campus.

"So, Karly, have you had a chance to check out the guys in our class yet?" My best friend Violet and I walk down to the Med Sciences cafeteria.

I reply truthfully, feeling a bit embarrassed at my admission. "I've been too focused on not getting lost, and on making it to classes on time."

Violet sounds wistful. "So you haven't noticed Clay Aldridge yet? Every girl in the class has eyes for him."

The name sounds familiar. "Honestly, I haven't taken notice of much else today other than planning out my semester." With three years of undergrad already behind me, I already know the importance of starting off the year running. I also know what the fallout being distracted by a man exacts. Been there, done that.

We walk into the cafeteria, and get in line. I watch as a group of girls is about to sit down together. Oh, and one gorgeous guy, who is looking straight at me. "Speaking of..." My voice trails off. "That wouldn't happen to be him, would it?" He seems familiar. I think we had some undergrad courses together. I was too busy being distracted by another man back then to pay much attention.

Violet looks in the direction I'm looking. She squeaks. "That's him! And he's looking straight this way!" Clay stands there, looking at me, as the girls around him sit down. He has dark brown hair, piercing blue eyes, and this endearing lop-sided grin on his face. I smile demurely at him, and he nods at me. One of the girls tugs on his shirt, and the spell is broken as he glances down at her, then slowly sits with the group.

Violet pokes me. "Karly? Earth to Karly?" I turn and look at her, then at the gap in front of me in the line up, and quickly walk ahead.

"Don't worry. Clay seems to have an effect like that on all the girls. He should be labeled an illegal distraction." Violet giggles. I watch Clay laugh and chat with the popular girls, and he doesn't look my way once. I wonder if I imagined the whole thing. He's already forgotten about me—if he really even noticed me in the first place.

I snap back to reality and the present, step through the door, and walk briskly to the ICU. Clay easily keeps stride with me. He asks me about the remainder of my med school training. "So you stayed with the accelerated program, too?" Clay has that serious look in his eyes again.

"Yes, I wanted to be as useful as I could, as soon as possible."

We enter the ICU together. "Karly, Clay." Dr. Romara, the intensivist who heads up the unit, acknowledges us with a nod as we arrive at the ICU specifically reserved for patients with COVID-19. "Really glad you're here. We've been short-staffed." Dr. Romara glides quickly past us, as she continues with her pre-round patient evaluations.

I pick up a tablet and start reviewing the patient list, both to get a general knowledge of each case, and to carefully analyze for any change in day-to-day trends, regarding measurements and conditions. Understanding the general patterns in each patient's chart helps highlight deviations from the norm, which could be early warning signs of more serious health issues.

When it's time for rounds, Clay and I wash up and put on our first set of Personal Protective Equipment: N95 masks, gloves, face shields, gowns, and head and foot coverings. I'm certain I'll feel like a boiled chicken by the end of my shift.

We begin rounds together as a team, going over the observations, needs, and progress of each patient. Each patient's treatment plan is discussed, any changes in their vitals or condition are clarified by the nurse, and goals and clarifications are given by the specialists on the team. The pharmacist adjusts medication calculations as needed. We also do physical exams of each patient.

In the first room, the team prepares Mrs. Johnson to be turned onto her front. A nurse repositions all the wires and tubes while we prepare the bed, position pillows, and ready Mrs. Johnson herself, who is sedated. By the time we're finished, she looks like a burrito.

The Respiratory Therapist directs us. "On three." She does the count, and we turn Mrs. Johnson carefully to her side. The ventilator tubing is adjusted, and we do the final turn. Clay adjusts Mrs. Johnson to relieve pressure points while I document the procedure and the other team members check tubing and devices. I can see how gentle and caring Clay is with the patient, and I smile to myself.

The entire process of turning the patient, between disinfecting, donning and doffing our protective equipment, and the actual turning, has taken 30 minutes. We continue with rounds, and finish four hours later. Clay says he'll grab me something to eat after meeting with his resident supervisor and will put it in the break room fridge for me.

Clay uses a mock formal voice, and pretends to pull out a pen and paper. "Can I take your order, Ma'am?"

I giggle. "A deli sandwich would hit the spot."

Clay speaks in his normal voice. "Any specific type?"

I give him a smile. "Surprise me."

Clay has a glint in his eyes. "So you like surprises?"

"Love them! They keep life interesting."

As Clay leaves for his meeting, I head over to mine. I became reacquainted with Dr. Jamar during orientation. I was full of trepidation at first, starting with a new supervisor, but I found him to be disarming, and he encouraged me to voice my opinions. I admired his thoroughness as well as his compassion for his patients as I observed his approach to patient care. I'm really happy with my assignment, as I highly respect him. I am sure I can develop and improve my skills under his supervision.

"So what were your thoughts today?" Dr. Jamar asks me regarding one of the patients I've been assigned to. We work through the list of patients on the tablet, while he continues to jot down notes on paper. I like the way he is open to my comments and suggestions without patronizing me or shutting me down. I feel like a colleague rather than like the student I had been up until recently. It's a new feeling that will take me some time to get used to.

Voicing my opinion has been difficult in the past, and I'm still pretty sensitive to other people's responses. Unfortunately, once you've been belittled, there's a tendency to clam up or just plain freeze. Although in my head I understand my opinions have value, I know it's a long road to actually *feeling* like my contributions are valuable. I'm still struggling with this, but can already see potential for personal growth in this area with Dr. Jamar.

Once we've reviewed the patient list, we walk over to the nurse stationed outside my first patient's room, where she can clearly see and monitor him. She has light brown hair swept back off her face in a ponytail holder. Curls that have fallen out of the elastic stray around her ears. She is very attentive, monitoring her patient.

"Hi there, I'm Karly. We met briefly on rounds earlier. How's Mr. Vaughn doing? Any concerns?"

"Maggie." She nods and smiles in greeting. "Nothing new. Jaime seems to be responding well to the convalescent plasma and antiviral meds. He's showing some initial signs that indicate he is fighting the virus." The nurse smiles. "It's encouraging when someone is having a good day, especially when it's someone so young."

I can only imagine what her experience has been like this last year. The initial survival rate from COVID-19 was 50% in this ICU, but has now increased dramatically by placing the patients in prone position and through various treatments. Some seem to be responding well to the plasma of survivors with antibodies that can fight the virus, others not so much. Newer anti-inflammatory drugs have also been very helpful in increasing the survival rate from this terrible disease.

Although most younger people don't become critically ill with the virus, there are those who do. My patient in Room 5 is only 24 years old; he's the same age as me. *It's good that he may be on the road to recovery. I truly hope he won't experience lung damage or damage to his other systems.* That's always a possibility with this disease. For those sick enough to warrant a bed in the ICU, the probability that the disease has invaded other systems of the body is high.

Part of my job is to update the family on Jaime's progress. I put through a call to them, returning an earlier message that was left. "Mrs. Vaughn?"

"Oh, thank goodness you called." She must be able to see I'm calling from the hospital's number. "How is he doing?"

"Jaime seems to be responding positively to the new treatment. He's made a bit of progress, but has a long way to go. As you know, there are risks with the treatment, but we'll do our best to mitigate them." I hope my message helps to alleviate some of her anxiety, but at the same time, I need to be cautious, as his prognosis is guarded.

"So he's finally making some progress." Mrs. Vaughn sighs as if a weight has been lifted off her shoulders. There is a pause in the conversation. "Thank you, doctor. For everything you're doing for him."

My heart is filled with compassion, I acknowledge her thanks, and am at a loss for words. Old feelings begin stirring up as my mind travels back to six months ago. *Didn't I express those exact words of appreciation back then? But then things went sideways and we lost her.*

I change the subject before I start to get emotional, as the feelings of loss threaten to grow. "I know this has been a tough road for you, Mrs. Vaughn, but how are you and the family doing?"

"Oh, we're getting by. We're used to the intermittent social isolation by now, but it's been difficult, knowing our son is so ill. It's been especially hard on Patrick. He isn't one to express his emotions, and I can tell he's just holding everything in."

They could use some support. I should put through a referral to the social worker to arrange counseling for them.

"Keeping busy distracts me, but sometimes the anxiety takes over and I just start pacing non-productively. That's when the fears start building inside me, especially at night." I can hear her sniffle.

My voice is soft and compassionate. "It sounds like you've been going through a lot." I hear the rustling of a tissue box and she sniffles again. "Did you have any questions about his condition or treatment?"

"Not at the moment. Patrick may have some questions, but he's outside working in the yard right now. I don't want to disturb him because it's a respite for him. Helps him to deal with everything." After a few more moments, her voice changes. As she speaks, she sounds like she has more control over her emotions. "Can we see our boy today?"

"Sure. Why don't I give you a video call when you and your husband are ready? Patrick can ask any questions he may have at the same time." I check my watch. "What time this afternoon would be good for a call back?" After confirming a general time frame, I let her know I can put in a referral to get them some counseling to help them through this.

"I think that would be good for us. Thank you so much for calling us and giving us the news." I say goodbye, put in a referral to the hospital social worker, and pencil in the call back time.

After the call to Jaime's family, I head down the hallway, and nearly bump into Clay. Clay smiles at me. "Hey. You ready for that break now? I got you a 'Deli Surprise'." He winks at me.

Again, Clay has surprised me. "You waited for me?"

He gives me that lop-sided grin of his. "Of course."

"Sure, I'm in between patients right now."

"Same here."

We head to the break room. As we pass through a door on the way, I feel his hand lightly graze the small of my back, and a fluttery feeling goes through me. As his hand brushes me there again in a subconscious gesture, I inhale sharply as a surge of tingling energy travels down my spine. *What the…? What's going on?* With so much physical distancing, it feels so odd to have someone in such close proximity. I shiver.

"Are you cold?" Clay looks concerned.

I smile up at him as we walk together. "No, I'm fine."

We enter the break room, and Clay holds the door open for me. He opens the fridge, pulling out both our wrapped sandwiches and a couple of bottled waters. We both wash up, then have a seat at the small round break table.

Clay speaks cautiously. "So, how are you doing?"

"Well, Jaime's responding well as you know from rounds, and I haven't had time to see my other patients yet…" I'm about to ramble on, but Clay's hand lightly touches mine. It's so brief, but it feels like an electric shock goes through me.

"That's not what I meant." Clay looks into my eyes, searching. It feels like he's piercing his way into my soul. I try to push my anxiety down so it doesn't rear its ugly head. "How are *you* doing, after everything that's happened?"

I put my sandwich down, feeling choked up. I open my water bottle, take a drink and force it down. "You mean the pandemic?"

I see in his eyes that's not what he means, but instead he hesitates and gives a contrary response. "Sure."

Does he mean…? But how could he know? I didn't think he knew I even existed until today. I decide to play it safe. "In general, I'm doing okay. That last year was pretty rough, getting everything done online, then as a student in my placement in Toronto."

I try skimming over the last year so I won't have to think about everything. To *feel* everything… "I'm really glad to finally be done, of course. I know we could have jumped in to fight this thing more fully earlier, but I figured I'd be more useful if I finished my training, rather than jumping in as a student."

Clay nods. "Same here."

A call from the premier went out a year before, asking for retired medical personnel, anyone with experience, and even students to assist with the situation caused by the pandemic. Within a day, 10,000 people in medical-related professions had responded online.

"I could have jumped in full-time to assist, but decided that I'd be more valuable to the health-care system if I finished up through the Accel program and became an intern. Besides, I was able to put in a good share of hours in my student placement, contributing there.

"I also volunteered with a group of med students to help sort protective gear from shipments that came in." It all comes out in a rush, then I suddenly remember I should breathe. *Why do I act so strangely around Clay?* I wonder if it's just due to the strain of the first day, adapting to a new situation.

Clay has admiration in his eyes. "Wow, you've certainly kept busy."

A fleeting thought crosses my mind. *I can't believe how quickly Clay wolfed down that sandwich. He must have been really hungry.* I feel a bit bad that he waited for me before starting lunch.

I pick up my sandwich. "What about you?"

"Pretty much the same as you. Instead of helping with PPE, I've been helping elderly folk with groceries so they don't have to leave their homes." Clay smiles. "Some of the elderly ladies are so sweet."

"I can imagine." I laugh, thinking of all the 80-plus older ladies being sweet on Clay. "It's really good of you to do that for them."

"It's the least I can do for those around me. I hope I'll have a greater impact here, though. I can carry a bigger workload and act more independently. My brother is going to take over picking up groceries for the ladies." I finish up my sandwich, and drink my water. "Well, shall we?" Clay gestures to the door.

We throw our sandwich wrappers in the garbage, then wash up. As we walk through the door, Clay's fingers brush my upper arm ever so slightly, that I think I might have imagined it. Again, it has me quivering. We walk out together, and part ways to see our assigned patients.

Clay
Afternoon, Mon., May 3, 2021

I was fortunate to be able to take a break at the same time as Karly on our first day together, since time can be unpredictable when dealing with such ill patients. I don't expect we'll have many more opportunities to chat at the hospital, as our patient load will be increasing as more cases come in. Breaks may be few and far between. *I want time alone with her. I just have to figure out how to get it.*

I set the thought aside and carefully tend to my patients' needs. I consult with the pharmacist, dietitian, physiotherapist, and other specialists throughout the afternoon and evening. I regularly check my patients to make sure fluids are balanced, I adjust anesthesia, and suction airways to clear them. I alleviate pressure points by adjusting pillows, adjust bedding, and administer eye drops.

I contact families of my patients to give them updates, and arrange for them to see their loved ones virtually. I chart and notate changes, and update other staff as I work with each patient.

I'm impressed with the nursing staff, as I find each of the RN's to be observant, thorough, and compassionate. They are the ones constantly monitoring the patients, and will be quick to notice any changes that need immediate intervention.

The evening flies by in a flurry of activity, and before I realize it, I'm nearly at the end of my shift. I finish charting for my final patient, and brief the night shift doctor on my cases. As my shift draws to a close, my desire to see Karly increases. I hope I can catch her before she leaves. I have an idea that might work to give me more time with her, and help her out in the process. I mentally cross my fingers as I go search for her.

Karly

Night. Mon., May 3, 2021

I'm packing up my things to go, when Clay finds me. He jogs up beside me in the hallway. "Hey Karly, how are you getting home?"

"Oh, I usually just Uber."

"Would you like a ride? I'm happy to drop you off."

"Are you sure I'm not out of the way?"

"You're downtown?" I nod at Clay's query. "Same here." He gives me that boyish grin of his.

"Okay, if it's not too much trouble."

"Oh, no trouble at all. Let me take your bag for you."

We walk out to the parking area, and to Clay's vehicle. He opens the passenger door of the black SUV for me.

"Thank you." I'm blushing. Clay smiles back through his mask. *He's so sweet.*

Clay jogs around the front to his door, then gets in. "A little chilly tonight." He rubs his hands together. He starts the car, and turns on the heat.

"Ohhhh, heated seats!" I feel the light heat start to intensify. *Sooooo warm!* "I looooove heated seats!" I sigh contentedly.

Clay laughs at my reaction. "They are pretty awesome, especially with our winters."

"Thank goodness we're through winter now. That second wave hit us all hard." I suddenly choke up, and look out my window. My anxiety levels heighten and my breathing becomes more rapid. *Oh no! Wrong train of thought. I need to steer back to a safer topic.*

"The weather is changing at least." I'm rambling on quickly. "Can't believe we had a snowstorm in April though!" I try to make my voice sound bubbly, as I stare out my window. I hope I've fooled Clay, and that he's oblivious to the torrent of emotion under the surface of my facade. I wonder if I'm about to have a panic attack. *Please not now. Not in front of Clay.* That thought only increases my anxiety.

"Karly." Clay's voice is gentle as he brushes my arm with his fingertips, then continues to stroke my arm. It's strangely calming. My anxiety level lessens slightly. "It's okay. You don't have to pretend. I know."

"You do?" I'm so surprised that I glance over at him without thinking. I try to wipe the tears from my face with my sleeve before he notices. He turns his head and looks at me. *How could he know? I didn't even realize he knew my name until today! He has to be talking about something else completely unrelated.* Clay hands me a pack of tissues, and I wipe the rest of my tears from my face.

"Yeah, my mom told me. She and your aunt worked in the same volunteer circles." The pieces finally click in place. He moves his hand to cover my smaller hand, and gives it a little squeeze. I feel his comfort, his warmth. I let his hand stay there. It feels like my anxiety is flowing out of me into a void of nothingness. I feel so calm.

"I see. Thanks." I wipe the rest of my tears from my face. I know now that I don't have to explain anything to him or hide my emotions. He understands that my grief is recent, and I don't have to pretend I'm fine when I have difficult moments during the day. I exhale in relief.

"If you ever need to talk about it, I'm here." I can tell Clay is absolutely sincere, that he really cares. He squeezes my hand again, then removes his. My hand feels strangely bare without his covering mine.

I nod and my voice comes out in almost a whisper. "Thanks, Clay."

We pull up to my apartment building, and Clay jumps out, jogs around to my door, and opens it for me, offering me his hand. His action endears him to me. It's a very sweet gesture. I take his hand, as he assists me out with all my belongings. He carries my bag for me, and guides me to the front door of the building with his hand gently on the small of my back.

We face each other in front of my building, standing in the darkness, under the overhead lights. Clay hands me my bag, his hand lingering as it touches mine to transfer my bag to me. I smile up at him. In a world with so many pressing concerns, gestures like the ones he's made today that show kindness mean everything.

"I'll pick you up for next shift." I'm about to protest, but he chides me. "Nuh-uh, no objections. It's actually safer for you and the team if you don't take an Uber." He does make a valid point. Less exposure to other people and surfaces that could be contaminated is better for our team overall.

"Thank you, Clay." My voice is soft, as I look up through my thick lashes into his eyes.

"My pleasure, Karly." He opens the door for me, and waits until I use my fob to open the inner door. I turn around and give him a little wave, then he heads back to the curb where his black SUV sits.

Clay
Night. Mon., May 3, 2021

I think about Karly as I drive home after dropping her off. I shake my head. *God, she's so beautiful.* I'm excited because I now have the perfect opportunity to spend a bit of time with her here and there, even with our busy schedules. I also like the idea of her depending on me to drive her to and from work.

I park and take the elevator ride up to my apartment, then go through my regular after-work routine laundering my clothes, disinfecting and showering. I pull on a pair of shorts and a t-shirt, dim the lights, and make some spiced chai. I grab a comic book for some downtime, and relax. At least...I *try* to relax. It's difficult to get Karly off my mind. I mindlessly scan the colorful pages until I'm done my tea, then brush my teeth and hop into bed.

I lay on my back, lacing my hands behind my head, as I stare up into the darkness. *I wonder what she thinks of me...if she even thinks of me.* Although we took the same training, we never connected the way I wanted to. She was so "occupied". I hope that we'll have time together, now that we've started our professional lives.

She seems to have matured over the years. She's not as bubbly as she was five years ago when I first saw her, but her vibrant personality still shines through. I think about the way I've always admired her, and about the times when I felt troubled around her. *Now that she's close by, I can keep an eye on her.* I finally drift off with a smile, as I picture her face looking back at me.

Karly

Early Morning. Mon., May 3, 2021

That night, I toss and turn in bed, unable to sleep. I check my alarm clock. *2:30 am. And I'm still awake.* I sigh.

I walk into the kitchen, and heat up some water for some rooibos tea. As I wait for the kettle, I try to trace back my thoughts to find what is troubling me and keeping me from sleep. I think about my day, my patients, my team members, everything that occurred during the day. No physical reaction in my body. Then I think about the one person my mind has been avoiding. *Clay.* And my body physically reacts with a fluttery feeling, a downward shot of electricity, and warmth in my core. *It's Clay. All Clay.*

So I analyze our interactions from today. His hand grazing the small of my back, his light touch in the break room, his touch of comfort when he covered my hand with his. And then there are his gestures of kindness. Picking up lunch, offering me a ride home, and the chivalrous actions he took have been so endearing.

I'm cautious about making premature assumptions, so I feel I'm left with one conclusion. I discount any other possibilities completely because I'm too scared to go there.

I'm super-sensitive to any physical touch right now, with the social distancing. That's what's happening here. I've been lacking physical affection and that makes me more sensitive to physical touch of any kind.

But at the same time, I wonder if I'm overthinking things. I can be very analytical at times, and usually it serves me well when it comes to regulating my emotions. However, it doesn't seem to apply when I get caught up in matters of the heart. Instead, I become a confused mess.

His kindness does make him extremely attractive to me as a person.

As my friends know, the number one quality I look for in my relationships is "kindness", and everything that comes with that: empathy, compassion, and generosity. If that isn't there, then the relationship is a "no go." The second quality is honesty. However, if it's a choice between kindness and honesty, I jokingly tell my friends to go with kindness first.

Instead of honestly saying, "That red dress looks hideous on you," I'd prefer: "Personally, I think the blue dress you wore last week looks beautiful on you. You should wear it instead."

My friends may laugh, but hey, it's true—I prefer it when kindness overshadows honesty. It is quite amusing how they quote me down to the last word though.

I pour the hot water from the kettle into my teacup, and my tea bag floats around near the top, infusing its flavor into the water, changing the color of the liquid gradually. *Just like the pandemic has affected us. Gradually diffusing itself through the population. Then as soon as we think it's under control, another wave hits. We need that vaccine, and soon.*

The long-awaited vaccine. It's still months away, and until that time this new world we live in will continue as is, with instability. Our physical health and economy are depending on that vaccine. Well, multiple vaccines that fight the virus in different ways. But it's more problematic than that.

If the wrong country or organization develops the initial vaccine, they could withhold it from other countries. *It's so disheartening that some nations' leaders still feel a need to feel "superior" to the rest of the world. Whether it's economically or because they possess something that other nations don't. I hope a collaboration of countries develops it for the benefit of the global community.*

Honey drips from a bottle into my tea, as I gently stir the hot liquid with a small spoon. It's now cool enough to drink without burning my tongue, and the tea is soothing. It feels like it's soothing my soul.

I sigh as I finally start to relax, while sipping my rooibos tea. I can taste hints of vanilla. Explaining away the surges of physical sensation and emotion around Clay has settled me down. It's simply due to my current lack of human connection. In addition, mindfully letting go of what I cannot control, the development of the new vaccine, has lifted a weight from me.

After organizing my thoughts, my emotions are more serene. My head is clear, my body is relaxed, and I'm ready to head back to bed. I place my teacup in the sink, walk down the hallway, and into my dimly lit bedroom. I lay down, turn off the light, and fall into a peaceful sleep.

Anonymous
Morning. Tues, May 4, 2021

I get up in the morning at 7 am, thinking about Karly and her smile. Although I'm tired from my late night working at the hospital, I'm looking forward to seeing her this morning and dreaming up plans that center around her. I grab some coffee as I speed out the door, not wanting to miss a moment.

After a brisk walk, I open my backpack and pull out my binoculars and a booklet on bird watching. I step onto a cement bridge over a rocky creek and ravine in downtown Mississauga. I'm unable to see Karly's apartment from my current vantage point since she's facing the Toronto skyline, but there are some nice parks nearby, perfect for "bird" watching. *Ha—"chick" watching.* I cringe to myself in a self-deprecating manner. *Some jokes are too lame to even call jokes.* Instead of rolling my eyes, I allow the anticipation of the morning to build up. Or maybe it's the caffeine high.

I walk to the closest local park around the other side of Karly's building to get a better vantage point, and attempt to find her balcony. I count floors, and because I know the layout of her building, I know which apartment line is hers. I focus the binocular lenses on her balcony door, but don't see any movement. *Well, she had a late shift last night, so I don't expect she'll be up for a while.* I'm more than happy to wait.

Although I'll be seeing her regularly at the hospital during her shifts, I just can't seem to get enough of her. She's both poison and sustenance to my soul. Do I believe in love at first sight? Maybe I do. However, I've also learned the hard way there is a fine line between love and hate.

I sit on a nearby bench, enjoying the cool morning breeze, relaxing while listening to the birds in the background. I pull out my notebook which has Karly's hospital schedule stapled inside and make notes on the people I've seen her come in contact with.

When I peer through my binoculars a bit later, I see Karly moving around her apartment. I reach into my bag and pull out my camera with telephoto lens, and start snapping pictures of her. I make sure that to anyone else it looks like I'm photographing nature. *Beautiful.*

Once the movement stops, I watch her apartment building door. *Ah, there she is.* She catches my eye, and I'm riveted. I snap another series of photos of her, then pick up my bag. *She's on the move.*

Thankfully my mask is shielding my face, and should help disguise me if I get too close. I don't intend on doing that, but instead plan on blending into the background. I'm just another person on a morning stroll, admiring nature. *Yeah, admiring "nature".* I chuckle.

I catch sight of Karly jogging down the street in my general direction, pony-tail swinging with every move of her beautiful body. I see her enter the park area and head to the trails. I set out in the same direction, with my camera at the ready. *We're going to be spending a lot of time together, Love.*

CHAPTER TWO

Karly

Morning. Tues, May 4, 2021

I wake up in the late morning, put on a track suit and running shoes, and go for a run. There are a number of people out jogging, walking, or taking their dogs out, and everyone tries to stay a safe distance from each other. Most of the people are wearing masks. I jog on the spot, waiting on the corner for the light to change, then pick up with my run.

It's another cool day, the sun is out, and I enjoy the feeling of the breeze whipping through the golden locks that have fallen out of my ponytail. Although it's a busy area, I recognize a couple of people and we nod to each other as we pass. My shoes are well-padded so the impact on the pavement is moderate, as I pick up the pace down a straight stretch of road.

I finally reach one of the local parks and turn in. I run past a large sign with a map, and onto a trail. Trees and greenery are all around me, as I run along the mulchy path. Just being in such a natural setting sets me at ease and relaxes me, and I take deeper breaths, inhaling the scent of the late spring. My mind clears and the endorphins are doing their job, making me feel light and free.

As I do the trail loop, I begin to feel uneasy, as if I'm being watched. I glance over my shoulder but don't see anyone there. The feeling of uneasiness doesn't pass, and I pick up the pace. As I come to the end of the loop, I burst out of the trail into the sunshine. I see people walking in the park. I'm back in public now, but my skin is still prickling with an uncomfortable feeling.

By the time I get home and shower, it's mid-morning. I prepare a stew in my pressure cooker, pull out some multi-grain crusty bread and cut two slices, then spoon out the rich stew into a bowl.

After it cools enough, I dive into lunch while reading updates to global news on my laptop.

After a few minutes in, I'm feeling irritated. *What right do government leaders have to disregard the advice of health experts, especially when they're doing it for political gain? Don't these people have any sense of morals or ethics?* I close my laptop, and try to change my train of thought.

My thoughts naturally gravitate to Clay. *What are the chances of us getting into the same hospital, in the same department, and on the same team? It feels so bizarre.*

I decide to call my BFF. She answers on the third ring. "Hey Karly!"

"Hi Vi. Whatcha up to?"

"Just doing some cleaning right now. I'm glad you called. I needed a break from the boredom. There's only so much to clean when you're isolated in your home." Violet sighs. "So what's new? How's life as an intern in the ICU?"

"Well, the hospital's organized with their screening procedures, the staff seems really supportive, and I know I can make a difference in the lives of the patients."

"You've got a tough job. I'm enjoying my position in Toronto in Emerge, although it's a bit nerve-wracking due to COVID. You would think there would be more variety of "normal" issues, but people seem to be staying away from the hospitals as much as possible. We screen every patient for the virus when they come in, and that's what the majority of people are coming in for. There's a separate admitting and waiting area for those coming in with COVID symptoms."

"Yeah, I was reading that even people who should be going to the ER for issues are skipping it. That's a real problem for serious cases. When people put off care like that, their condition ends up being so much worse." I find myself shaking my head at the thought.

"Well, at least the people with 'non-emergency' issues who often end up clogging the ER are using the public health line to get answers to their problems."

"True. But I worry that people who should be getting care are putting it off."

"You're definitely right. Too many people are afraid of contracting the virus in the hospital, unfortunately."

"By the way…" I hesitate. "I was wondering—do you remember Clay from med school?"

"Do I remember him? Girl, who doesn't remember him? He had girls hanging off him for years. It's odd though, because regardless of rumors, I don't think he really dated much during that whole time."

"Excuse me? Some of us were actually focused on our studies, and didn't have time for dating."

Violet laughs. "Well, he could have had any girl he wanted, at any time. Quite the charmer."

"Mmhmm."

"Some people called him a player, but I think he just has a friendly personality—he was friendly with everyone, regardless. Very kind and affectionate. So why do you bring him up?"

I can tell Violet is curious. "Well, he's on my team in the ICU."

I hear silence for a few moments and wonder if the call has been dropped. "Wow." Violet puts on her best announcer voice: "Everyone, meet the medic formerly known as Karly, winner of the lottery for the widely coveted Most Eligible Bachelor!" I laugh at her silliness. But now Violet is intrigued and wants to know more. "How in the world did that happen?"

"I don't know. He lives in Mississauga, and there are only three hospitals here, so I guess that could account for his placement. He offered to drive me home last night."

At first, Violet sounds surprised. "He did? Well, he's always been a gentleman. If he suspected you didn't drive, it's natural he'd ask you. Did you go with him?"

"Yes. You know, he's different than I imagined him to be. Most guys with girls hanging all over them are cocky and arrogant. He's so gentle and kind."

"Well, girl, time to get in the game. It sounds like he meets your first criteria. Please let me live vicariously through you instead of through reality TV? Please, pretty please?" Violet uses her best pleading voice.

I laugh. "It's not like anything is going to happen between us. We're coworkers now, and super-busy. It's nice to have someone from our med class with me, though. Listen, I have to get some laundry done and do some basic adulting before work tonight. Talk to you later?"

"Sure, Karly, keep me updated. You can fill me in on all the juicy details tomorrow!" I hang up, laughing. Violet always puts a smile on my face.

I throw a load of laundry in while reflecting on our conversation. I feel my cheeks heating up, thinking how Vi was teasing me about Clay, implying we could be something more than just friends. I'm curious to know what he thinks about me, but at the same a bit fearful. I don't want to go through another nightmare of a relationship, so I try to put him out of my mind.

Clay

Afternoon. Tues, May 4, 2021

I smile, looking forward to picking Karly up tonight, thankful I was able to convince her to travel to and from work with me. While it's only a twenty minute drive each way, it will give me some time to get to know her in person, instead of just from afar. I secretly hope we'll be traveling together from now on. *I feel so drawn to her.*

I finish washing the dishes, leaving them to air dry on the counter, walk to the living room, and grab my phone to check for texts. I see a reply from Justin. I flop down on the couch and read his text.

Justin: "Yeah, Mom and Dad want to chat. Zoom. Whenever."

I type out a reply to our ongoing conversation. Me: "Sounds good. Send me an invite." I turn on the remote, flipping from station to station, watching anything that catches my interest. I'll admit it's difficult to concentrate when you have someone "special" on your mind.

I turn off the TV, and pick up my phone again. I lay lengthwise on the couch, and look up new research studies on COVID-19. I read through abstracts for a while, checking out any relevant studies to ICU care in detail. Lots of new global studies have been popping up everywhere since the pandemic started. By now, a lot of the smaller studies have been either been verified or disqualified by larger studies that have used more random sampling.

Although we've learned a lot about the virus over the last year, there is a lot that we still don't know. For example, why does it seem to trigger secondary symptoms in some patients? *They still aren't sure why it sometimes triggers cardiac inflammation in very young patients. That's a major concern. That and the universal issue of excess blood clotting which is occurring in many patients.*

I check the time, and realize it's time to finish getting ready for work and get out the door. I put on my wristwatch and gloves, grab my bag, shoes and coat, and head out the door, energetically. *Time to pick up Karly!* I smile to myself.

Karly
Night. Tues, May 4, 2021

Clay swings by to pick me up for our 14 hour night shift. He gets out of his car, smiles at me, gives a mock bow, and sweeps his arm. "Your chariot awaits, m'lady."

I laugh at his lighthearted gesture and he opens my door for me. "Why thank you, kind sir." Clay retreats after closing my door, and soon we're on the road.

"So how was your day, Karly?"

"Pretty good—just catch-up stuff around the house mainly. How was yours?"

"Same. Got a lot of work done around my place. Productive day, anyway." Clay glances over to me with one of his captivating smiles, before focusing on the road again. I can feel my pulse quicken, and this time it's not due to anxiety or physical touch. The realization surprises me and makes me blush. *Okay, maybe my theory was wrong.*

I clear my throat. "Did you read the latest news about the vaccine?"

"Yeah, it's still a ways off, but things look promising from the different agencies on the varying vaccines. It looks like they're making some progress in the clinical and human trials."

"I hope they're successful. It's not always possible to come up with a vaccine that will work for everyone." I mentally cross my fingers.

"I'm glad we have somewhat effective treatments for some patients, but it will be a relief when the vaccine comes out."

"Interesting news about the serology tests that show who's actually had the virus without symptoms. They're showing there's a time limit before a person can become infected again. It's shorter than expected. That means booster shots will be on the horizon when it comes to the vaccine. Also, less severe cases seem to have a weaker immunity to the virus."

I felt dismayed when I first learned of the time limit of the effectiveness of immunity to the virus for those who had already had it. If people can be reinfected with the virus fairly quickly, then it's more evidence the "natural herd immunity" argument is invalid, and it would make returning to "normal" life take even longer. It would mean herd immunity could only be obtained with a vaccine and only temporarily without additional shots.

"That was a valuable test when it came to confirming who to collect plasma with antibodies from. In theory, it was originally supposed to help us know who was able to safely go back to work with less worry about reinfection. However, with the time limit on immunity to reinfection, the test's purpose changed." Clay waits at an intersection for the light to turn green.

"Lots to think about with all the medical changes. With the CURA units coming in next week our workloads are going to be even heavier. A great solution for expanding the amount of beds in the COVID ICU, but I worry about the staffing. Will there be enough doctors to handle the influx of wave three patients?"

"Don't worry about it too much, Karly. Just focus on what's in front of you and on your own patients."

I know Clay is right, and ironically my father would say the same thing. I need to stop worrying about the big picture, and focus on my part in all of this. But it's still difficult to quell the anxiety of the overall global situation, situation at the hospital, and in my own life. I worry about my own family and friends who I've only seen in video chats for months now.

I didn't even get to hug her before she died… I fight the wave of sorrow welling up inside of me. *I can't go there right now. I need to focus on today and doing my best work during my shift.* I clear my throat, trying to refocus my mind. "You're absolutely right. I need to stay focused." I resolve to do just that, and mentally start preparing myself for my shift.

Clay glances over at me, unspoken questions in his eyes after hearing my tone of voice. I know he can tell I'm dealing with brokenness, but he decides not to say anything. I feel relieved. Instead we drive in a comfortable silence.

After arriving at the hospital, Clay parks the car, and I notice the overhead light flickering in the darkness. It makes patterns of shadows on the pavement intermittently. *Just like us. We're in the darkness, but we see the flickers of light. The future won't be so bleak, once things are under control. Control. Will we ever truly have control? We lived in an illusion before the pandemic struck, thinking we were in control. This has been such an eye-opener.*

"What are you thinking, Karly?" Clay and I walk to Diagnostics to be tested.

"Just about how I used to feel like I was in control of my life, but that control was all an illusion."

Clay nods, understanding.

"But I'm learning to let go of the things I can't control. It's difficult for me though, you know?"

Clay looks at me with compassionate eyes. "I think that realization that we don't have full control over our lives and futures in this day and age has floored a lot of people. Everyone's world has been flipped upside down, and most people are still reeling from the changes and the losses. Some of us still yearn for control we don't currently have, and will do anything to regain some semblance of control." I glance up as Clay speaks with an odd tone, but he doesn't elaborate further.

We enter Diagnostics for testing, and when we get the "all clear" we head up to the ICU. As we enter the unit, we see that things are a lot more hectic tonight than they were twenty-four hours ago. The day shift debriefs us, updating us with what has transpired with each patient.

Twenty-four hours can bring a lot of changes in the ICU. Three more patients have been admitted to the ICU, which means we're at maximum capacity. We knew this was coming, and I hope we're prepared for what the third wave brings our way.

During the night, one of the ICU nurses calls a Code Blue. I've just finished up a procedure with a patient, and rush to the code as soon as I can. I disinfect, don new protective gear, and after my N95 mask is checked, I enter the room. Clay is at the foot of the bed, running the code. Meds are being administered by the nurse on the left, and the Respiratory Therapist is at the head of the bed. I stand on the right, ready to administer chest compressions as needed.

"Two minutes, Doctor."

Clay gives orders to the team. "Pulse check." Compressions are stopped and the patient's pulse is taken. The cardiac monitor shows an erratic pattern. "V-fib. Continue compressions. Charge defibrillator. Going to shock."

We continue the cycle and get ready to shock the patient. The patient's body suddenly lurches. The team continues CPR. As I do compressions, I hear a crackling sound and feel a rib crack. I keep going, until the next pulse check is called.

"Administer 0.5 milligrams epinephrine."

CPR continues, and an ECG is ordered. No movement. After 30 minutes, Clay asks for any objections to stopping the code. No one objects, and the time of death is called. The room clears out as Clay performs the death exam.

My PPE goes into the biohazardous waste, and I clean up so I can return to my patients. My eyes have unshed tears in them. *That poor man.* I go back to my patients and work until the end of my shift.

Clay
Early Morning. Wed, May 5, 2021

The sadness hits me once the adrenaline is no longer pumping through my veins. Life and death situations trigger me to hyperfocus—it's almost as if the world is in slow motion, but I'm able to operate at regular speed.

Even though death is a natural part of life, it's difficult to let go. After doing the death exam on the patient, I pick up my tablet and read up on the man's profile. It's something I'm determined to do before contacting the family members of the deceased. Although I'm aware of his medical details, I want to discover who he was as a person. It's up to me to put the pieces together to learn who he was.

The man who just passed away was in his 70's and lived a full life. He loved and was loved by others. He is survived by three children and seven grandchildren. He leaves behind a wife of 45 years of marriage. As an occupation, he built and ran his own construction company, turning ownership over to his two sons after he retired. He was in good shape, especially for his age, but he was no match for the virus. The news that he has passed may come as a shock to his family.

As the doctor who ran the code blue, it falls to me to make contact with the family. I hate having to do this over phone call instead of in person. There is so much more that can be detected in body language that is undetectable during a phone call, and the personableness is not there while on a call. I reluctantly pick up the phone, and call his oldest son, listed as his first emergency contact, to break the tragic news.

Anonymous
Early Morning. Wed, May 5, 2021

As I put down the phone, I clear my mind, and think about the current situation on the second floor. It's been a stressful night as the hospital cases add up, keeping me constantly on my toes. The demand is pressing, and I've been constantly back and forth, grabbing supplies and checking to see if what's needed is available. Keeping PPE in inventory is vital, and the supply is sometimes tentative.

My mind wanders to Karly and I see her walking further down the hall, turning a corner. I know where she is at all times, her schedule, who she's with, and when she's alone. Soon she'll be mine to toy with, like a cat plays with a mouse. *Karly will soon be right where I want her. Right underneath my thumb.*

I walk into the supply room to prep the PPE. Once I'm finished, I'm ready to go about my next task. But before I start, I scoot down the hallway in the direction Karly went. I pass the door to the room she's in, make eye contact then rapidly turn away, and she calls out to me. "Clay!"

I don't acknowledge her, and walk straight by as though I hadn't heard her. I know she's watching me through the large glass window. Resentment builds inside me. *Let her think I'm ignoring her. She deserves to hurt, to feel the rejection.* I continue to walk around the ward, making sure the staff is stocked with PPE and well-prepared for the next inevitable emergency.

CHAPTER THREE

Karly

Morning. Wed., May 5, 2021

"So what are you doing tomorrow?" Clay looks at me as he and I walk out of the hospital into the sunlight. Tomorrow is our day off, and then we have a 14 hour day shift following that. That's assuming we don't get called in on our day off.

I still haven't figured out why he treated me so coldly earlier. *Maybe he was having difficulty dealing with emotions after the patient's death?* I decide not to bring it up.

"Groceries tonight or tomorrow, adulting, and chilling around my apartment." It's been a pretty intense couple of shifts, and I'm looking forward to some down time before the craziness starts again.

"Do you have anyone to take you for groceries?"

"Nah. I usually just walk there and Uber back home. I know what you're going to say, but I don't want you to go out of your way, Clay."

Clay smiles mischievously. "What if I told you that I need to pick up groceries, too?"

I laugh and shake my head. "Seriously?"

"Yeah, might as well go together. In fact, why don't we swing by there after we shower and change clothes, since it's already midday?"

I give in to him. *Who can resist that smile?* I shrug my shoulders. "Sure, it beats going in the evening or tomorrow." Clay drops me at home for half-an-hour then picks me up once I'm showered and changed. His damp hair glistens in the sun as we walk outside in the parking lot.

When we arrive at the grocery store, we put on our masks before heading inside. We pick up the basics as we go through the store, and I hover around the chocolate in the junk food aisle.

"Chocoholic?"

"You bet." I grab two bars, one orange flavored dark chocolate, the other spicy dark chocolate.

"You like that stuff?" Clay points to the spicy bar.

"It's really good. You'll have to try it sometime. Have you ever had an Aztec mocha?"

"Aztec mocha? What's that?"

"Basically a mocha with cinnamon and a pinch of cayenne pepper. It gives a kick. It's similar to the chili chocolate."

"Sounds interesting. I'll have to try that. I love chai, so sounds like something I'd be into."

Back home in the parking lot, Clay pops the trunk and starts taking out the heavier groceries to carry up to my apartment for me. I pull out the remaining lighter items. "Thank you so much, Clay. This has made things tons easier for me."

"No problem, Karly. My pleasure to give you a hand. Besides I'm a pro at this. Remember all the little old ladies I shop for?" He smiles with his laughing eyes.

I'm feeling mischievous and decide to tease him, so I try to sound offended. "Hey! Are you saying I'm a little old lady now?" I pout at him.

Clay's eyes grow big. "No, not at all!" I can see the blush in his cheeks as he starts eyeing me head to toe.

"Riiight." I'm enjoying his flustered expression.

Clay is insistent. "No, I definitely didn't mean it like that." It's more than just a quick glance, and he lingers as his eyes roam over certain areas. Suddenly, he seems to realize what he's doing. He turns away while blushing an even deeper shade of pink, and I chuckle silently to myself. *I usually hate being eyed like that. But I don't mind Clay looking at me.*

Then the realization hits me. *Yikes. I actually like it when he looks at me like that!* Now it's my turn to blush. Thankfully, Clay is avoiding looking at me, so I'm hoping he doesn't notice.

We exit the elevator on my floor, and walk down the hall. I set my groceries down and unlock my door. We walk into my apartment. "Soooo… This is my place."

"Nice place." Clay smiles, glancing around, his arms still full of my groceries.

"Here, you can set them down here." After quickly disinfecting, I clear a section of the counter off for him to set the groceries down. Instead of leaving the groceries on the counter, after washing up he starts taking items out of the bags and putting them in the fridge.

"Oh! You don't have to do that."

"Well, I do 'full service' grocery delivery." Clay winks at me and I giggle.

"And what is included in this 'full service' delivery?" I feel playful as I wink back at him.

"Well, what would you like to be included?" Clay has a mischievous grin on his face.

I'm at a loss for words. *Is he flirting with me? Or just being playful?* I feel the electricity coursing through my body again. I try to think of something to say. I glance at the kitchen counter and spy the coffee maker. I pull out a random idea. "Ummm...you get to be the barista?"

Clay laughs. "Sounds like fun to me!"

After the groceries are put away, Clay makes himself at home in the kitchen, and tries to figure out my single serve coffee maker.

He asks me for a demonstration. Clay jokes with me. "Since I've been promoted to barista, I need a bit of training in my new position."

I walk to the coffee maker, and Clay stands behind me to watch. I take a pod out of the drawer, flip up the lid and insert the pod, then press the start button. "See, simple enough." I spin around and bump into Clay. I didn't realize he was standing so close to me. He grasps my arms to stabilize me and smiles, shyly. I look up through my lashes at him, while he gazes down at me, his eyes dark and hooded.

After a moment he breaks eye contact. "Okay, my turn." Clay reaches around me to replace the coffee cup and takes a pod with the other hand. He cages me in the process. I inhale sharply, feeling our proximity acutely, our chests so close to each other's. But Clay doesn't seem to notice. He seems to be focused on the coffee maker. *Um...did he intentionally mean to get this close?* Then my denial kicks in. *He probably doesn't realize it. A guy like him wouldn't be interested in me.* I feel a touch of confusion. *At least I don't think he would be?*

I have no choice but to turn around and face the coffee maker, or I'll be face-to-face with him, up close, which feels really awkward. His arms are on either side of me, trapping me between himself and the counter. Clay flips open the coffee maker, places the pod in and presses start. The espresso starts to fill the bottom of the second coffee cup.

"Great." My voice breaks a bit, since Clay is in such close proximity to me, his front to my back. I can feel his body heat even though he isn't even touching me. I feel his breath on my neck as he leans down—to watch the coffeemaker I assume. *His lips are so close to my neck. I wonder what it would feel like if he was to kiss me there…*

My heart rate quickens, and I feel blood rushing to my cheeks. I feel a pulse of electricity fly from my waist downwards. *Why am I feeling these sensations? It must be the close proximity thing again.*

Once the espresso is done, Clay moves his arms to one side of me to take the two mugs, while I get the vanilla soy milk from the fridge. There's no indication that his mind was travelling down the same path as mine.

He was just concentrating on making the espresso, I guess. I feel relief, but at the same time I'm a bit disappointed. Confusion plagues me. I try to focus on what we're doing, instead of on fleeting fantasies.

"So this is an automatic frother that heats up the milk while frothing it. It's so much easier than using a steamer. You just pour the milk in and press the start button. The tiny whisk attachment froths up the milk."

"Wow, super-easy." Clay pours milk for the first mug into the frother. "You have a seat while your new barista froths the milk." Clay gives me a lop-sided smile, his eyes bright. He really is enjoying this.

"How much cocoa powder and cayenne do you usually put in for the Aztec mochas?" He starts searching the cupboards until he finds the items.

"A tablespoon of cocoa powder and an eighth of a teaspoon of cayenne. Quarter teaspoon max. Oh and half a teaspoon cinnamon. Plus some sweetener."

"I'm liking this. I don't need to watch the milk while it froths and heats." He stirs the cocoa, cayenne, cinnamon, and sweetener into the espresso. Clay looks a bit more closely at the frother. "Oh, Starbucks? I didn't realize they made these. I'm going to have to get one."

I stand up and walk to the fridge. "Just grabbing something to go with our mochas." I heat up some cinnamon rolls from the store in the microwave for fifteen seconds each. I put them on two plates and place them on the kitchen island beside each other. I settle myself on one of the bar stools to chat with Clay.

We joke around while the milk froths twice. Clay brings the finished mochas to the island, and sits on the stool next to mine, turning his body so we can chat comfortably. My eyes widen with a realization. "This is actually the first time I've had anyone over for coffee in months."

After the second pandemic wave hit, the social distancing guidelines tightened up again. Even though restrictions were loosened again later, I was so busy in the accelerated med program, and dealing with the tragedy that had struck our family, I didn't have time for or the interest in a social life.

"Hey, have you forgotten who the barista is? I'm having you for coffee at your place." Clay's eyes twinkle and I laugh.

I feel amused. "Well, I'm really happy you've invited me to join you at my own place, Clay. Although my place is a bit untidy." I look at the pile of papers stacked on the dining room table.

"Untidy? You should see my place." Clay pauses for a moment. "On second thought—you shouldn't see my place." We both laugh.

"Well, one thing my mom used to say when I was self-conscious about my place was: 'I'm here to see you, not your house.'"

Clay takes a sip of his mocha, then cautiously approaches the subject. "How is your family, by the way?"

"Well, we have weekly family Zoom meetings to catch up with each other. Things are pretty much the same. Dad's been working at the Oakville Hospital, and my mom is busy at home teaching her students online." I take a breath. "Katie has taken over my aunt's old position, volunteering at the local Food Bank." My voice quivers slightly, but I'm able to keep my words even. Clay places his hand over mine, and gives me a gentle squeeze. His compassionate eyes are searching mine. The kind gesture causes my eyes to tear up.

I decide to open up to Clay. I clear my throat before continuing. "My aunt's death was difficult for all of us to handle. Especially since we weren't able to be there to comfort her as she was dying. We all felt so helpless and guilty for not being able to be there for her physically. We had virtual visits, but of course it's not the same."

Clay nods and his thumb gently caresses the back of my hand. I shift the conversation slightly, objectifying the topic, so it's a bit easier to talk about. "I understand how the families of our patients feel, not being able to be there physically for their loved ones. There are so many complex emotions, and there's a feeling of incompleteness. Lack of closure."

Clay nods, his thumb still tracing circles on the back of my hand. "Being able to be there in person physically for someone is something we all took for granted." Clay gives me a significant look. "It affects us more than we care to admit."

"There are so many things we used to take for granted."

"I think a lot of people's eyes have been opened. Instead of viewing life as a rat-race with everyone competing against each other, they're now realizing that the important thing is caring for each other."

"So true."

Time flies by as we chat, and my tummy starts rumbling. "Did you want to stay for lunch, Clay? I have lots of sandwich stuff here."

"Sure, I'd love to." Clay and I set about making lunch together. I'm glad he seems to feel at home in my place. It's so nice to have someone over to do simple everyday things with.

"Oh! What about your groceries?" I realize Clay's groceries are still in the car trunk.

"It's okay. It's cold enough out that it shouldn't be an issue."

"The joys of living in Ontario." We both laugh.

After lunch, Clay and I hang out and watch a movie. I think we've both been starving for the company. We sit on the couch with popcorn and start watching an action flick.

Suddenly, my eyes snap open. Clay and I are leaning against each other in the middle of the couch. We must have drifted off to sleep. I don't want to move, because I'm so comfy, curled up beside him. I close my eyes for a minute, savoring his warmth and soothing presence.

Clay
Afternoon. Wed., May 5, 2021

My eyelids grow heavy as I sit on the couch, watching The Mummy with Karly. I've seen the movie several times, and still enjoy it. I feel myself drifting off...

"Karly?" I watch as a good-looking older guy in a suit walks by the bench I'm sitting on, calling out to one of the girls. She whips her head around to see who's calling her, and I gasp. Her face is vibrant, stunning, and so full of life.

"Geoff?" She smiles. "Come sit with us." Karly is sitting on a blanket on the grass, with a group of friends, eating lunch. She pats the spot next to her.

"Uh, not in my suit," he says, scrubbing his hand through his dark brown hair. Karly stands up and I hear her introduce Geoff to her friends.

"Hey guys, this is my boyfriend, Geoff." Karly blushes,shyly. Her classmates greet him warmly. I can tell that Karly's girl friends are taken with him. In all fairness, he is a physically attractive guy. However, he seems distracted and aloof.

"Karly, maybe we could go for a walk?"

"Oh, sure." She picks up the rest of her lunch and her book bag and says goodbye to her friends, while Geoff takes her hand in his. She and Geoff chat as they walk across campus. He seems like a serious guy. A bit intense, maybe.

"Hi there, I'm Michelle." A girl my age is standing in front of me, holding out her hand in greeting. She looks to be of oriental descent. "These are my friends, Sue and Andrea."

I stand up and shake hands. "I'm Clay." They're not the first to approach me during orientation this week. I've met a lot of friendly students here at U of T.

"So what are you studying?" Michelle asks me, slowly removing her hand from mine.

"I'm in pre-med. I just transferred in this semester."

"Cool. Want to join us for lunch?"

Everything fades and my mind jumps ahead in time.

Karly's sitting a few seats to my left in the lecture hall, and I can see something is wrong. She hasn't been her normal lively self for days. I'm tempted to go up to her to strike up a conversation, but I don't want to complicate her situation and cause ripples like before...

My mind shifts further back to an unpleasant encounter.

"I'm warning you, Aldridge. Stay away from Karly." I can tell Geoff is dead serious as he intercepts me on the way to talk to her.

My mind shifts forward again.

"Michelle, I do enjoy your company, but I can't see us ever becoming more than friends." Michelle's face along with all the other girls' faces dissolve in front of me. All I can see is the face of the one girl I keep being drawn back to. *Karly.*

Her smile is like sunshine to me, brightening my day, no matter how bleak it may seem to be at the time. But what I'm drawn to most is her genuineness. I see it in her eyes, the way she talks to others, and through the important questions she asks our professors during class. She's down-to-earth, caring, dedicated and will make an excellent physician.

My mind shifts forward.

I see her in the lineup in the cafeteria. I've caught her eye, and I nod to her. I must have been staring, because the girl to my left pulls on my shirt and reminds me to sit down. The next time I look up, Karly is gone.

My mind travels through the blur of med school to today.

Leaning over Karly in front of the coffee maker, puts me so close to her. I inhale her soft scent that contains hints of jasmine. I'm so darn close to her. My lips hover near her, and I forget myself. My lips brush her neck, trailing downward with gentle kisses. I encircle my arms around her waist and hold her close to my body, swaying slightly. She sighs softly, and relaxes fully in my arms.

She turns her head towards me, and my lips brush hers. She responds, turning her body so she's facing me, and I cradle her face with my hands. I touch my lips to hers, holding them there. I gently suck on her lower lip, then kiss her softly. As I lay my lips again on her full mouth, my tongue touches her upper lip and she parts her mouth.

Karly's hands are around my neck as our kiss becomes more intimate. I just can't get enough of her. My tongue touches hers, and the electricity between us amplifies. As our kiss deepens, so does the intensity.

Suddenly the room shifts and we're lying down together on a soft surface. I grasp her hair, and she inhales sharply. Her hands are now under the back of my shirt, and I'm holding her tightly to me as we passionately kiss. My fingers are running down her spine under her shirt, caressing her back.

Then she's lying on her back and I'm leaning over her, my hands stroking her face and hair. I pause for a moment, "God, you're so beautiful." I search her face, and I can see she has eyes only for me. There is so much tenderness and longing in them that my heart overflows.

I know she's the only woman for me. I've known it for years. She captured my heart long ago. My lips are drawn to hers, and I can no longer hold back the passion I feel for her. *Just being near her is purely intoxicating…*

Things become a blur, then I snap out of my reverie, slowly becoming aware of my surroundings. But the feelings remain.

Karly
Afternoon. Wed., May 5, 2021

I feel Clay stirring beside me. *I must have fallen asleep again.* I open my eyes, and see Clay looking down at me with an adorable sleepy expression on his face. He wears a crooked smile, and looks amused. He leans his arm on the back of the couch, and gently rubs my back.

"Have a good nap?"

"Mmmhmm…" We stay in this position for a few minutes. Then I slowly and reluctantly put my legs on the floor and stand up and stretch. "I really needed that nap. I usually take one after the night shift."

Clay stands up and smiles at me. "That was the best sleep I've had in ages. We'll have to watch more action flicks together like that." We both laugh, and I feel my face flush. "Thanks for having me over for lunch, Karly. I really enjoyed it. You're great company. I feel so relaxed around you."

"I enjoyed having you over, Clay." I look up into his eyes and he smiles affectionately at me.

At the door, after Clay puts on his shoes and coat, he puts his hand on the small of my back. I'm unsure if he means to hug me, so I just stand there. He smiles down at me and says goodbye, as he gently touches my cheek with his finger and thumb. "Bye, Karly. I'll pick you up for next shift." Then I close the door softly behind him.

After Clay leaves, I draw myself a bath and my muscles relax even more in the hot steamy water. I give my hair a deep conditioning treatment and relax for a bit in the bath. Sometimes it's the little things that make the difference when trying to keep stress levels under wraps. Having a soothing bath is such a wonderful feeling. When I'm done, I put my hair up in a towel, then get ready for my family's Zoom meeting. It will be so nice to see the fam.

I log in and join the meeting, and see that everyone was able to make it. I notice my dad looks tired, but otherwise everyone looks healthy. "So how have your first days as an intern been, Karly?" My dad looks at me with a smile.

"Similar to when I was a student, but with more responsibility. It's been really busy. I've been familiarizing myself with the status of each case before rounds, and getting to know the members of the care team better." I think of Clay. *Some more than others.* I feel myself blushing.

"It's about to become even busier. Thankfully, we received a heads up from sanitation that there is a surge in local cases. The sensors placed there are indicating rising levels of the virus in the local population. The CURA pods have arrived at the GTA hospitals, fully equipped. Each pod will be able to take an additional two COVID patients each."

"That's great, Dad! Our ICU is already at max capacity and this will make a big difference."

"Having the negative pressure CURA units will keep the virus from spreading while the patients are being treated. This is great news for the province."

"We should be able to manage the third wave much better than the second wave."

"Well, we don't anticipate this to be as bad as the second wave, since flu season is over now. I just wish the CURA pods had been ready when the second wave hit. It would have made things a lot easier for us."

I don't want to dwell on the "what ifs". Taking that mental path would lead me on a downward spiral. It's not like my dad to dwell on them either. If anything, he's always reminding me that we can't change the past, but we can change the future.

I need to stay focused on the present. I use a subtle redirect. "Well, we have them now, and that's the important thing." Dad chuckles. He knows exactly what I just did and why. I shift the conversation slightly. "How are they going to deal with the long-term care homes?"

"They've decided to go with CURA pods as needed, and the military will be in charge of transportation and setup. The pods will be ready to go wherever there is an outbreak, whether it's to a specific facility or to be assembled as a field hospital. This way the virus will be contained, the patients will have the care they need, and many won't have to be transported elsewhere to be in quarantine. This will lessen risk for the patients. It also means that hospital ICUs will have a higher percentage of cases that originated from community transmission."

"What about staffing for the pods at the long-term homes?"

"Specialists on call will be brought in, along with extra staff. In a worst case scenario, the military themselves will provide medical personnel."

I nod. *Sounds like they have a viable plan in place this time that can be executed quickly. It's been a long time coming.* I turn my attention to Mom, who's been patiently listening, very interested in what's happening on the medical front. "How's the online teaching going, Mom?" The five of us chat together for an hour, Katie filling us in on her volunteer work, and Mitchell on his paramedic duties as part of a specialized COVID team.

Mitchell shares his recent experiences. "People are going from okay condition to extremely poor condition in a matter of hours. They're able to breathe by themselves but then within a few hours need to be intubated. We're seeing this pattern of rapid deterioration over and over again. There is little warning, and we're usually called in when someone is struggling for breath." Mitchell is also living and working in Mississauga in connection with Trillium Healthcare's three hospitals. It's nice having him nearby, with the possibility of running into him at Credit Valley Hospital.

Katie seems to be feeling under a bit of pressure, due to taking a summer semester of online courses, in addition to her volunteer work. "The food bank is still having difficulty meeting demands. People are really struggling right now due to the economy and so much job loss. We're hoping the government will pass approval for more funding soon so we can meet the needs of communities." Katie has become passionate about how she's contributing during the pandemic, and for me it feels bittersweet. She's providing a connection to my late aunt's world and a continuation of her legacy, but it's also a reminder of our family's loss. Living with Mom and Dad makes it possible for her to continue with her schooling while investing a large amount of hours into volunteering to help our community.

After our Zoom meeting, I check my emails. I see the subject line "Thinking of you, Karly", from "Guess Who", at an email address I don't recognize. A small smile plays on my lips, thinking it could be from Clay. I open the email and there's a brief note with a link to a YouTube video.

Missing You. See you soon.

I click through the link to the music video.

...I saw an angel, of that I'm sure.
She smiled at me on the subway, she was with another man,
But I won't lose no sleep on that 'cause I've got a plan.
You're beautiful. You're beautiful. You're beautiful, it's true...

I blush as I listen to James Blunts' song "You're Beautiful". I leave the song on as I tidy up my living room. A smile plays on my lips as I think of Clay.

Clay

Evening. Wed., May 5, 2021

I randomly flip channels, watching bits and pieces of this and that, while eating a bowl of maple pecan ice cream. My feet are up on the coffee table—my mom would kill me if she saw that. Well, she would at least give me a lecture about how that's not the way her boys were brought up. Although respect and manners were ingrained in us, I allow myself certain concessions.

I'm flipping stations to distract myself. *Karly.* Although my hands were tied back in med school, I'm thinking about pursuing her now. I know what I want. *I want her. But can I really balance things with her, given the circumstances involved?*

I'd overheard Karly talking about applying for a local placement near home. I knew the odds were good that we'd end up in the same hospital if I applied in Mississauga, since there are only three hospitals here, all run by Trillium Healthcare. So I surreptitiously copied the application details I'd heard her voice to Violet, and here we are.

We were both placed where there was the biggest void, where we were needed most during this crisis. I feel grateful that we're on the same team, as it will give us some time to get used to working together in a professional setting. And now, traveling to and from work together gives us the opportunity to spend time together on a more personal basis.

Karly, you are truly one of a kind. I've never met anyone like her. I start to doubt myself. *What if I screw this up?* But then my confidence overrules the thought. *All I have to do is follow the plan.* My lips curl up into a smile.

Anonymous
Evening. Wed., May 5, 2021

Although I'm usually rigid about my "self-imposed rules", I allow myself some flexibility of thought. *If I do this right, then I'll have what I've been wanting for years. Karly is perfect in her current state. Perfectly difficult, which means she's perfect to break. I just have to be cautious and be patient.* Patience is definitely one of my virtues.

Since I now see Karly regularly, I'll be able to keep tabs on who she interacts with while she's working, and guide things in my direction. We're in such close proximity to each other all the time now. I'm able to stay close to her and monitor her when I'm not involved with other tasks.

One thing I'm disliking is all the male attention Karly seems to get. I can see the way they all look at her. With longing in their eyes, whether she notices or not. They all want her. *Well, they can't have her. She's mine.* I'd push them all away from her, but it would create problems if I came across as too possessive. *No, I have to be cautious and work subtly.* Although I still don't know exactly how to proceed with my end game, I plan to start by taking things slowly and drawing her unknowingly into my web.

CHAPTER FOUR

Karly

Morning. Thurs. May 6, 2021

The following day flies by as I get all my food preparation done for the week. Now that my work schedule has been established and I'm back in a routine, I'm on a planning stint. I lay out everything I need to do on a weekly basis in my day planner. I establish a time for groceries, regular laundry, food prep, cleaning, and anything else that needs doing. I take advantage of the day off to be productive, since I know I may be called in constantly, once the surge hits.

In the evening, I sit down to watch the news, but it's a mistake. *Why don't they stop the political posturing and deal with things in the best interests of the global community? This is so ridiculous. They should be focusing on reports of medical experts and updates on potential vaccines and treatment.*

I turn off the TV and decide to read a book instead. Shortly after settling down to read, I get a call from Violet. "Hey Karly!"

"Hey Vi. How are you?"

"I just got off a long on-call shift. I did get a couple of hours sleep in between calls, though. So I'm a bit wired."

Where does she get the energy? Those shifts can be brutal. "Wired or weird?" I laugh.

"Both, I think!" Vi's laugh rings out over the phone. "So tell me, any new news with Clay?"

"Nothing much." I feel reluctant to say anything. "He took me for groceries."

"Oooo!"

Out of the blue, I suddenly feel defensive and my response is a bit too rapid and insistent. "It didn't mean anything. He was going anyway." I neglect to tell her about having lunch together, the feeling I had when he was in such close proximity making coffee, and how we fell asleep, leaning on each other in the middle of the couch.

Violet must be able to sense my reluctance to talk about the subject. "Well, keep an open mind, okay? I don't mean you should read stuff into things, but be open. Not all guys are like Geoff."

Ugh...why did she have to bring him up? Dating Geoff during my second year in undergrad was a nightmare. Unfortunately, it took me a while before I saw what he was really like. An established young entrepreneur at twenty-five, his achievements distracted from his character deficits. He put up such a good front he even had my family deceived.

I was only twenty, but afterwards I felt like a fool for falling for him. As a perfectionist, he eroded my self-esteem. It got to the point where I believed him when he said no one could love someone like me. I become aware of Vi's voice again as she repeats herself. "Okay?"

"I'll try to stay open minded." But deep down, I'm fearful of falling into another abusive relationship. *It took me a couple of years of therapy to start believing in myself again.*

I need to stay focused on my job. But I know it's a cop-out, focusing intently on my job just to avoid being hurt again. Diving into work or studies is my defense mechanism for self-protection. It's why I've never looked at another man since Geoff. "Okay then."

I can sense that Vi doubts I'll let myself be open to anything other than a platonic friendship with Clay. She knows me too well. *Now she's going to start pushing the issue, every chance she gets.* I, too, know *her* well. After we hang up, I relax into the quiet of the evening.

Morning. Fri., May 7, 2021

The following morning, I'm up early, getting ready for work. The hospital's going to get busier and busier over the next while. I think of Clay. *He's such a bright spot in my day.* I realize I'm excited to see him. *Hmmm...maybe I'm more excited than I should be.* I pull on my shoes. *Stop it, Karly, he's just a friend and coworker.*

I'm downstairs in the lobby when Clay pulls up to my building. It's still dark outside. Clay walks over to the passenger side and opens my door for me. I hear soft music playing on the radio. *He is such a gentleman, opening my door for me.*

"Thank you, Clay." He makes sure I'm in, then closes my door. We comfortably listen to music on the way to work. Clay seems to have something on his mind, but I decide not to press him.

We arrive at the hospital and start our shift. The intensivist makes an announcement as we prepare for rounds. "We're in the process of admitting new patients to the CURA units." I hear murmurs of relief in the room. Although I wasn't an intern at the time of the second wave, I saw first-hand the hospital overcrowding and stress during my Toronto placement as a student. *This time we're better prepared.*

On our rounds, we come across a 38 year-old patient with no other underlying conditions. "The patient suddenly became very ill and had a high fever. Labs indicate he has cytokine storm syndrome."

Cytokine storm syndrome. The name fills me with dread. The body's immune system ravaging the body's healthy cells, triggered by an overactive immune response brought on by COVID-19.

The intensivist nods in agreement with the pharmacist. "We'll treat with anakinra then. Hopefully that will reduce the hyper inflammation." It's a delicate balance, since the immune system needs to be suppressed so it doesn't destroy the patient's lungs, but at the same time, the immune system needs to be able to target the virus.

"After monitoring the patient for response, we'll know if extracorporeal leukocyte modification is needed instead. For those of you not familiar with what that is, it's a type of dialysis in which we reprogram the white blood cells to alter immune response. The goal of treatment is that when those blood cells return to the body, they will fight hyper inflammation rather than promote it.

"If we go that route, we'll stop the anakinra during treatment and treat in combination with an antiviral?" He looks at the pharmacist for verification, and the discussion shifts to specific medications.

Later on in the day, I dash down the stairwell to the back parking lot and take a quick look at the CURA units, so I can understand what we're looking at when the influx of patients pushes us into overflow.

CURA stands for "Connected Units for Respiratory Ailments". It was a concept developed by architects and engineers who wanted to help during the world's time of crisis. There was such a shortage of ICU beds globally, and they wanted to offer assistance. It all started with one prototype, then took off from there.

As I look around the parking lot, I see white shipping containers that have been repurposed as negative pressure rooms that can each contain two patients each. Patients can be monitored by the nurses through the large windows inserted into the lengths of the containers as well as through instrumentation. I see the equipment being prepared for the mini-ICU rooms and realize the full potential of the setup.

Instead of just using tents where COVID-19 can easily spread from patient to staff, each room is a negative pressure room, meaning it's completely isolated and the virus can't contaminate anything outside the room. It's a perfect quarantine setup. Military personnel can set up the units in different configurations, depending on whether a whole hospital is needed, or just extra ICU rooms. It's anticipated that the beds will fill up fairly quickly at our hospital, and I'm grateful there is a pre-emptive solution to overcrowding.

Once I have a general idea, I head back up the stairwell to the hospital ICU. I pick up my hospital mail, and read through it. I open a white envelope and there's a note inside that says, "You're beautiful." I can feel the red blossom in my cheeks and my face quirks into a smile. I tuck it safely into the bottom of my bag, thinking it must be from Clay.

Clay
Night. Fri., May 7, 2021

On the drive home, Karly tells me she got a good look at the ICU expansion, namely the new CURA system. "I'm really impressed with the concept and setup. The shipping containers are easily transported worldwide, and there is so much potential to meet the individual needs of specific communities."

I listen to her description, as she continues. "Not only is it convenient, but the biocontainment filtration system eliminates most of the hazards we would normally face in a tent or quarantine camp setup." Karly is visibly excited as she speaks, vibrant and animated, with eyes aglow. *So beautiful. She's so passionate about her work and the difference she can make in people's lives.*

I can feel myself falling for her. She captured my attention those first days I set eyes on her so many years ago. That intrigue has only been growing within me. The way she cares for people in general pulls me in and makes me desire her more. My heart aches for her.

I can feel the corners of my mouth tugging upwards. I could listen to her all day. Karly always brings out a smile in me. *I think she brings out the best in me. When I'm around her I want to be a better, more noble person. She motivates me to try harder.*

"Clay, are you listening?" Her face looks inquisitive as she engages my eyes.

"Of course. I'm just trying to imagine the setup the way you've described it to me. It sounds like an amazing system, something that can also be used in poorer nations of the world to help with treatment of patients. It will keep health care workers safe."

"Exactly!" Karly becomes even more animated. *I just love seeing her like this.* "This could revolutionize healthcare and make a difference globally, preparing the world to deal with future pandemics."

"Definitely. It's a great solution to the ICU bed shortage many nations are now facing." I look over at her. She draws out another smile from me.

We have so much common ground. I want to hold onto her tightly and never let her go. I try to stay focused on what she's saying, but my mind drifts and all I can think of is being with her. *But what if she doesn't want me back?* I feel a pang of anxiety. *I'll have to deal with that problem if it arises.*

Karly
Night. Fri., May 7, 2021

When I get home I check my laptop. I've received another email from "Guess Who?" with the subject line "See you tomorrow".

I smile as I open the email. *Wow, Clay's fast. He only just dropped me off.*

I see you.

I check out the video and listen to the lyrics.

Oh, can't you see you belong to me
How my poor heart aches with every step you take
Every move you make and every vow you break
Every smile you fake, every claim you stake, I'll be watching you.

I feel confused and shocked as I listen to the song. It's an old song from the 80's called "Every Breath You Take" by The Police. It's not the type of song I would expect Clay to link me, and I'm unsure what he means by it, if anything. The lyrics make me feel uncomfortable. I feel uneasy.

Maybe he just enjoys the guitar arpeggios; the rhythm and melody are very catchy. Or maybe he's referring to our patients, how we're having to watch every breath they take. *Ah, that might be it.* It might have another context that I'm just not clueing into.

However, there's something about the email itself that bothers me, but I can't put my finger on it. Something tickles in the back of my mind. I close the uncomfortable email and forget about it as I go about my evening. I feel completely worn out from my shift, and get ready for bed before I pass out from exhaustion.

Anonymous
Early Morning. Sat., May 8, 2021

It's 2 am. I can't help myself, the urge is overwhelming. I pick up the phone and dial Karly's number. I hear her sleepy voice as she picks up. "Hello?" She sounds so small and vulnerable.

I lower my voice to a whisper. "Karly, you're beautiful." I feel both admiration and spite.

"Clay? Is that you? Is everything okay?"

I feel perturbed as a multitude of emotions bubble under the surface. I whisper, "Everything's fine. Always remember: I see you."

"ICU? I don't understand."

I gently hang up, still feeling disturbed.

Karly

Early Morning. Sat., May 8, 2021

I'm asleep when I feel my phone drop out of my hand onto the mattress. I startle and pick it up. "Hello? Hello?" But there's no answer. I pry my eyes open and check the screen. I'm not on a call. Maybe I was just dreaming.

I quickly go to the history, and see through my clouded eyes there was a call from a private number a few minutes ago. *It was something about the ICU? The Intensive Care Unit?* My mind swirls as I drift off again. My hand lowers to my mattress and my phone settles there. Within a minute, I'm sound asleep.

CHAPTER FIVE

Karly

Afternoon. Thurs., June 3, 2021

The next three weeks pass by as if we're living in a whirlwind. We're taking in more patients because of the CURA beds, but we always seem to be short-staffed for one reason or another.

I feel like the stress is taking a toll on me as I'm subjected to case after case of COVID-19. It's because each case isn't just a "case". It involves a human life that hangs in the balance. Sometimes we do everything we possibly can for patients, and it's still not enough.

Each death affects me, and occasionally I find myself at home in tears for what seems to be no reason. Thankfully, our team is supportive of each member and we've been growing closer with each day that passes. We look to each other for support.

"Thanks, Maggie." Today's been a particularly difficult day, and I'm thankful I have someone so understanding to talk to. We're both teary-eyed as we break our hug. Things are subdued today, as we deal with not just loss of life, but also life sentencing. Some patients will be sentenced to a life of long-term care, unable to look after themselves, but stable enough to leave the hospital.

Most people think of this disease in terms of whether a person lives or dies from it. However, they overlook the permanent disabilities that have been caused by this terrible disease. It's not a black or white situation. There is suffering, which I guess you could term as the grey area. It's extensive, and can include organ damage, stroke, neurological damage, and many more disabling conditions.

Maggie grabs a couple of tissues for us. "Hang in there, Karly. You're doing a great job."

"Thanks. Just talking things out and getting the feelings out can be so helpful. I feel less stressed now."

Maggie grips me on the shoulder and gives me a squeeze. "We'll get through this together. It's been a long road, but we'll make it through this."

Things would be a lot easier if I wasn't getting so much hot-and-cold from Clay. Whenever I run directly into him he's friendly, but from a distance he won't acknowledge me. I would suspect his hearing or sight possibly being an issue if it wasn't for the fact that I've caught him staring directly at me with steel cold eyes. I don't know what's up with him, but it makes me feel uneasy.

Clay
Morning. Friday, June 11, 2021

Karly and I are growing closer day by day. The more I get to know her, the more I admire her. I admire her tenacity, her commitment to her patients, and the positive energy she brings everywhere she goes.

My feelings for her keep growing, and although I'm trying to be patient, I feel such an urgency. *I need to stay in control, not just of my feelings but of the whole situation. I'm falling too fast.* This wildfire inside me could consume me if I'm not careful. *I need to hold back.*

It's difficult not knowing if Karly will reciprocate, so I try to keep everything platonic with her and not push. There are bonding moments where we sometimes will hold hands or give each other a hug, but I'm trying not to do anything that might push her away. However, it seems that can't be avoidable. Sometimes I feel her pulling away from me, and I don't know why.

Where we are at now is mostly comfortable, although we do have awkward moments. *I need to just enjoy each day I have with her.* Because when I'm not with her, I feel like I'm going crazy with need for her company. I just wish I could have her completely to myself. *I want her to be mine so badly that it hurts.*

Karly
Evening. Tues., June 29, 2021

It feels like I've been working nonstop, so much that one week has blurred into another. I exit my patient's room and remove my gear, and I'm welcomed by an amazing, mouthwatering smell. My tummy starts rumbling. "What's up? Something smells amazing."

One of the nurses smiles. "Volunteers and a local restaurant sent over meals for us. They know we're receiving an influx of patients, and want to pitch in as much as they can."

"That's very thoughtful of them." I feel like I'm beaming inside. My heart has been lifted. It's not just the meals, although a lot of the ICU staff skip meals because they are too busy to take a break. It's that people are thinking of us, and appreciate our efforts. We all pour our hearts and souls into our work, and to feel that we are being recognized for the sometimes heart-rending work we do, means so much. I check on my patients, then later find a few minutes in between consultations to heat up some dinner in the break room.

While I'm waiting for the microwave, one of the nursing students pokes her head in the room. "Hey Karly." She walks into the room.

"Oh hi, Samantha." I smile at the cute, bubbly nursing student. Her straight brown hair is in a french knot as usual, tendrils framing her face, and her blue eyes are stunning.

"I was wondering. You're good friends with Clay, right?" I think about my relationship with Clay. *We're so much more than friends who just hang out with each other. Apart from Violet, he's become my closest friend and confidante over such a short period of time. Being with him feels*

like I'm with family, I'm so comfortable with him. But what are we exactly? How do we define our relationship?

"Sure. What's up?"

"Well, I was wondering. Could you put in a good word with him for me?"

I'm confused and taken aback. "A good word? I'm not sure what you mean."

"He doesn't seem to know I exist. Maybe mention me and see what he says?"

It dawns on me. *Ohhhh, she's interested in him.* Suddenly, the image of the two of them together, talking and laughing, has me feeling jealous. *Jealous?* I feel surprised at my emotion so I rationalize. *It must be because I'm afraid of losing his friendship, if someone else comes along.*

"We usually don't talk about that type of stuff. He'd know something's up if I mentioned you." *Plus, we've spent so much time together and he knows me so well, he can often read me like a book.*

"Ah, okay." Samantha looks crestfallen.

I feel kind of bad for her, so give her some friendly advice. "He's pretty easy to talk to, you know. Just start a conversation with him and see where it goes." Inside I'm cringing, but I don't know why. I take my food out of the microwave and sit down at the small table.

Samantha brightens. "Really? Thanks, I'll try that." She walks out the door, back to her station. *I never took her for the shy type, but maybe she feels that way with men. Or maybe it's just with Clay.* That feeling of jealousy gnaws at me again. I decide to analyze my feelings while I take my first break in days. Lately, I seem to be a bit of a confused mess when it comes to Clay.

Our boundaries define our relationship. Our relationship doesn't define our boundaries. It's the best way. But then I question myself. *Is it really* the best way? *What does that make us then? What are we exactly?* I chew on my pasta slowly, in thought. *It's the only way to keep my sanity, and to protect my heart. After Geoff—well, I don't want to go through that again.* And I know it's true about my sanity. Dealing with anything more complicated right now would overwhelm me.

Evening. Friday, July 16, 2021

We've been run off our feet all day, non-stop, as usual. Although the third wave seems to have now peaked, according to the epidemiologists, it doesn't mean things are dropping off in the ICU. *It feels like we're trying to avert crisis after crisis, going from one Code Blue to another, some overlapping each other.*

It's one of those hot, humid summer days, and even with air conditioning, the atmosphere in general feels stifling. Add that to wearing full PPE, and it feels nearly unbearable at times. But I stay focused on my patients. What they are going through is much worse than the circumstances in which I need to function.

After putting on a new set of protective gear, I turn around too quickly, and collide with Clay. He catches me by both arms and stabilizes me before I take a tumble. Clay looks concerned. "You okay, Karly?" Our face shields touch as we lean our foreheads towards each other. My heart is pounding and my breathing has accelerated.

Recently, I've realized I have strong feelings for Clay, and out of desperation I've buried those emotions, forcing myself into a type of denial. But they threaten to push the boundaries I arbitrarily set, and it scares me to death. As a result, I've pulled away from Clay emotionally.

Does he not realize what he does to me? We're not even actually physically touching, and he has a hold on me. I push the thoughts away and set my feelings aside. I stuff them deep down with the double-edged fear, both the hold he has on me and fear of loss of our friendship.

I feel paralyzed because of my worry that he will eventually try to control me like Geoff did. *What we have now is great. It's non-threatening and encourages me. I don't want that to change.*

Later on when I'm alone, I reflect on our friendship. *What I have with Clay is a truly special friendship, and I won't jeopardize that for any reason. The last thing he needs is some love-struck girl with a crush on him. God knows he's had enough of those during his life. I'd rather not become a statistic. It would be so painful if he started avoiding me because of my feelings. It would be even more painful if we got involved and our relationship ended up like it did with Geoff.*

That's when my subconscious decides. I hear my own voice in my head. *Nothing will ever happen between Clay and I. What we have right now means too much to me.* I'm so determined to preserve what I have with Clay, that I try to avoid him while I have confusing feelings for him. I'm also subconsciously pushing him away because I'm afraid he'll reject me if he finds out, and because I need to protect my heart.

When I check my phone later, I see there's an email from "Guess Who" with the subject line, "Premonition".

Thought you might want a listen.

The YouTube link is to a song by Maroon 5 called "Animals". I've always loved the group, but again I feel confused as to why Clay would send me this particular song. It does have a great beat to it and a really cool melody line. But the lyrics... It makes me feel alarmed and I feel like distancing myself from him even more. The red flags are going up.

Baby I'm preying on you tonight, hunt you down, eat you alive, just like animals...

...Yeah you can start over you can run free, you can find other fish in the sea.

You can pretend it's meant to be, but you can't stay away from me.

I blush as I listen to the lyrics—they sound so aggressive and possessive for Clay. *Is that how he really feels inside? There's a real problem if he does. I obviously made the right decision deciding to push him away.* My mind is screaming "red flag!" all over the place.

But maybe I'm reading too much into it. I should talk to him about it. I'm not sure if he's just sharing random songs or if they have personal meaning to him. *I feel almost creeped out though—the last two songs describe things from a stalker's point of view. And he seems to be ping ponging all over the place emotionally with his hot-and-cold act at the hospital. It gives me a feeling of instability in our relationship.* I put it out of my mind for now, but plan to ask him about the song later.

Clay
Evening. Sun., July 18, 2021

I feel Karly pulling away from me, and I wonder what has caused this change. It feels as though she's closing herself off. *That's not good at all, especially with all the work stress. I don't like seeing her withdraw like this. We all need our space from time to time, but there's an undercurrent here—something else is going on in that mind and heart of hers.*

She seems to be conflicted. Maybe she's fighting her feelings, having an internal struggle. Whether it's about our relationship or something else, I want to be there to keep an eye on her. But it feels like there's this "weirdness" between us sometimes. Things seem to be going great, then she pulls away, as if I've done something that upsets her. I'm not sure what's going on, but am determined to get to the bottom of it.

Karly

Evening. Fri., July 23, 2021

I'm finding it's very difficult to avoid Clay, since we still drive to work and back together. When I get into the car, I ask Clay to turn the music on, because I'm so afraid of conversation with him and accidentally spilling out the truth about my feelings.

After driving together like this for a week, Clay finally confronts me as we arrive at my apartment after work. "Mind if I come in?"

I freeze. "I don't think that's a good idea."

Clay audibly inhales. "Look, Karly, I know you're under an incredible amount of pressure right now at work, but you don't have to close yourself off to the people who care about you." He gently brushes the side of my cheek with his knuckles as he looks into my eyes steadily. His light touch triggers me and I feel the endorphins, mixed in with the fear of my own feelings for Clay, the fear of losing him, and the fear of being controlled by him. The fear must have shown itself in my eyes.

"What are you so afraid of, hun? Why are you shutting me out?"

I close my eyes so I won't reveal anything else. Clay gently places his hands on my cheeks and his forehead touches mine. It's a replay of the other day but without us wearing our protective equipment. A replay I've seen in my mind a thousand times since then, but without the gear, as we are now. It's like deja vu.

Clay gently touches my nose with his own. And then it happens. He gently brushes his lips against mine. My fear rises to the forefront. "Clay." I whisper as I sit up straight, stiffening, as I face him. "I don't want things to change between us. Things are comfortable the way they are." I open my eyes and as I do my eyelashes flutter.

Clay moves his head away from mine, and I see a flash of disappointment in his eyes. But only for a millisecond. "It's okay,

Karly." He looks at me earnestly. He gently raises my chin with his fingers, tilting my head so he's looking deeply into my eyes. "You don't have to run from it."

At that moment I can see in his eyes that he knows. I feel a surge of fear course through me. He knows I have feelings for him and it terrifies me. At the same time I feel mortified with embarrassment. I'm also afraid because the emails I've received give a glimpse of a controlling, stifling personality. My reaction is flight.

I gently move Clay's hands away from my face and study his eyes. I can see his emotions reflected there, desire, want, care and compassion. But once bitten, twice shy. Under no circumstances am I going to risk this relationship going in the same direction as the one with my ex, Geoff. I need Clay, but as the caring friend he has been, not as a controlling boyfriend.

I realize he must have feelings for me, too. My heart is ecstatic that he does, but my head believes those feelings need to be nipped in the bud. It's an inner struggle, but fear wins out. I keep my voice level, and am surprised when it doesn't shake. "Clay, I think we need some time apart."

I can see shock and disbelief in his eyes briefly, then hurt. Then his eyes seem to go void of emotion. "If that's what you think you need." I take a deep breath. I hate to do this, but it's necessary. In a world spinning out of control, I'm so afraid of losing what little control I have left, over my heart and over my self-imposed boundaries. I push Clay even further away, in an attempt to regain some type of control.

"Don't worry about picking me up for our next shift." I'm determined to keep resolve, which is extremely difficult when I'm around him. I see another flash of hurt in his eyes, but he quickly recovers and his eyes show nothing.

He gives me a smile that doesn't touch his eyes. "As you wish." He quickly opens his door and gets out to open mine. As I get out of the car, I search his face, but don't see anything there. He's covered his emotions completely. I watch from the lobby as he drives away before I head up to my floor.

As soon as I've twisted the lock and attached the chain, I slide down my apartment door to the floor, tears pouring out of me. My head lowers in my hands. As I sit there, all I can think of is that I've hurt Clay badly. *I'm trying to save our friendship and at the same time protect my heart. But then why does it feel like my heart's been torn in two?*

Clay
Evening. Fri., July 23, 2021

As I drive home, I think about what just occurred. I feel a sadness and an emptiness wash over me. *Karly completely pushed me away. There was so much fear in her eyes.* I wrack my brain, trying to figure out why she responded to her own feelings with such fear. *Or does she see me as possessive?*

She has feelings for me. I can see it in her eyes, and no matter how much she tries to deny them, I know they're there. I worry about her shutting me out of her life completely. I think about how that makes me feel on different levels. There are the natural feelings I have for her, as well as the emotional pain that comes with her rejection and distance. It's a dance between excruciation and exhilaration. It always has been.

I think I may have revealed too much, and that feeling of imagined pressure might be the reason why she's pulled away. She's been spooked. I sigh, resigning myself to what I believe is the best course of action. *I'll plan to withdraw for now, and let's see if I can hold to that.*

CHAPTER SIX

Karly

Morning. Fri., July 30, 2021

The weight of this job over the last three months has taken a toll on me. Dealing with such ill patients and their families has been heartwrenching. But it's the memory of my aunt that makes me determined to help other families dealing with the devastation of COVID-19.

My family wasn't sure if I'd be able to handle this type of work, since her death was so recent. However, I feel that because there is still a rawness to my grief, I'm able to connect more with the families. I want to do everything I can to alleviate my patients' ailments, but also to support the families with the empathy and compassion they need. *Someone did it for our family. Even though it wasn't enough, because we couldn't be with her, it still made a difference.*

Eight of the CURA units have been filled with 15 new patients. Things are still hectic, and the pace doesn't seem to be abating. We've lost several patients with DNR orders, and my heart breaks more with each loss. Since the last time I talked with Clay, I've resorted to sleeping in an on-call room with a pager, instead of heading home after shifts. Although I miss the feel of my own bed, I'm desperate to try to help these patients. And to be honest with myself, I'm trying to run away from my feelings by immersing myself completely in my work.

And now another new patient has been admitted to the hospital and is in the ICU. Little Jeremy has been diagnosed with COVID-19. However, it's not the disease alone that has put him in the ICU. It's the accompanying symptoms that mimic toxic shock and Kawasaki syndromes.

"Patient is five years old, and suffering from abdominal pain, gastrointestinal symptoms, and cardiac inflammation. He will be transferred to SickKids Hospital in Toronto as soon as they have a pediatric COVID bed available for him."

I look through the window at the small body lying on the bed, hooked up to monitors and tubes. I can feel unshed tears in my eyes, waiting to be released. *Focus. Focus on how to help the patient.* I glance around the room, and I can see I'm not the only one affected. We're all worn down and weary, and the presentation of this case is pushing our personal limits of what we can handle emotionally.

Later I lay on the bed in the on-call room, while images rapidly fly by my eyes. When I finally fall into a deeper sleep, I dream about a child with dark hair, a happy child playing outside on the playground in the morning light. He runs onto a field where he plays with a golden retriever, his dad helping him throw a red frisbee for the dog to catch. I see the boy running on the beach with his mom, wiggling his toes in the surf, laughing freely.

And then I see a small coffin.

I jerk up in bed, throw on my shoes, and dash to the ICU. I find myself pleading. *Jeremy! Please, no!* I rush to his room—and it's empty. Tears start to overwhelm me, streaming down my face. I feel desperation. I've lost control over my emotions.

"Karly?" One of the nurses approaches me from behind. It's Maggie. "Little Jeremy was transferred to SickKids." She looks up from her paper, and sees my face. "Are you okay?" Although I feel relief, so much relief, the tears won't stop coming. Maggie grabs me a box of tissues and holds it out to me.

"Sorry, I thought… I thought something had happened to him."

"No, he was just transferred as planned. Want to talk about things?"

I wonder where this lady gets her strength from. She's seen the same horrors as myself and for much longer, yet she is always supporting others around her. Maggie is a rock. "I think I'm okay. I just jumped to conclusions too quickly."

"Sometimes it's hard not to, with what you've seen since you've been here. Are you getting enough sleep? You're looking exhausted."

"I'll be alright."

"Well, if you need to talk with someone, I'm here, and there is also counseling support available."

"Thank you, Maggie. I'm good now." I smile at her, and put my tissue in the garbage, then wash my hands. I figure since I'm up now, I should check on my patients.

During the week, I rarely see Clay apart from rounds and procedures. On occasions when I do, Samantha is always in the vicinity. I feel a twang of jealousy peal through me.

I run into Samantha in the hall. "Hey Karly, have a moment?"

I have to get my charts updated, but of course my priority is to get info on patients' current statuses, so I stop to talk with her. "Sure, what's up?"

"I just want to say thank you."

I look at her with a blank expression. "For what?"

"For the advice you gave me about Clay. I think he's interested in me." She smiles at me with that million dollar smile.

"Oh." I feel numb. "I'm happy for you. I, uh, have to write up some updates now. Bye." I rush to my on-call room. I tell myself it's to work on the charts, but really I just need to get away. The numbness fades and my chest is tight. A tear trickles down my cheek. *Why does my heart feel like it's breaking?* I feel like my whole world is crashing down around me.

I finish up the charts, have a shower, wash and hang up my underclothes to dry, change into my spare set, then crawl into the small bed for a bit of shut-eye. I've been averaging three hours of sleep a night over the last week, since I started sleeping at the hospital.

A few hours later, a new patient coming into the ICU needs to be put on a ventilator. The patient is sedated, an intubation box is placed over them to minimize exposure, and the Respiratory Therapist uses a GlideScope to intubate the patient. I start an arterial line for blood pressure readings and to test for blood oxygenation levels.

I wash up, then before I have a chance to breathe, there's a Code Blue. I'm briefed as I arrive. "Patient has had a stroke from a large blood clot. 7.4 mg tPA injected." The nurse continues to listen to the baby monitor used to track what the team is doing inside the room.

I don my protective gear and get ready to enter the room. Clay is running the code, and I'm surprised to see him since I've lost track of our shifts together. "Infuse tPA dose 66 mL per hour." I mentally cross my fingers and hope this dissolves the clot completely. However, according to the CT scan, it doesn't. A neurologist is called in to remove the clot using a stent retriever while a hematologist stands by.

After the procedure is finished, we doff our PPE and debrief. A couple of minutes into the debriefing, I start feeling lightheaded. I notice Maggie glancing at me, with evaluating eyes. I'm feeling woozy. *Why is Maggie looking at me like that?*

I listen as the neurologist drones on but am not hearing him. Suddenly, the room starts spinning, and everything turns black. I hear Maggie yell. "Grab her!" I feel strong arms grasp me, cushioning my fall.

What feels like an hour later but is really only a couple of minutes, I'm sitting in a chair with my head between my knees. The neurologist is still there, as is the rest of the team that dealt with the blood clot. Clay is crouched down in front of me, looking very concerned. Maggie brings over a glass of water, and Clay hands me the glass. "Here, drink some water." I take a few sips.

"She's been pushing herself too hard. It's likely exhaustion, but she should get checked. She's been sleeping at the hospital with a pager, rather than going home."

"I'll look after it." Clay helps me down the hall, so the group can continue their debriefing without distraction.

Clay elevates my feet on another chair, and tries to talk to me. "What have you been doing to yourself, Karly?" He's crouched in front of me again, his voice is soft, and he looks at me with caring eyes. They are pleading with me. "You've got to look after yourself and get some rest."

Clay looks closely at me. "I can tell you haven't slept properly for days." His fingers lightly brush my cheek as he sweeps a lock of my hair behind my ear. Clay takes my blood pressure and makes sure I'm hydrated. "I want you to go and lie down for the rest of your shift, and I'll come find you afterwards." I begin to protest.

"Uh-uh. Doctor's orders." He sees my stubbornness and knows I won't follow through. "Here, I'll walk you there and come check on you in an hour."

As we walk to the on-call room, I feel petulant and confront Clay about control issues. "You're being controlling right now, and it feels like you're trying to live out those songs you sent me. Stop trying to control me."

Clay stops in his tracks, looking confused. "What songs?"

I stop and look into his eyes to evaluate his response. "In your emails. The links. You know the ones from 'Guess Who'?"

He looks at me strangely. "Karly, I haven't sent you any emails with song links in them." He pauses, thinking. "Are they going to your hospital email or your personal email?"

"My personal email," I say slowly. It seems he knows nothing about them. We resume walking. "I also received a note in the hospital mail, with one of the song titles." Now I'm beginning to feel a bit panicky and sick.

"That sounds concerning." He looks worried. Heck, I'm worried now too.

"I... yes. Two of the songs are about stalkers." I take a deep breath. "I need to think about this and sort it out in my mind. I also received a phone call in the middle of the night. The voice was whispering something to do with the songs—I can't remember what exactly. At first I thought he was talking about the ICU, but then I realized afterwards it sounded more like 'I see you'. Like he was watching me, like in that song. I was half asleep and thought it was you as well."

Clay looks dismayed. I'm assuming it's at the implication I thought he was involved, but his expression quickly changes back to concern. My head feels like it's going to explode, between the anxiety about the emails and other contact, and thinking that Clay had anything to do with it. A lot of my fear about Clay was based on my assumptions, which means I have a lot of rethinking to do. I need to sift things through in my mind and sort out my thoughts.

"I think you should go to the police, Karly. This is serious if the guy is phoning your cell and knows where you work." I don't say anything. It's too much for me to process right now. "Do you still have the note?" I nod. We walk in silence. I'm relieved that Clay doesn't push the issue. I just have too much on my mind right now.

We arrive at my on-call room, and I unlock the door. Clay watches as I get my things ready for my shower, then heads back to the ICU. After my shower, as I lie down on the small bed in the on-call room, I'm left alone with my thoughts. My mind is a jumble and racing. Images are flashing a mile a minute in front of my eyes due to sleep deprivation.

I feel confused about everything. About Clay. *Why do I feel such a pang of sadness when I think of Clay and Samantha together? I made it clear to him I didn't want things to change between us. But if he and Samantha are together, where does it leave our friendship?*

On top of all that confusion, I need to process how the emails have affected my view of Clay. They've eroded my trust in him. Apart from those emails, I haven't seen much indication that he's a controlling person. He's more so a supportive, encouraging person. But I've already pushed him away and into someone else's waiting arms. Have I made a mistake? I feel troubled and for the next 20 minutes I lay there, restless, not knowing what to do.

Clay
Night. Fri., July 30, 2021

My concern for Karly has been growing lately, and after what's transpired today, there's no way I'm going to let this go. *She's so sleep deprived and exhausted she doesn't know which end is up. She's clinging to control, since her whole world has been flipped upside down, and feels a burden of responsibility that's not hers to carry. I need to intervene, no matter how stubborn she may get. I won't take "no" for an answer.*

I feel wary about the emails and the way they may have affected Karly. I feel I'm walking a thin line, and need to be careful. I don't want her to think I'm a controlling ass and bolt again. I work on my notes, then head over to Karly's on-call room when I'm finished.

Karly
Night. Fri., July 30, 2021

I must have fallen asleep, because the next thing I'm aware of is Clay sitting down beside me on the small bed in the on-call room. "I'm taking you home, Karly." Clay is firm in his resolve. "As your friend..." Clay looks pained for some reason. "...I can't let this continue." *Friend.* Sleep threatens to overtake me again. I don't know why, but hearing the word from Clay makes me feel sad. I'm so exhausted I don't have the will to resist. I feel so confused, but I know I have to keep going, working.

As I lay there on my tummy, Clay rubs his hand over my back. *It feels so relaxing, so comforting.* "Karly, you're shouldering much more of the burden than you should."

"But the patients... If only I had been there for my aunt... There might have been a way to save her." My tears are falling freely now, dampening the sheet below me.

"You're 'bargaining', Karly." It's as though Clay's words strike me in the heart. I know they're true. I'm bargaining, trying to change the outcome of the past by my actions in the present. Clay continues the hypnotic rhythm, as he traces his hand over my back. The tears continue to flow, and I feel a kind of emotional release, for the first time in weeks.

After the tears stop, I'm between that place of asleep and awake. I vaguely feel Clay's arm wrap around my back, and his gentle kiss on the top of my head. He strokes my hair, brushes his fingers on my cheek. I start to wake a bit with the sensation. "C'mon, Sleepyhead. It's time to go." I just want to lay there and sleep. "Don't make me tickle you now." Clay has amusement in his voice.

"No tickles." I'm muttering, but I still don't move.

Clay rolls me over onto my back, then scoops me up in his arms. "I'm taking you home, even if it means I have to carry you." He sounds even more amused. I open one eye to peer at him. He has a twinkle in his eye.

"Okay, okay. Put me down." I'd never live down the mortification I'd feel if another staff member saw him carrying me out of the hospital like that. I stand on my feet, wobbling a bit, steadying myself with my hand on the bed, while Clay gathers my things together.

In the parking garage, Clay shuts the car door, and I lean back, shivering. He turns on the heat and within five minutes my body is warm, relaxed, and drifting off. In the distance, I hear a car door close, a rush of cold air on my skin, then drift off again, feeling weightless. I hear the beep of a fob from somewhere, then hear a key turning in a lock.

I feel each foot freed from the constriction of my shoes and socks, some tugging at my clothes, a blanket being placed over me. Then I feel weightless again. I feel something soft on my back, and my eyes flutter open.

"Shhhh." Clay lays me down gently. He brushes my damp hair off my face and kisses my forehead softly. I feel my lips forming a contented smile. I fall into a deep, dreamless sleep.

Clay
Night. Fri., July 30, 2021

It feels so right, having Karly stay with me so I can look after her. She looks so peaceful and content while she's sleeping. *I can't believe she was sleeping in one of the on-call rooms all week.* I shake my head. *She needs a proper rest so she can recover.* I can't help but feel a tinge of anger.

I throw in a load of laundry, then shower and disinfect in the bathroom. I brush my teeth, then make up a bed for myself on the couch. I lay down, resting on my elbow, and play with the remote, trying to find something interesting to watch. I'm wide awake. Having Karly so close by, sleeping in my bedroom—well, I feel pretty wired. *I just hope she doesn't get upset about the clothes…*

I switch the laundry over, and continue to watch TV until the wee hours. When the laundry is finished, I fold the clothes, then lay down on the couch again. I feel myself nodding off a few times, and shift my position so I'm now lying down.

I see Karly lying in my bed, soft golden curls splayed on her pillow, as I look down from the ceiling. Suddenly, I'm beside her on the bed, leaning over her, stroking her hair and touching her face with my hands. Her cheek leans into my hand, and she plants a kiss on my palm.

"Good morning, Mrs. Aldridge." *Oh, the thrill that gives me to call her that.*

"Good morning, Mr. Aldridge." Karly smiles at me through sleepy eyes.

She puts her hands around my neck and draws me down to her face, and into a long, tender kiss. Our lips separate, and I stare into her beautiful eyes. I can see the longing there, the desire she has for me, smouldering embers, ready to burst into flame at any given moment. I run my hand up her side, underneath her only garment, a royal blue, satin nighty. She quivers, and I can see those embers being stoked, before I lean in to kiss her once again.

I've only ever dreamed of this—her wanting me as much as I want her. I run my thumb along her abdomen, and brush my knuckles up against her side, while we are engaged in a deep kiss. She pushes me onto my back, so she's now above me, and my hand grasps her hair with my left hand, while my right hand strokes her cheek with my thumb. I pull her down to me, into my strong arms,

enveloping her in the love and passion I feel for her. *My Karly.*
Forever mine…

I must have fallen asleep with the TV on, because I'm awakened
by the morning news. I yawn and stretch, taking a minute to orient
myself. I tiptoe down the hallway to check on Karly. She looks
adorable, lying on her back with her arms bent. After placing some
items on the bed next to her, I quietly leave the room and close the
door, hoping to not wake her.

I spend the day doing things as quietly as I can, to avoid waking
up Karly. *Wow, she must be exhausted. She's slept the whole afternoon*
away. I think about my dream from last night, and how much I've
grown to want her. *I want her to be mine.* I start cooking breakfast for
dinner, something I always prefer to eat right after waking up. I
think that Karly might prefer the same.

Karly
Evening. Sat., July 31, 2021

I must have slept the entire next day away, because I wake up
and I can tell by the light it's evening. I still feel sooo tired, though.
I lay there, staring at the ceiling, trying to focus my eyes. Suddenly,
I realize I'm not in the tiny on-call room anymore, and the
memories from last night come back to me of Clay insisting I go
home. But I'm not at home either.

I sit up suddenly and my blanket falls off my chest, revealing
my bra. I gasp for a moment, then see my clothes from yesterday,
neatly washed and folded on the other side of the bed, along with
my overnight bag. *Clay must have washed my clothes for me as a*
precaution, to prevent contamination. But that means he took them off me.

I can feel the blood rushing to my cheeks. I realize why he removed them, and that he's seen much more than underclothes in our profession, but that doesn't stop me from blushing.

I take my bag into the ensuite. I turn on the tap and wash my face, feeling the warm water renew me. When I'm finished brushing my teeth and am back in my clothes, I wander out of Clay's bedroom, to the smell of bacon. I walk to the kitchen, and see Clay cooking breakfast. Breakfast at dinner time.

"Oh hey!" Clay's eyes light up when he sees me, and he gives me a welcome smile. "How are you feeling?"

I yawn. "I still feel so tired I could sleep for a month."

We both interrupt each other. "Just so you know—"

"By the way—"

"Ladies first."

He seems a bit anxious. I wonder if he's worried I'll freak out about my clothes. "Thank you for bringing me home with you and looking after me." Clay looks relieved. "I'm sorry I worried you like that. You don't have to worry about a repeat."

"I'm just glad you're okay, Karly." Clay turns off the stove and puts bacon and eggs on two large plates. Then he opens the oven and uses a towel to pull out a tray of pancakes.

"You made pancakes, too?" My mouth drops open. "And they're banana chocolate chip!" I laugh. "You're spoiling me."

"You need to be spoiled sometimes. Especially when you've had a week like the one you've just had." Clay puts a few pancakes on each plate, then we sit at his kitchen table to enjoy breakfast for dinner.

"So what were you about to say when I interrupted you?" I pour maple syrup on my pancakes.

Clay blushes. "Oh. I um...threw your clothes in the wash last night."

I feel a bit mischievous. "It's okay. As long as you had your eyes closed while taking them off me, I'm good with it." I look at Clay with an innocent look on my face. He halts and stares directly at me, looking guilty. I can see him blushing harder. Inwardly I'm laughing at how cute he is, all flustered. I can't hold it in any longer. I start laughing. "You should see your face, Clay. Don't worry about it. I trust you. It was the logical thing to do to avoid contamination."

He exhales with relief. "I was worried you'd be weirded out or something."

"Of course not. It's all good." I smile to put him at ease. "I would have done the same to you if the situation was in reverse."

A smile quirks on his face. "Yeah, as if you could ever carry me." I look over at his 6' 2" frame, and chances are, I'd never be able to lift him, let alone carry him.

I clear the table and do the dishes while Clay walks into the living room and checks Netflix. "Want to watch a movie tonight?"

We have a low-key evening with popcorn, then Clay takes me home. He insists on walking me up to my apartment. I unlock my door, and we stand in the frame to say goodnight. "I'll pick you up in the morning for work. I've missed having my traveling partner with me." Clay smiles, tucking a lock of my hair behind my ear.

I've missed him, too. "I'll see you in the morning then. Goodnight." I'm about to close my door, but Clay doesn't move out of the frame. Instead he draws me into his arms. He cradles the back of my head with his right hand, holding me close to his chest and rocking me slightly. I start to feel fluttery feelings again in my abdomen.

Calm down. It's just one friend giving another friend a hug. He's just been worried about me. No need to read into things. He got the message last week that I want to be friends only. Plus, it looks like he's now seeing

Samantha, so that's an added boundary to keep things in check. I'm like a sister to him.

Clay plants a soft kiss on the top of my head, then brushes his hand down my arm as we draw apart, lightly touching my fingertips. He whispers."Goodnight, Karly."

I watch him as he walks to the elevator, then I close my door. *It seems like things are back to normal and Clay's all about friendship again. But why does that thought leave me with pangs of longing? I can't seem to get my head on straight. My thoughts and emotions are all over the place.* I'm still exhausted from my work marathon, and fall asleep as soon as I crawl into bed.

CHAPTER SEVEN

Karly
Night. Sun., Aug. 1, 2021

I'll always remember the following day as the beginning of my descent into hell.

Things seemed back to normal with Clay, distance but not too much distance, and that part of my life was sorted out. But after the phone call I received late that evening, time suddenly stood still.

I'm near the end of my shift and I've briefed the night doctor on my patients. I've finished charting and am about to pack up to go home for the night when I get the call. My phone rings, and the ringtone indicates it's my dad calling. "Karly, Honey. You done your shift?"

"Hi Dad. Yup. What's up?" I feel a stream of anxiety shoot through me. I already know by my dad's tone of voice that something is off.

"Put me on video."

I activate the cam on my phone, and can see Dad sitting in front of the cam in his regular clothes at home. *That's odd. He's scheduled for a shift at the Oakville Hospital right now.*

"Karly, we need to talk in private."

"Okay, Dad." I head over to the break room which isn't being used, and pull the door shut.

"Have a seat." I sit down in a chair. This can't be good. My anxiety level has just increased several notches. I feel a headache coming on. "Karly, your mom started to feel ill, and she tested positive for COVID today."

"No! That can't be right!" I suddenly feel choked and the pressure builds up in my forehead. My breathing becomes rapid and I start hyperventilating. I lower my head beneath my knees.

"Karly, slow down. Breathe with me. In through your nose. Now out through your mouth." My dad repeats the process several times with me, until I get my breathing under control. He knows that I suffer from panic attacks, which is why he had me sit down to inform me of my mother's condition.

"How bad is it?" The tears are now streaming down my cheeks.

"She was feeling under the weather and fatigued earlier this week, then started to feel better as the week progressed. But today her condition rapidly deteriorated over a period of hours, and Katie brought her in to be tested. She's been admitted to the regular COVID ward. She's fully conscious and breathing on her own at a regular rate, but she was ill enough to be admitted. She's currently being given additional oxygen, but no need for intubation at this point."

I try to put things in perspective. *She's breathing on her own and in a regular ward, not the ICU.*

"Think of it this way, Kiddo. She's under observation, so if things start to go awry, she'll get help right away. It's better than her staying at home and not having fast access to treatment. Plus, I have access to regular updates about her condition from colleagues." I hear what he's saying, but we've already experienced one COVID death in the family, and the panic wells up inside me again.

"Katie and I are at home in isolation. Our first tests came back negative. If our second tests are negative, we'll be cleared to get back to where we're needed. Mitchell's fine, of course, since he hasn't had contact with us." I feel completely drained by the end of the conversation. I get up, and walk out of the room as if I'm in a daze. *Mom has COVID.* I'm still in disbelief.

"Karly?" Maggie runs into me in the hallway. "You're looking a bit pale." I know she's been concerned about me since my fainting spell two days ago.

"Just found out my mom has COVID." My voice sounds far away, emotionless, as though it isn't really my voice. Maggie sits me down, elevates my feet on a chair, and gets me a glass of water. It's like another case of deja vu. We just went through this earlier this week. I feel like I'm a robot. My consciousness is far away, but my body is just going through the motions. I'm staring far off into the distance. At what, I don't know.

I think I hear Clay's voice off in the distance. "Karly?" His voice sounds closer now, and suddenly I'm startled back to reality. My eyes clear, and I see Clay crouched in front of me. "Karly." I'm able to focus on his face. "You've had a bit of a shock. Our shift is over, and it's time to head home."

I nod my head. "I'm going to gather your things together, then we'll walk to the car." I nod again. Clay gathers my things, helps me into my coat, and walks me to his car. He opens the door and buckles me in, then drives me home. He parks in the Visitor parking, which is odd. He normally just lets me off at the front door. He pays for parking, puts the ticket in the dash, then comes to help me out of the car. He takes my hand and leads me to my building.

I fumble with my fob; my coordination is off. I feel like the air has turned to a thick liquid which is impeding my actions. We get off the elevator at my floor, and Clay has to unlock my door for me since my hand can't grasp the key properly.

Clay leads me into my apartment, and has me go into the bathroom to remove my clothes. I'm still in a daze, and walk out of the bathroom in my bra and panties. I see that Clay has stripped down to his boxer briefs, and is getting the washer ready for a load.

He glances over, and looks startled by what he sees. "You forgot to put on your robe, Silly." Although he looks away, ever the gentleman, the corner of his mouth quirks up into a bit of a smile. Clay retrieves my clothes from the bathroom, and starts the washer.

He then tells me to join him in the bathroom. Clay helps me to disinfect my hands, and he does the same. Although I'm not "all there" cognitively, my body seems to be keenly aware of Clay's proximity to me, and the fact that we're nearly naked.

Clay and I shower in different bathrooms, and I walk out of the master bedroom in a towel. Clay has finished in the main bathroom and is in the living room, also in a towel, since his clothes are in my washer. He looks over at me from his spot on the couch.

"Hold me, please."

Clay looks at me skeptically. But he walks over, takes me into his arms and holds me close to him. Several minutes pass by.

"This isn't working. Our bodies... It's too much for me." Clay seems a bit shaky. He lets go of me and runs his hands through his hair. He seems frustrated.

"I need you to hold me, Clay."

He thinks in silence for a minute. "I have a better idea." Clay scoops me up and carries me to my bedroom, gently laying me down on the bed, and pulling the sheet and duvet over me. He lays beside me on top of the covers, then holds me close, with the covers between us serving as a barrier. I force my towel out from under the sheet and drop it on the floor beside the bed. Clay lets out a startled laugh.

He pulls the sheet up to my chin. "That's better." Clay seems satisfied with this arrangement. He leaves the lamp on so he can observe me. "How are you feeling?"

"I still feel like I'm in a trance. Not as numb as before though."

He holds me close and strokes my back. I know he's hoping that the physical contact will help me reconnect with the present. I feel safe in Clay's arms, less overwhelmed, and the physical contact is helping me to reorient myself. I see him shiver, then he leans over to grab the spare blanket at the bottom of the bed for himself. He resumes holding me, watching me, and eventually I start to drift off to sleep.

Clay
Early Morning. Mon., Aug. 2, 2021

Being the one to hold her and comfort her is an amazing feeling. I don't want to miss a second with this woman. So I stay awake, holding Karly, stroking her hair and face. I kiss the top of her head while she sleeps. *She needs so much tenderness. But can I give it to her?*

My feelings for her are all over the place, possessiveness and anxiety, fear of rejection, and conflicting concern with contentment. My emotional whiplash is confusing to say the least. Especially when combined with the building and warring emotional intensity in our relationship.

I feel so torn between my own needs and desires and what I think she needs. I'm not sure how to proceed with things, so decide then and there to go by instinct. At this moment, I'm just going to give my mind a break from this internal tug-o'-war.

Karly
Morning. Mon., Aug. 2, 2021

I wake up the next morning, safe in Clay's arms, and for a moment I'm confused. It takes me a minute to remember the circumstances of the night before. Then it all comes back to me. *Mom has COVID. Clay brought me home and took care of me. He stayed with me.* I can't help but feel flooded with warm feelings for this man who has been so caring and thoughtful towards me. I watch as his eyes open, and he looks into mine, stroking my hair with his hand.

"Good morning, Sweetheart. How are you feeling?"

I analyze my feelings. Things don't feel as overwhelming as they did last night. I still feel a considerable amount of anxiety, understandable under the circumstances, but I also feel something warm. Like I'm not alone in this. "I feel comforted, just lying here in your arms. It's helping the anxiety dissipate."

"Then we can stay like this as long as you need." Clay pulls me tightly to him, as closely as he possibly can with the covers between us, and kisses me on the top of my head. I feel so safe and secure. This is exactly what I need to get through this. After laying there together for a time, I pull away slightly so I can look at Clay's face.

"You okay?"

I nod. "Thank you, Clay, for being here for me when I've needed you the most. This week has been overwhelming for me."

"Of course. I plan to always be here for you. After all, what are friends for?" He smiles at me. Pain briefly flickers through his eyes, but is gone so quickly I might have imagined it.

I think about how his comfort would have made such a difference to me last year, during my ordeal, and I'm just happy he's here now. I don't take him for granted, I never could, after weathering the storms alone when my family couldn't be in close proximity to me. "You being here for me means more to me than you know."

"And *you* mean more to me than you know." He playfully taps his finger on the tip of my nose and I laugh. Then he tickles me until I'm at his mercy, and we get up for the day. The dark clouds don't feel as black as they did yesterday.

When I'm done in the bathroom, I walk out and see that Clay has made breakfast with Aztec mochas for us. After breakfast he wets his hair down and borrows a comb and some gel while I clean up the dishes. *Clay's been here for me in a way that no one else could have been.* I feel overtaken with feelings for him, in response to his caring, loving attitude towards me. My heart feels full, even within the current circumstances.

My dad has been texting me with updates on my mom. She's stable and doing well, still receiving oxygen and incredibly fatigued, but hasn't taken a turn for the worst. He says she seems to be in good spirits today, even with her sickness and exhaustion. *Thank God.*

I let Clay know how my mom is doing. He smiles as he runs a comb through his hair. "That's great news! Let's hope she makes a full recovery without complications." Clay looks over at me and seems to be gauging how I'm doing. "Would you be okay if I go home until tonight's shift? I have some things I need to get done, and need to connect online with the fam."

"Of course."

"Keep me posted on how your mom's doing, and if you need me for any reason, don't hesitate to call and I'll be right over. I can be over within five minutes if you need me."

"Thank you, Clay. For everything."

He pulls me close to him and I rest in his arms. Little rivulets of water are dripping on me, traveling down from his hairline, and I giggle. "What are you giggling at?" His tone is good-natured and light.

"I'm having another shower right now."

"Oh really? You know you want one, don't you?" He laughs as he shakes his hair to try and get me wet, but I scoot down the hallway. He runs after me, and catches me from behind, rubbing his damp hair on me. He swings me around, my legs flying outward.

"Stop!" I'm dying with laughter and so is he. He stops and we take a breather. I don't remember the last time I've laughed so hard. Life has been so somber, morose. But laughter is very freeing, and I don't feel as wound up with tension anymore.

"Alright. I'm headed out and will see you soon. Try to stay out of trouble, Trouble." He winks at me, flashing me a goodbye smile, then leaves.

That afternoon, I make some calls and get in contact with mental health at the hospital. I book an appointment with a therapist for later in the week. Although I'm feeling okay right now, the amount of stress and my physical reactions over the last few days are sure signs I need to get in to see someone.

Seeing a therapist on and off over the years has been incredibly helpful for me. I was prompted to see my first therapist by my parents during the time I was dating Geoff. I started becoming moody, my grades were slipping, and my self esteem was at an all time low.

It was at that time I learned how to trace back my feelings to their origin. I learned how to use a process called CBT, Cognitive Behavioral Therapy. That's when I discovered that Geoff was the one eroding my self worth, and that it was a toxic relationship for me.

Therapy enabled me to see I could stand on my own two feet again. Boy was Geoff pissed, when he could no longer manipulate me through guilt or by triggering feelings of low self esteem. He was frantic when he lost control over me, to the point where his behavior was becoming more and more erratic and his displays of anger were spilling out when other people were around.

I think back to that time, over four years ago. "Geoff, I'm going to kindly ask you to leave." Geoff was looking back at me wild-eyed in disbelief, as my father firmly escorted him out of our family home.

The argument had started shortly after Geoff arrived, in the entryway of all places. He'd made a snide comment, a subtle putdown, and I stood up for myself. Geoff became irate, and not realizing my father was in his home office, his behavior started getting out of control. It wasn't his first time becoming explosive, just the first time my father had witnessed such an extreme outburst of Geoff's anger. It was at that point my parents realized what had been going on behind the scenes. I finally broke down and shared with them the things I'd kept secret for months, thinking they wouldn't understand.

Although Geoff hadn't physically harmed me, he was becoming more forceful and controlling, and it was apparent to my parents that things were headed in that direction. They supported me fully as I made a clean break with him, and my dad made it clear to him that he wasn't to approach me again.

Therapy helped me to get through it, and to reclaim my life. In the same way, therapy helped me through my aunt's illness and to come to terms with her passing. And I am sure it will help me now.

My phone rings, and I see it's Violet. "Hi, Vi."

"Oh, Karly, I'm so sorry to hear about your mom. I called as soon as I could." I had texted Violet a couple of hours before, but I'm unsure when her shifts are, so wasn't expecting her to call right away. "How is she doing?"

"She's doing okay in the regular COVID ward. Dad says she seems to be in good spirits regardless."

"That sounds like your mom. She's always so positive. Hang in there, Karly. She's an incredibly strong person." I can hear a flurry of activity in the background, and urgent voices. "Have to run—I'm needed in the ER. Keep me posted." Violet ends the call. She's right, my mom is a very strong person, as I've seen over the course of my life, and she's a fighter.

During the evening, I reflect on my performance in the ICU, and review what I want to achieve. *Lately, I feel like I've been a liability to my team. I want to go back to being a valuable asset.*

Although I've felt like a burden to my team this week, I know it's because of extenuating circumstances. Exhausting myself to the point of burnout, the emotional stress of the job, finding out my mom has COVID, and life stress in general have all built up to overwhelm me.

At least I'm now getting proper sleep, thanks to Clay's "Intervention". I'm taking steps to get more self-care: sleeping at home, booking an appointment with a therapist, and opening up to people around me again. I didn't realize how closed off I'd become.

I make myself a nice dinner, then begin preparing for the night shift. When everything is ready, I sit down to chill for a bit with the movie "How to Lose a Guy in 10 Days." The movie takes my mind off things for a while. I think about some of the romantic comedies I've seen, and think about how getting the lines of communication crossed can spell disaster. *I wonder if I should explain to Clay all the reasons why I reacted the way I did, when I distanced myself from him. Or should I just leave it?*

I've never gone into detail with him about my relationship with Geoff. Clay knew that Geoff and I were an item way back, but he doesn't know the reason why I broke things off. *Maybe Clay would understand better why I freaked out and pushed him away. My trust crumbled away during my experience with Geoff, and although I've been healing, it's still fragile. I also have such a fear of losing what Clay and I have together.*

But it might be better to let sleeping dogs lie. *Clay probably wouldn't want to discuss it anyway. I saw the look of pain in his eyes. It would likely do more harm than good.* I decide not to approach the subject with him since things seem to be going smoothly between us after I insisted we keep our boundaries. However, if he brings it up, then I'm open to talking about why it's so important to me.

The realization hits me. *I trust him more than I've trusted anyone for a long time. He's so caring and considerate, and goes out of his way to help me. He hasn't let me down so far, and every day we grow closer to each other.*

The thought about staying away from the subject is reinforced when I check my email later that evening and see "Guess who" with the subject line "Song about us". I cautiously open it.

Pushing me away.

The song is "Apologize" by OneRepublic. Given my current situation with Clay, I feel like I've been slapped in the face.

I loved you with a fire red now it's turning blue,

And you say sorry like the angel heaven let me think was you.

But I'm afraid it's too late to apologize, it's too late.

By the last chorus of the song, the tears won't stop flowing. The guilt comes pouring back as I think about how I pushed Clay away. *I know I messed things up with him. Does he really forgive me deep down? Or will those pained feelings of rejection I see in his eyes always be there?*

I give myself a dose of self-talk while I shake my head. *The email isn't from Clay. It just happens to fit how I fear he feels about me, in the middle of this mess we're in right now.*

But then in my upset emotional state a disturbing train of thought hits me. *Or could these emails actually be from him?* I breathe in sharply. *Could he have lied to me?* I stare at the email on my screen as the song ends, and my eyes blur over and my lower lip trembles.

I wipe my tears away and my eyes start to refocus. I lean forward to have a closer look at the message, and quickly inhale, then hold my breath. I release it as a huge sense of relief hits me. I realize what it is that's been bothering me in the back of my mind since I received the previous emails. In small print, at the end of the email, it says "Sent from my iPhone". *But I know that Clay has a Samsung.*

The revelation hits me more clearly. Clay's not the one who's been sending me the emails. That I can now be sure of. I realize my fragile sense of trust has been teetering over the edge again, making me unsure, and susceptible to doubting the word of others. Making me doubt one of my closest friends.

Oh no. I had already pushed him away, partly because the emails had become so disturbing, and I was just about to again—all because of my trust issues. *I need to focus on facts. I know for sure Clay isn't the one sending me these emails because he has a different phone.* I wipe my face with my hands, catching the residual moisture left by my tears.

I think about the email itself and wonder if it's some unknown creep, or if it's someone I know who's been sending the messages. I don't know what to think. Between the intermittent emails, phone call, and note left at the hospital, there definitely is more to this than randomness. Could someone actually be stalking me? But if they are, why have they targeted me specifically? It's not like I'm a celebrity or anyone noteworthy. *Please just be random pranksters. I have too much stress in my life to deal with anything else right now.* But I have a sinking feeling this is more than just pranking.

I start to question myself about Clay and have a growing feeling of desperation. I know I've pushed him away because I've been afraid. *But he's the one I want.* The thought startles me as I feel a jolt that brings me out of my denial. If only I was willing to try again at some point. My finger and thumb pinch the bridge of my nose while I hash this out in my mind. I don't know what to do, I'm so confused. But then I remember the boundary called Samantha. My heart sinks. I don't know if that boundary makes me feel relieved or regretful. Maybe a bit of both?

And now with this song in my head… *Is it "too late"? I pushed him away because I was scared. Has he shut out the possibility of romantic feelings for me and looking for that elsewhere?* Although I don't know their relationship status, I know Samantha's pretty set on him. And she's a flawless beauty, so perfect. *He'd have to be crazy, or crazy for someone else, to not go for her.*

I sigh audibly. Clay has my head spinning and these emails are messing with my head. On top of that, with mom being ill… Well, I feel like a total wreck—frustrated, full of apprehension, and afraid. My mind is all over the place. I'm a ball of anxiety, or a spring so wound up that the pressure is too much for me to handle. I'm just overwhelmed by everything going on in my life.

I put my elbows on my desk, head in my hands. I allow myself to cry angry, hot tears. After a while I just feel sadness. Then I lift my head and breathe deeply. I know that a lot of what I feel is due to what I've experienced at the hospital, triggered by current things in my life. I need to find a better way to deal with the emotional stress that comes with my job.

My mind goes back to personal things in my life. Namely my love life...or I should say my *non-existent* love life. *If I told Clay my reasons for pushing him away, how would he really react? Life is so short—I see our human mortality every day. Maybe I owe it to both of us to at least try to have a conversation about that night.*

I receive a text from my dad, just a quick update on mom's condition, which is the same as the last update. No change. Her lung x-rays look decent, so that's a relief. I text the info to those who've asked me to keep them updated on her status. The rest of the afternoon whips by, and I try to keep myself distracted so I don't dig myself into a deep, depressing, emotional hole.

When Clay drops by to pick me up for the night shift, I feel very nervous. I can tell Clay senses my tension, because he keeps things formal on the surface. Otherwise, we drive in silence.

"Soooo, what's on your mind, Karly? You seem awfully quiet this evening."

"I've just been thinking a lot about things in general, my life, my relationships, you."

Clay arches his brow. "Well now I'm intrigued. What have you been thinking about me?"

"Life's so short, and I owe it to you to tell you why I reacted the way I did a few weeks ago."

Clay's face contains subtle evidence of pain, but he's careful to hide it. "It's okay, Karly. No need to explain. We're all good." Clay looks over at me and smiles.

"No, I want to explain." Clay drives in silence, waiting for me to continue.

I take a deep breath. "I was afraid." Then I sigh, as if I'm releasing a build-up of emotional energy. Keeping my eyes forward, staring at the road ahead of us, I begin to share my thoughts and feelings with Clay. "I was in a relationship a while back…"

"Geoff?"

I nod my head. "He seemed like the nicest guy at first. He even won over my parents." I take a breath before I continue. "During the relationship he eroded my self esteem, demeaned me as a person." The muscles in Clay's face tighten as I see his jaw clench.

"At first it was with backhanded compliments which made me feel insecure about myself. Then later it became more direct. It was so gradual, that I didn't realize what was happening. I'm fortunate I was only in a relationship with him for a year, but the damage it did to my self worth was real."

"That was during the year I transferred in. I remember how vibrant you were during first semester, and how desolate you seemed later. I thought it was due to the break up. I had no idea what you were really going through."

I stop Clay, my hand touching his arm. "Wait a sec. You remember me? From undergrad?" All I remember was struggling through that year with Geoff, then the extra year it took me to get back on my feet. My studies hung in the balance, and I was an emotional wreck.

"Of course. How could I have not noticed you? You were the prettiest girl I'd ever seen, so full of life." As Clay turns towards me and gives my arm a light squeeze of comfort, I see that his eyes hold a tenderness I've not seen in them before. "And you've become such a beautiful, capable woman." I feel a bit choked up at his words and the sincerity with which he's spoken them.

We pull into the hospital parking lot, put on our masks, and walk to the entrance. I can tell Clay is processing what I've just shared with him. I surprisingly feel better now that I've talked to him about things. *One of the main differences between Clay and Geoff, is that Clay builds me up instead of tearing me down.* That's when I realize I should be looking at the differences between the two of them, not the similarities. I should be evaluating differences in character, instead of assuming that every man is the same, and will hurt me the way Geoff did.

The shift that night is a particularly difficult one, with two deaths in the ICU. Both patients had been with us for over a month, and it's difficult to see those under your care pass away like that. We did all we could for them, but it was still not enough. In the end, I held one patient's hand while the priest said last rites over the video call with the family.

I feel a helplessness wash over me. Like we're fighting a war with only the info at the tip of an iceberg, and the rest of the iceberg of information is vital to our survival, but hidden from us. But that doesn't make it any less deadly.

It's so true. Many governments saw the tip of the COVID iceberg, but instead of altering course, thought they could sail right past it. They believed that the iceberg would "miraculously disappear". *Politically driven asses. We're being continuously assaulted by waves of this disease, but all they care about is their political standing. And it's not like they're doing a quality job, it's mediocre at best. They're completely ego-driven, and people are suffering because of it.*

At the end of my shift, I search for Clay, which is odd because he usually finds me first. I stop short as I hear his voice and Samantha's in the break room. They laugh about something, and I feel a pang of jealousy shoot through me. *I did this to myself, when I pushed him away.*

I take a deep breath and walk into the room. Samantha is stroking his left arm while giggling at some private joke they've shared. I feel annoyed. To be fair and to his credit, although Samantha is hanging all over him, I do notice he makes no move to reciprocate her advances. He has a friendly aura around him, and I can't tell if there's anything more there.

Clay turns to face the door, and his eyes seem to light up when I enter the room. He cracks a big smile, one side of his mouth higher than the other. That lopsided grin threatens to steal my heart.

"Well I'm off. See ya." Clay addresses Samantha and she gives him an adorable pout.

"See you Wednesday, Clay." She gives him a cute little wave. My heart sinks, because Wednesday is our day off.

I try to hold back from saying anything, but my curiosity gets the better of me as we exit the hospital. "So what's up on Wednesday?" Clay gives me a guarded glance as we walk to the car. My heart sinks even lower, since he won't talk about it. We've never really talked about current relationships with other people, and I'm guessing this is the new norm. He wants some semblance of privacy, so it's his turn to set boundaries. We walk in silence.

"Rough shift, hey?"

I nod. "I was with one of the patients as she passed this morning."

Clay looks down at me and puts his hand on my lower back in concern. "You alright?"

I nod. We arrive at the car and he's about to open my door for me, but instead he draws me into a hug and holds me, rocking me slightly, side to side. I feel such a heaviness, a sadness. Usually an embrace from Clay lifts me, helps me feel as though I'm not alone and that others will share life's burdens with me.

But this time the tears flow, and I feel such a pang of heartbreak. Not only am I grieving from the painful shift and loss of patients, I'm now grieving the loss of "what could have been" with Clay. *I'm too late. I pushed him away, and now he's pulling away from me.*

I know our friendship will change after this. I'm losing my closest friend who I've been through thick and thin with, in a time of world turmoil. We've weathered this horrible tragedy together, supporting one another through the many losses in our work. *I should have allowed myself to trust him. I should have let him in.* As the words go through my head, I think of what my dad would say to them.

"'Should' is not a word in your life dictionary. It means you've failed. Instead, substitute it with the word 'could' which means you can learn from your experience. Otherwise, you'll carry regrets with you throughout your life, burdens you don't need to carry." I change my self-talk. *I could have allowed myself to trust him. I could have let him in.* And following my father's principle, I am determined to learn from my experience. If there's ever another chance with Clay... But now is the time for me to let go.

The tears I shed no longer come because of the agony of loss; they are a washing of my soul. They are clearing out all the mistrust, the hurt and heartache, and the fear that have kept me hostage all these years. For the first time I feel hope for the future, whatever it may bring my way. I vow to be true to myself, and to unravel the intricate veil of defense mechanisms that has forced me to lie to myself for self-protection. I'm determined to set one foot in front of the other, and create a pathway for myself.

I'm now ready to let Clay go. I sniffle, then pull away from his chest and smile up at him. He's still holding me gently, and I can see the care and compassion in his eyes. This wonderful man will always have a place in my heart. He cherishes all those around him, and cares deeply for them.

"Thank you, Clay." He rests his face on my head for a minute, then opens the car door for me. We both climb into the car, and I open the glove box, searching for a tissue. *No tissues there.* My mind barely registers that there's an iPhone sitting in Clay's glove box.

He pulls out a pack of tissues, and I'm distracted when he starts dabbing my face. I laugh. "I can do that, Silly." I playfully push his hand away. I grab the box of tissues, and dry my face and blow my nose. We listen to music on the way home, and when I say goodbye to Clay, I feel like I've been lifted out of the depths, and ready to face the rest of the day. But first it's naptime for me.

Anonymous
Afternoon. Tues., Aug. 3, 2021

The desolation and frustration inside me just keeps building. *Why did she push me away like that? The better question is why did I let her push me away? I should be fighting for what's mine, what we could have together.* I feel angry with Karly over her rejection, but also angry with myself for letting her push me away. The chasm between us might as well be miles.

Women have always thrown themselves at me, but it doesn't matter. They hold no interest for me. All I want is Karly. She's the only one I've wanted for years. She makes me feel alive, and awakens feelings inside me that I barely recognize. Intense feelings of want and desire. Every time I walk by her in the hospital, when I work beside her—it all just adds to the tension I feel. I feel like I'm going to explode if I don't act on it.

I sip my hot coffee and make a face. It's bittersweet, which characterizes my entire experience with Karly. Her rejection is paramount and the anger keeps building up inside me. *When will this charade end? More importantly,* how *will it end?*

Karly

Evening. Tues., Aug. 3, 2021

I'm awakened in the early evening by the beeping of my phone. It's a text from my dad. "Mom's condition is the same, she's on antiviral meds. Katie and I have been cleared—our second tests were also negative. Love you."

I breathe a sigh of relief. *I don't have to worry about my dad or Katie anymore. Mom's doing okay.* But I know how quickly things can go downhill with this virus, so I still need to cope with that pocket of anxiety within me.

After doing some adulting, I settle down to browse Netflix, and have a quiet evening. I try to settle the anxiety within me, and dive into The Lord of the Rings trilogy. I usually watch the whole series through once a year, and right now I need the respite from my internal and external burdens.

I get through The Fellowship of the Ring during the evening, but am too tired to go on to The Two Towers. I yawn and decide to get to bed. *I'll watch the other two movies tomorrow. That will force me to physically rest on my day off, and take my mind off whatever Clay's up to with Samantha.*

Time flies by on my day off, as I binge-watch the remaining eight hours of the LOTR trilogy. I decide to go for a run, since the evening is so nice. I shower and have dinner, lasagna using a fresh pasta roll, that I had made and frozen ahead of time. Then I spend the remainder of the evening reading a mystery novel on my apartment balcony, enjoying the nice summer weather. *Today has been a day just for me.* I feel relaxed, well rested and rejuvenated, ready to tackle the remainder of the week.

Morning. Thurs., Aug. 5, 2021

The next morning, Clay picks me up for work. He's oddly quiet, but is still the polite gentleman I know. In contrast to how I feel, ready and raring to go, Clay looks exhausted, maybe even a bit morose? It takes all my willpower to not pry.

But willpower alone isn't enough. I suddenly blurt out the words. "So how was yesterday?"

Clay gives me that guarded look as he looks over at me. "It was good." He doesn't give anything away with his expression or his eyes. Then he turns on some soft tunes. He clearly doesn't want to talk.

Things are already hectic when we arrive at the ICU. Although we're finally starting to flatten the curve due to social distancing measures, it won't curb our workload for weeks to come, since we are the "last line of defense" for COVID patients.

I run into Maggie in the hallway. "Karly, you're looking well."

"Thanks, Maggie. I'm feeling tons better. You're looking great yourself."

Maggie smiles at me and squeezes my shoulder as I walk by. It's so wonderful to work with supporting, caring people. *This tragedy has brought out the best in so many people. I've been a witness to true humanity, the default of human nature.* I prep for rounds, and although things have been hectic already this morning, I feel at peace. I'm at peace with myself, and with the universe.

Today is a monumental day. Jaime has been extubated and will be moved to the regular COVID ward. He responded as well as could be hoped to the treatment, and he is one of the few that will eventually go home. Over a period of months, he will be able to reclaim his life as he recovers. The thought gives me joy, and brings tears to my eyes.

All those who leave the ward, mostly under sadder circumstances, either through death or a transfer to a long-term care facility, will be remembered by those of us who work here. *We are the ones who sit with the patients, looking after their basic needs, easing their discomfort, acting as family, since family can't visit. We provide them with human touch and comforting words, even though they may never remember due to their sedation or coma.*

It's a terrifying job, playing such a spiritual role in these patients' lives. Physically caring for them while trying to touch their souls. I pray that my connections with my patients have been meaningful in some way. Some will never wake up, and ours is the last connection with humanity they will ever have. But days like this one, when Jaime takes his first step towards going home, fill my heart to the fullest. Although Jaime will never remember his time in the ICU, I will always remember him.

The day flies by, with updates from my dad regarding Mom's condition. She's still stable, but needing some oxygen to boost blood levels. She's in good spirits as usual. As long as I can remember, she's always been positive. She's an optimist to the core. I feel very much that way today. It's like I experienced some type of epiphany a couple of days ago. My mind cleared and the shadows that have been haunting me for so long have dissipated.

I rush past Clay later in the afternoon. He really does look exhausted. He looks up from the chart he's examining, smiles and nods. We both continue our separate ways. *This is a foreshadowing of things to come. Ships passing in the night. But I'm okay with it now. I may have lost him, but ultimately he deserves happiness and fulfillment, regardless of who he is with.* A pang of sadness threatens to choke me up, but I breathe deeply and focus on the future. *I'm no longer in shackles and life has been breathed into me for the first time in years.*

Things wind down in the early evening, and dinners have been delivered today, by one of the local restaurants in coordination with volunteers. I head into the break room, and to my surprise, I've arrived when they are still hot. I usually have to microwave them because I'm too busy with duties.

I sit at the break table, and open the styrofoam container. *Veal parmigiana! Wow!* I begin eating this amazing meal, savoring the flavors and texture with every bite. I'm usually a fast eater—comes with the territory—but I'm determined to enjoy every mouthful. Halfway through my meal, Samantha drops in. "Mind if I join you?" She takes a meal from the counter.

"Sure. Go ahead." I gesture to the empty seat. We eat together, talking about patients, upcoming changes in provincial health policy, and the pandemic in general.

I'm floored by what she says next. "Clay was amazing yesterday."

Huh? The thing is, there's no hint of maliciousness, like she's trying to rub anything in or flaunt her relationship with him. But my zen has been shattered.

Samantha goes on to praise Clay. "He definitely has a magical touch..."

Is she just clueless? Or does she usually talk like this about her relationships? I don't know how to respond. *Ohhh, maybe she thinks of me as a girlfriend she can confide in.* I tune her out, nodding at the appropriate spots, and can't wait to get out of the break room and out of the conversation.

Then she starts talking about Dr. Jamar and how the two of us would make a cute couple. I'm cringing, not just because of her flippant attitude, but in memory of Dr. Jamar's reaction when I politely refused to go for drinks with him. Since that time there has been underlying tension in our professional relationship. I don't think he was too pleased with my refusal.

She jumps from subject to subject like a Mexican jumping bean. But she always bounces back into discussion about Clay. She's obviously infatuated with him. I politely say goodbye, in disbelief of what I've just heard about her relationship with Clay.

Regardless of my resolve to live my future not based on my past, I feel almost a fury build up inside me. *I really thought Clay was starting to have feelings for me that night weeks ago.* It feels like a lifetime ago. *They obviously weren't serious feelings if he could easily go from me to Samantha in such a short time. Maybe I misread him and pushed him away for nothing. And the way she talked about him…*

I don't know whether to grit my teeth or to sigh in resignation that my self esteem has taken another serious blow. *I wasn't really that important to him that way, maybe not at all. Again it's my fault for pushing him away and running. Another casualty of that ugly thing known as fear. But I need to just let it go.*

That evening, Clay and I listen to music on the way home. I'm not interested in talking, and he looks too exhausted to even make conversation. He lets me out at my apartment. "Goodnight." Clay doesn't look back as he jumps in the car and drives away.

So it's going to be like this from now on, is it? I sigh audibly as I make my way to my apartment. Even with my resolve, my thoughts and emotions keep ping-ponging all over the place. *I'm glad I have a therapy appointment tomorrow. Hopefully that will help me regain my sanity.*

CHAPTER EIGHT

Clay

Morning. Tues., Aug. 10, 2021

We're in the middle of great global difficulty, but it only motivates me to work harder. A lot of the front-line healthcare workers are exhausted, run-down, and have seen terrible tragedy. I'd like to think that it hasn't affected me as heavily, but to be honest with myself, it's hit me hard. But this is what I trained for, what I decided a long time ago to devote my life to—taking care of the well-being of others.

Another one of the doctors at the hospital has taken ill with the coronavirus, so I've stepped up, and am taking on as many extra shifts as I can manage. It's exhausting me completely, but it's my turn to step up and try to make a difference. Immersing myself in my work has kept me sharp and focused, and doesn't give me time to dwell on the situation with Karly. It gives me a break from coping with conflicting feelings.

Although the physical exhaustion is something I had expected upon graduation and becoming an intern, I didn't expect it to be so difficult emotionally. But then, when I entered med school I never expected we'd be hit by a pandemic, and illness with such a high fatality rate. This pandemic is so contagious, has a worrisome death toll, and has incapacitated patients and made them gravely ill. It's like nothing I ever expected to see in my lifetime, at least not in Canada. I've thought about participating in Doctors Without Borders or with another organization at some point that deals with third world countries with higher threats of contagious diseases. But I feel like I'm dealing with that type of urgent situation right here, right now.

So I work, then sleep, and make sure I remember to eat when I can. I've taken to carrying around trail mix in my bag during the day, since I usually don't have time to take breaks during my shifts. I know the craziness is just temporary, and that we'll all get through this. The general infection rate has fallen, and if we've really passed the peak of the wave, it's just a matter of time until the cases in the ICU start declining again.

Karly
Afternoon. Fri., Sept. 10, 2021

Days have flown by, and we know now that the third wave has definitely peaked and we're on the other side. The numbers of hospital cases have been declining as we go into the fall, and we no longer have as many patients in the ICU CURA beds. A couple of doctors who were off sick due to COVID are now back.

I have another online therapy appointment with Dr. Mazik. I'm very comfortable with her, and she is helping me to gain insight into my thoughts, feelings, and actions. I talk about the possibility of entering into a future relationship at some point, in light of my previous experience with Geoff.

I waffle back and forth for part of the session, feeling unsure, and lacking confidence in my decision-making. I know it's partly because of the decisions I made in the past regarding dating Geoff, and partly because he brought out so much self-doubt in me. That self-doubt is resurfacing as we discuss moving forward and the possibility of entering into a future relationship. I express my feelings of self-doubt to the therapist.

"Well, one thing to consider, is that the next time you consider a relationship with someone, you'll be going in 'with your eyes open'."

"What do you mean?"

"When things happened with Geoff, he conditioned you gradually to accept his abuse, whereas next time you know what signs to watch for."

"True." As we continue to talk through the session, I start to feel reassured. I get to the point where I feel I might be ready to try entering into a relationship, and that it could be different this time.

"Just remember. If the relationship constantly triggers a lot of negative feelings, then it might not be healthy. Especially if it causes you to view yourself in a negative light."

I nod my head, feeling a bit more confident, as I reflect. "But if it's the opposite and builds me up over the long-term, then it's a different situation." Then I suddenly feel deflated, as I remember the current situation. "There's another issue."

"What's that?"

"I think the person I'm interested in may have moved on and might be with someone else now." It hurts to think about it.

"Well, you've said you're good friends with this person and know them well. What approach do you think would be best for you to take?"

"When we don't talk about stuff, things tend to build up and create a wall between us. When we talk about issues, the tension clears. Our best times together are when we've been open and honest with each other." I think about when I explained to Clay about why I'd pushed him away. "It's emotionally freeing." After the session, I feel the need to clear the air with Clay so we can move forward in our friendship.

Morning. Tues., Sept. 14, 2021

Clay and I have finished working the night shift. We're on our way home.

"Hey, you need groceries or anything?" I think he might just be asking out of politeness, so I hesitate to answer. "I need groceries myself, so want to go with me?" Clay smiles at me cautiously.

"You're sure it's not too much trouble?"

"None at all."

"Okay, let's go together." Clay looks relieved for some reason.

Later we arrive back at my apartment, and go through the old routine. Clay seems to be enjoying putting my groceries away, then decides to play barista, like he did the first time he helped me get groceries. This is the first time in a while things have felt like the "old normal" for us, and I wonder if I've completely misread something or am just cuckoo for coco puffs.

We sit down for coffee, and for the first conversation we've had in what feels like ages. We're away from the whirlwind that is the ICU, and finally have a chance at a decent conversation.

"So how is your mom doing?"

"She's doing well, actually. Dad thinks she'll be discharged soon and able to recover at home. He's going to move into the trailer in the driveway so he can continue working at Oakville Hospital, and Katie will look after Mom in the house."

"That's great news, Karly. I know she gave you quite a scare."

"Well my fears from my last experience with my aunt carried over. I've been trying to face my fears from the past as I step into the future." Clay nods thoughtfully at me, as though what I just said holds particular significance for him.

"So anything new?"

"Well, I started seeing a therapist after I found out my mom had COVID. She's helping me sort out my head a bit." I smile at Clay as I sip my hot drink. "So what about you? Anything new you want to share?" I double-wink at Clay, but he looks at me oddly.

"Nothing really. Family's good—we're in touch online like yours is. Nothing's changed since we last talked about stuff."

"Oh come on, Clay, you don't have to hide it. I know about the two of you."

"Wha...?" Clay looks thoroughly confused.

"You and Samantha? Dating? It sounds like you've been up to... a lot." I say 'a lot' because the alternate words feel as though they are poison. I want to keep the conversation amiable. I want openness with Clay but feel impatient, and though I try I can't keep annoyance out of my voice. As a result, I give off mixed signals. Clay just looks at me, bewildered.

"You've been seeing a lot of each other. Don't bother denying it, Silly." Although my words are light, I know I'm speaking more forcefully than I mean to. My tone has a tinge of bitterness to it, since there is so much emotion packed behind my words.

Clay looks at me as though I've grown a second head. He's hesitant when he responds. "I don't know what she's told you, but the only place I ever see Samantha or ever will see her in the future is at work."

Now it's now my turn to be confused. "Then why all the secrecy?"

"The secrecy?" He looks confused at my question. I can see when it suddenly dawns on him what this is all about. The look on his face confuses me even more. "Karly. I've been taking extra shifts at the hospital because they're so short-staffed."

"What?" I speak slowly as I'm trying to process what he's saying. "Then why hide it from me?"

"You overdid things. Remember when you were sleeping at the hospital, barely getting three hours sleep a night?"

I feel my face flush. Looking back, I feel a bit sheepish.

"Well I wasn't about to let you know there were other shifts that needed filling. After your fainting spell and then the news about your mom, the whole team was reluctant to say anything, since we knew your anxiety was through the roof and you'd just keep working yourself to death."

There's a pause in the conversation as we both process things cognitively. I can see the wheels turning in Clay's mind as he sorts things out. For that matter, I can feel my own wheels turning, trying to process new information.

"Is that why you were so exhausted all the time?"

"Karly, for a while there, I was sure I was a zombie and not really alive. I was dead on my feet."

All the silence, the distance, most of it makes sense now. "What about the times you saw Samantha? They were only when you were working at the hospital?"

"Yes, we had some overlapping shifts."

It dawns on me that I misconstrued a lot of what Samantha had said to me in conversation, so it fit what I suspected was happening between her and Clay. But nothing had ever happened between them. "I thought you were falling for her." My voice is soft.

Clay shakes his head, like I don't 'get it'. "No, you don't understand, Karly." Clay runs his hand through his hair, as if he's exasperated. He closes his eyes, then seems to have made a decision. He opens them again. His blue eyes search mine, and Clay seems to settle on something he sees in them. "I just need to know one thing. Are you going to shut me out again? Because if there's any chance you will, then we're not going to have this conversation." I can see he's dead serious.

I'm curious, interested, and intrigued, all rolled up into one. "It's okay, Clay. I promise I won't shut you out."

"Promise? No matter what I say?"

"No matter what you say. However, things could get really complicated if you're about to admit that you're an axe murderer."

He laughs, and then smirks. "Well, the axe isn't my first choice of weapon..."

I fake-slap his arm and he scoots back and off his stool in pretend avoidance. "You goofball." We both laugh as we have a light moment. It feels like old times. I take our empty coffee cups and place them in the sink.

I pick up the conversation from where we were a few minutes ago. "Okay, so you said you aren't falling for Samantha. I'm surprised—she's gorgeous, and seems so perfect."

Clay is shaking his head. He looks at me, eyes piercing to the depths of my soul. Suddenly, I flush. I feel so naked in front of him, as though my soul has been stripped bare. Clay's hands come up and they cup the sides of my face. He strokes my cheeks with his thumbs, and brings his face close to mine. We touch foreheads. "Karly." Clay whispers my name. "It's impossible for me to fall for anyone."

I feel a bit confused, wondering about all the reasons why he can't fall for anyone. *No way! He's not about to say he's sworn to celibacy or something like that, is he?*

Clay walks over the window, then back. He looks like he's trying to formulate what to say. He stops in front of me, encloses my hands with his, and looks down at them. He then tilts his head, and focuses on my eyes, as though he's trying to make a final decision, what to say. I clear my mind of speculation, and gaze up into his eyes in silence. I know this is an important moment, and I hold my breath.

Clay speaks softly. "The reason why it's impossible for me to fall for anyone. It's because I'm in love with YOU, Karly. It's always been you." I see Clay's eyes searching mine, but the full impact of his words hasn't hit me yet. I'm still not comprehending what he's just said to me.

Finally I have a delayed reaction to his earlier words. I feel shock rippling through me as I stand there, stunned. Clay's confession of love has completely blindsided me. My mouth is open, and I look like a guppy.

"I've wanted to date you for years. But you were in a relationship, and later I didn't want to be the rebound guy. When we hit med school, both of us were swamped."

I'm still trying to process everything. *I thought he was interested in Samantha. She's beautiful, perfect in every way. How could this amazing man be interested in me to this extent, let alone fall in love with me? He did just say that, didn't he? That he's in love with me?*

I stand there, not knowing what to say. My mind is blank, and even if it wasn't, my mouth wouldn't be able to form words anyway. But it doesn't matter that I can't form words, because suddenly, Clay's mouth is on mine. I find myself falling into his kiss, his gentle, but persistent kiss. He releases my lips for a moment, as he looks hesitantly into my eyes, then kisses me gently again. He draws my body close to his, holding me close.

I can now feel his love, an echo of his passion, as the kiss becomes something deeper. It's as though a dam has sprung a leak, but he's holding back the torrent of water behind the wall. Clay's lips slowly stop, and he softly kisses me on my nose, then my forehead, before pulling me into his chest. He holds me close to him, his hand stroking my back, rocking me slightly.

"Karly." I can feel his voice rumble in his chest. "You don't know what you mean to me. What you do to me." After a few minutes in his arms, I lean backwards from his chest. His face changes and looks unsure as he searches my eyes. Then he sees the reassurance he's been looking for. His thumb strokes the corner of my mouth.

"Then show me." I look up at him through my long, thick lashes. Clay tilts my chin up, and touches his nose to mine. He cradles the back of my head, and sweeps his lips over mine, teasing me. His lips settle on mine again, and his tongue gently flickers, causing my lips to part.

This time, I can feel the dam crumbling, as his passion starts flowing more intensely. I'm carried away in the rush of it all, being drawn downstream. Then suddenly I'm drowning in his kiss, and I don't know which end is up. Clay cups my bottom with his hands and lifts me up, and my legs instinctively wrap around him, as he carries me and lays me down gently on the couch. He kneels on the floor, and brushes a tendril of hair behind my left ear as he continues to lean over and kiss me.

Clay undoes my top button while tracing his lips down my jawbone, sweeping them onto my neck. His left hand is underneath my neck, and his right arm wraps around my left side and underneath my back as I lay on the couch. *I feel so secure, wrapped up in his love.*

He pulls on the collar of my shirt slightly so he can get to my collarbone, and traces his lips along it, peppering me with tiny kisses. Then he shifts position on the floor, moving his head further away so he can look at me. He brings his right hand up, and strokes my shoulder with his thumb.

Clay looks down at me. I can see his eyes are full of awe. "Let me look at you." He inhales sharply as his beautiful, blue eyes gaze down upon me. We both watch each other, in silence. "You are so beautiful. You are mesmerizing. I could stare at you for hours."

My eyes are wide as I look up at him. *I feel so vulnerable.* I don't understand why he feels this way about me, but I look into his eyes, and see my reflection. It's the love and care for me, mingled together with my reflection, which causes him to see me as he does.

This new step we've taken in our relationship, crossing a bridge that has brought me out of my denial, feels so natural. But it's also something so new and unexpected, that I'm thankful Clay isn't the type to rush things. We can just enjoy every moment of the "now".

PART TWO

CHAPTER NINE

Karly

Early Morning. Wed., October 13, 2021 (Day 1)

I walk from the ER into the stairwell, after assisting with a cardiac patient. Since the ICU has now eased up, I've been scheduled to take on a few 24 hour on-call shifts. Clay is concerned that I'll overdo things again, but I've promised to listen to him and heed his advice if I'm starting to look the worse for wear.

Canadian Thanksgiving was two days ago, but neither Clay nor I had time off. However, Katie sent over lots of leftovers, so we had our own little celebration the following day. Clay's parents would have sent something as well, but they're back west for a couple months, leaving Clay to drop by and look after things at their home.

The two of us recounted things we're thankful for, mainly for life itself and the health of our families. We've seen so much death in the COVID ICU and I have my own recent experiences with COVID threatening my family. Life is transient, and needs to be protected and cherished.

During our candle-lit dinner, Clay looked deeply into my eyes. "Karly, I propose a toast to us. I'm so thankful to have you in my life." We touched our wine glasses together as we shared our own private Thanksgiving dinner at my place on Tuesday.

However, before dinner had even ended, we were already in each other's embrace, sharing a gentle, romantic kiss. I was sitting sideways on his lap, my legs over one of his legs. His hands were stroking my hair and my hands gently cradled his cheeks. During our soft kiss, a heightened sensation of electricity ran through my body, swirling and building with each additional moment of our connection. Then Clay pulled me to his chest. I let out a gentle sigh. "Never let me go, Clay. I never want this feeling to end."

He held me more tightly, enveloping me in his arms, and kissed the top of my head to reassure me. "I'll never let you go, Sweetheart. Never." He touched his nose to mine, his face crinkled in a smile, then he planted a soft kiss on my forehead. It was a very special, intimate moment with Clay, the man I was falling more in love with every day.

Since Clay and I have different shifts, I'm now Ubering to work. It will be okay though, because we've been spending a lot of time together since our relationship transitioned a few weeks ago. I've told Clay he doesn't have to make up excuses to see me. I think that's what he had been doing before, in order to maintain contact with me. *It's so cute that he would do that.* I smile as I think about it.

We're still taking things carefully with our family members and friends, even though lockdown restrictions have been loosened. The threshold in our province is less than 200 new cases a day to bring a loosening of restrictions. Currently, we're at about 75 new cases a day in Ontario. But still, we want to be cautious overall and do our part to contain the virus, so it's not like we're going to house parties or anything that extreme. Just a small visit with my brother Mitch, or coffee at Vi's apartment.

Mom was released from the hospital a couple of weeks ago, and is recovering at home with Katie's assistance. She seems to be doing well, both physically and emotionally. She's one tough cookie, packed with optimism to boot. Although Dad is living in the trailer in the driveway, they have been spending time together, talking through the window from a distance. Dad should be moving back inside any day now.

I'm still smiling as I leave the stairwell, and walk down the hospital corridor towards the on-call room. I feel metallic smoothness in the indentation below my neck. Clay was so sweet, he gave me a silver heart locket and chain last week, with tiny photos of the two of us inside. He's definitely a romantic at heart.

I try to stifle a yawn, but am not very successful. It's been a long shift and it's now past the wee hours of Wednesday morning. I've been continually paged through the night to assist with internal medicine in different departments around the hospital. Now all I'm thinking of is getting a bit of shut-eye before the next call.

I walk into the on-call room, finally getting some time to lie down. *I hope I can get some sleep before I'm paged again.* I drop onto the small bed in the on-call room, kicking off my shoes, exhausted from the constant flurry of activity. Within a minute, I'm out cold.

Anonymous
Early Morning. Wed., October 13, 2021

Today's the day I take back control. I won't let her rule my life any longer.

At 6:30 am, I push the empty wheelchair along the corridor, until I reach the door I'm looking for. I check the hallway to verify no one's there, take out my set of hospital keys, careful not to jingle them, and quietly unlock the door. I enter with the wheelchair, and silently close the door behind myself.

I can hear Karly breathing evenly, so I know she is asleep. It takes a minute for my eyes to adjust to the darkness. My teeth are gnashed together, and I'm trying not to shake. It's time to steel myself and take action against the demons of my tormented psyche, once and for all.

Then I see her there, lying like an angel on the small bed. That switch flips again in my brain, and my breath catches. The song, "It's Too Late to Apologize" stops replaying in my head for the first time in weeks. Suddenly, my mind is quiet. It's the "push and pull"

that keeps us on the path to self-destruction. But what if I could eliminate that once and for all?

All my plans for her fly out of my head as I watch her sleep, looking so sweet and helpless. The words, "I saw an angel…of that I'm sure," from the song "You're Beautiful" pop into my head. The sentiment I feel is strong and overpowering. My drive for requital seeps out of me, and in its place I feel a softness.

I worry my lip with my teeth, going over things all at once in my head. I decide right then to diverge from my plan and go in a different direction. *Why merely evoke fear, when I can eventually have everything?* I move next to the bed, but my shoe squeaks on the floor. Suddenly, her eyes flutter open.

"Is someone th…?" But I dart to the head of the bed quickly enough and cut her off before her eyes can adjust to the lighting, smothering her with a chemical-dampened towel. She struggles against me, unsuccessfully. Her eyes, at first wide, eventually close, and she's now pliable.

I wheel the chair over, and gently lift her, placing her in it. I cover her with a blanket and gently manipulate a beanie with hair attached onto her head, similar to what some cancer patients wear. I drape the blanket around her shoulders and over the back of the wheelchair in a way that helps to keep her chest upright, even with her head sagging. I place a surgical mask over her face. I grab her personal items and place her bag underneath the blanket.

I quickly check the hallway before exiting with Karly in the wheelchair. She just looks like a sleepy patient, being wheeled from one department to another. With her remarkable eyes closed, different hair color and length, and her face and body covered, she is unrecognizable. I myself blend into the background as usual, in scrubs, mask, and surgical cap. I push the wheelchair into the elevator, keeping my head down as I hunch over, pretending to carefully observe the patient in my chair. We travel to the ground floor.

I go through the motions of adjusting the wheelchair, while waiting for the next person to enter the hospital. Then I walk Karly past security. The guard is too busy screening the newcomer to acknowledge me, and I continue out the door.

In the parkade, I load Karly into my vehicle, carefully laying her down on the back seat and buckling her in. Tinted windows will keep her out of sight. I fold the wheelchair and place it behind the back seat. I go to the driver's seat, throw on a jacket, buckle in, and swap my surgical cap for a red baseball cap. I drive out of the parkade after paying with cash.

I drive northeast on Eglinton, then southeast on Mississauga Rd. It's a good thing the trip is short, because Karly is starting to stir in the backseat. I peer backwards and see her shivering. That's to be expected with the inhalant I administered.

I pull into the garage, click the remote control so the door shuts, then rush to open Karly's door. After the door fully closes, I scoop her up easily, then head inside the house and downstairs with her. I can tell she's cramping up, and I grab the bucket I left downstairs just in time. I place it in front of her before she vomits. I kneel on the floor behind her, tuck the fake hair into her cap, and hold her body in a kneeling position over the bucket as she retches.

Karly

Morning. Wed., October 13, 2021

I'm disoriented, nauseated, and retching, kneeling in a dim room, on what feels like a tiled floor. My head feels like it's literally swimming, as my vision rotates and swings in a random pattern. I'm being held firmly from behind with one arm around my waist, and another has vertically been placed along my sternum, but I'm unrestricted enough to lean over the outline of a bucket as my stomach reacts. The large hand splayed on my chest is supporting me as I bend forward and throw up.

"Where am I?" I force the words out in between retches, but it comes out as a loud broken whisper. My throat feels cracked, and my head is pounding. I try to recall something, anything from earlier, but I can't wrap my head around anything, as things continue to spin and I feel nauseated. I start to panic.

"You're safe. Let's just get through this nausea," a voice whispers in my ear. I feel myself relax slightly.

Over the next hour, the cramping in my stomach lessens, and I stop retching. "Let me go, please," my throat is still dry and it almost sounds like I'm barking.

"I'm going to let go of you in a minute to get you some water and something to rinse your mouth out, okay?"

"Okay," I croak back. I'm gently set down so I'm sitting on the floor. I can finally feel the blood flowing back into my legs. As the sensation of pins and needles invades my legs, I'm beginning to feel like I've been bruised from all the kneeling. My head is still swimming, and the pounding hasn't let up. I close my eyes and wish the floor would swallow me up, put me out of my misery.

I'm handed a tiny cup with some green liquid in it. "Mouthwash," the man's voice whispers. I rinse my mouth out, gargle, and spit into the bucket. I repeat this a few times until the awful taste from before lessens.

"Water," he says, voice barely above a whisper as he hands me the glass. I gladly take it and swallow the soothing water. My throat feels cooled by it. "Would you like more?"

"Yes, please." My voice is still hoarse as I sit there panting. He walks over to the dresser where a half-full pitcher of water is sitting. I'm still feeling dehydrated, and I gulp down the first half of the next glass readily. Then my pace slows and I start to feel sluggish. The bit of clarity of thought I was regaining disappears completely.

Anonymous

Morning. Wed., October 13, 2021

Karly slumps into my arms within the next 15 minutes. I'm hoping that drugging her water will help her to forget the pain and discomfort I've had to put her through today to get her here. It's an odd thought, very ironic, considering all things. After seeing her earlier, inexplicable feelings of warmth and affection replaced the iciness and anger I've felt towards her. I never expected myself to react that way.

The irrepressible rage inside me had previously come to a head, after observing her so closely, especially recently. It had brought me to the point of wanting to torment her, just like she's been tormenting me, every day, for years. Years of wanting her, with only a temporary reprieve of her wanting me in return.

The last several weeks have driven me to the point where I couldn't stand it any longer. Losing her is not an option. But after seeing her lying there in the hospital on-call room, and shockingly being flooded with so much raw affection for her, I recalculated my position. I decided to approach this in a different way, and aim for a more satisfying and long-term result.

I carry Karly over to the hospital bed while she mumbles, and I lay her down softly on top of the blanket. I lie down behind her, and spoon her, wrapping my arm around her waist. She's talking to me, not quite incoherently but able to form words, and it endears her to me. I remove her cap, pull down my mask, and kiss her on the back of her hair. I then kiss her on the nape of her neck and stroke her hair. Feelings stir deep within me.

"I wish. I wish I was—a butterfly," Karly announces, and my mouth twitches.

"You do?" I whisper into her hair, then press my lips to her again.

"Yes. I can see colors in patterns swirling right now, but they're dark." She waves her hand in front of her face, as if she's trying to see it. "Oh, my wings must be covering up my hands." She hesitates. "Wait, maybe I don't have hands." She sounds as if she's in awe as she talks.

I sigh, feeling something akin to contentment for the first time in a long time. "Come closer little butterfly." I pull Karly right up against me.

"But I need to fly away." She squirms in my arms.

"Shhh," I whisper to her. I hold her tightly until she stops squirming. I feel her breathing slow down and become even, and I can tell she's drifted off to sleep. I could do anything I want, since I have complete control over her, and she's so helpless.

It's all about control, isn't it? But I desire something completely different from her than I did originally. I do know that after seeing her, I would rather *have* her fully, than have her merely be in fear of me. *But although I no longer want to torment her to gain power over her, I still desire to dominate her, body and soul. An ultimate control that will resolve my feelings of powerlessness when it comes to her. It will right the wrongs on the ledger.* I don't want to move. I set my watch alarm for two hours from now, in case I fall asleep, and just enjoy the feeling of having her body pressed into mine.

Clay
Morning. Thurs., Oct. 14, 2021 (Day 2)

I walk into the station, noting the RCMP officers are all wearing masks, some N95. Even though the third wave has flattened and cases are down, as first responders officers are often called to scenes where there is a high risk of contracting coronavirus.

I feel anxious and jittery. I anticipate that part of this meeting will be to update me on the start of the investigation, and the other part will be to interview me for more information. "I'm here to see Officer Duane Saunders, please. He called me in to meet with him."

"Name?"

"Clay Aldridge."

The officer at the desk nods and gets up to escort me to the office. He knocks on the door labeled "Officer Duane Saunders, Major Crimes" and opens it wide. "Clay Aldridge here to see you." Officer Saunders gives a curt nod, and the desk officer gestures for me to go inside.

"Hi Clay, nice to meet you. You're the one who filed the missing person report, am I correct?"

"Yes, that was me."

"You reported Dr. Jileski missing when she didn't come in to work?"

In Ontario there's no wait time to file a missing person's report, so I had filed it as soon as I could.

"I realized she wasn't at home or work, with her parents or with her best friend, Vi. I had a really bad feeling, and acted according to my intuition. I know Karly well. Firstly, nothing apart from an emergency would stop her from coming into work. Secondly, she was isolating due to the virus so wouldn't have been off anywhere else.

"I didn't know she was missing at first. Although we worked together on the same ICU team for weeks, Karly had just switched to 24-hour on-call shifts. The ICU is no longer swamped with COVID cases. As a result, she was scheduled to do two 24-hour on-call shifts with a 10 hour break in between."

The officer scribbles something on his notepad, then looks at me sympathetically. "Yeah, you guys have had a real time of it lately. How are you holding up?"

"I've been doing okay. Dealing with the patient deaths is the most difficult part."

The officer nods. He changes the subject. "Are you and Karly close?"

"Yes, we've been close friends for a few months now, and we've developed a romantic relationship over the last few weeks. We went to school together years ago, but didn't cross paths often."

"What were her habits like?"

"Well, I usually drive her to and from work, but I was doing day shifts when she was on her first on-call shift. I saw her briefly during the day, then I was off for the evening. I came in the following morning, and figured I must have somehow missed her. But then I didn't see or hear from her for the entire day. Then she missed her second on-call shift, which was supposed to start last night. That's not like her at all. She would never miss a shift like that. Later I went by her place since she wasn't picking up her cell, but she didn't answer her door."

"Has she been under a lot of stress lately? Enough to overwhelm her?"

"She was going through a lot, especially a month or so ago, but the team encouraged her to slow down. She started to see a therapist through the hospital, and she seemed to be doing better." The officer makes a note.

"Relationship stress?"

I start to feel uncomfortable as his eyes bore into me. "Not really."

"Any possibility that she just needed to get away from all of the sickness and death?"

"No, none. She's very responsible and has a high level of personal integrity. She would never do that to her patients, and she would never risk her career in any way. But back to what I was about to say. I usually drive her, but when I don't, she generally uses Uber to get herself to and from work."

Officer Saunders writes in his notepad.

"This is very helpful." He takes a deep breath and goes back to the previous line of questioning. "Is it possible the stress pushed her over the edge to the point where she might harm herself?"

I could feel my eyes widening. It hadn't even crossed my mind. "No. No way." I shake my head adamantly. "She was finding the team to be supportive, and she was taking steps to deal with her stress, like seeing her therapist and opening up to others about her feelings. I honestly couldn't see Karly doing anything like that."

Officer Saunders nods as he takes notes. "So I'll update you on what we'll be looking into right now. First of all, we'll try to contact her through her phone. I'll contact her family and have them check her apartment with an officer. They'll be asked to phone around to other family and friends.

"If you could phone anyone she could possibly be with, that would be helpful. Also, if you could let us know what her social media accounts are, we may need that information in the future. Most people show up within the first 48 hours, but we don't take chances."

I nod.

"If there's anything else you can fill me in on that will help with this investigation, please let me know. Here is a card with my direct line." The officer hands me a card, and I shake his hand.

I drive from the station to the hospital for my next shift. I feel emotionally exhausted from worry. *What am I going to do with you,*

Karly? I run my hands through my hair, with anxiety and frustration.

I place my belongings in my locker as I get ready for my shift. I attempt to dial Karly's cell number, yet again. *What did she do with her phone?* I'm pacing because I'm so nervous and restless.

I hear a muffled ringing sound coming from one of the lockers. I walk over to the locker where the ringing is coming from and see that the locker is Karly's. Hands shaking, I dial again to make sure. Sure enough, the ringing in her locker begins again. *Everyone knows she wouldn't leave her phone behind. I need to call hospital security, and also get hold of the officer on her case.*

Officer Duane Saunders
Morning. Thurs., Oct. 14, 2021

I contact Karly's father, Dr. Jileski, and verify he doesn't know her whereabouts. After checking Karly's apartment with the spare key, discovering she's not there, and that her purse is missing, he calls me back. I ask him to contact anyone he knows she might possibly be with or who may have information on her whereabouts, other family members, friends.

I hope this is just one of those situations where a missing person is found right away, has lost track of time or has confused their work schedule. That would be the best case scenario. Otherwise these situations can get bad, really quickly.

Right after I get off the phone with her father for the second time, I receive a call from Clay. He sounds vaguely detached.

"Security just opened Karly's locker at the hospital and found her phone and purse inside with her wallet. They're doing a sweep of the hospital, and covering every inch of the grounds, to see if she could possibly still be here. She would never leave her phone and purse behind. She usually Ubers when I don't pick her up, so she would need her phone for that."

My instincts kick in, and in my mind the case has just escalated. "Clay, would you happen to have the number for scheduling? We need to find out when Karly was last seen during her shift." Clay gives me the number, and I start doing follow-up to sketch an initial time-line.

The hospital has records of each time Karly was paged. A woman gives me the information I need. "I see she was called to the Emergency Department at 5:14 am for a Code Blue. I can give you the name and number of the attending physician if that would help?"

I follow up with the attending, and find out Karly left the ER around 6 am. *So that leaves two hours until her shift ended.*

Karly
Afternoon. Thurs., Oct. 14, 2021

I wake up confused and disoriented, not knowing where I am. My head is pounding so hard I feel it might explode. The physical pressure of the pulsation makes it impossible to focus on anything else. I try to push myself into a sitting position, and that's when I notice I'm in a hospital bed with a gown on. *What happened to me and where am I?*

The pounding dissipates slightly, enough to see a glass of water on the table beside my bed in the dim light. I take it and greedily gulp down the water. As it flows down my parched throat, I try to quell my anxiety. *Am I ill? Why am I here?* I carefully place my feet on the floor, and attempt to walk, focusing on staying balanced. I find my chart at the end of the bed and shakily look under the "Treatment History and Medical Directives".

Patient presented with hallucinations and paranoia. Diagnosed with COVID-19 with neurological and gastrointestinal symptoms. Headache, nausea, vomiting, confusion.

I stand there trying to read my chart and feel myself paling. *Well, it would explain the vomiting and the weird experiences I've been having. Everything's a mess in my head.* I'm fighting the dizziness and nausea that is overwhelming me, but am unable to get through much more of my chart before my vision blurs. I look around my hospital room, trying to focus my eyes. My anxiety level rises only slightly after reading my diagnosis. *Must be the dose of Xanax noted on my chart that is keeping my anxiety in check.*

It seems they've put me in a private room in the regular COVID ward, without any other patients. I wonder if my extended health insurance is covering the private room costs. I'm surprised they'd even have that much extra space in the busy ward for me to have a private room. My head still pounds, so I replace my chart and go back and lay down on my bed. I close my eyes as I vaguely register there's a camera on the ceiling across the room.

I feel something cool on my face, and realize someone has put a cold compress on my forehead. I must have fallen asleep. My headache is no longer as extreme, just a mild thumping. I don't seem to have anything noticeable in the way of respiratory symptoms, but based on my chart, it seems the virus has spread to my other systems. That concerns me. A lot.

I lie there, fatigued, exhausted, mind swirling. Again, I drift off to sleep.

Officer Duane Saunders

Afternoon. Thurs., Oct. 14, 2021

Officer Lauren Friezen walks in at the end of lunchtime, late due to her morning dental appointment. "Hey Duane." She tosses her purse on her desk as a gust of wind ruffles her short, dark hair. The outer door slams shut.

"Lauren." I nod at my partner as she joins me in the main area of the precinct. "So how was it?"

"Okay. Just nice to get it over with. Now I'm good for another six months." She flashes an exaggerated smile at me with her pearly whites. I finish my apple, then aim the core at the garbage. It's a three-pointer. "Good shot."

As soon as she settles in and joins me at the table, I start briefing Lauren on the Missing Person case. Lauren's a good officer, and I've been happy to train her. She's got good insight with the job, especially when it comes to female victims. I'm glad I have her on this case with me.

I call over to the hospital beforehand, to make arrangements for a tech to meet with us. Then the two of us drive over and walk into the Hospital Security Department to view their camera footage. "Let's start with 5:50 am, ER. We're following Dr. Karly Jileski." I lay her photo on the desk in front of the tech, and pull up a chair. I point to the screen. "Okay, let's follow her."

We watch as Karly exits the department on one camera, and travels up the stairwell on another. Her destination is one of the on-call rooms. There's no action after that and we fast forward. I see movement. "Stop! Back up." The security tech stops fast forwarding and rewinds the footage slowly to the beginning of the segment. He plays the recording.

A man in scrubs, surgical cap and mask, pushing an empty wheelchair, has stopped at Karly's on-call room. The security tech,

Lauren and I all look intently at the screen. The unknown man uses a set of keys while glancing down the corridor, and pushes the wheelchair into the room. It's frustrating because he keeps his head down low.

We fast forward again. A number of minutes later, we see him come out with a woman in the chair. Between his mask and reflective glasses, it's impossible to get a good look at his features. However, I'm able to get a general height and vague weight estimate, which at least gives us something to go on.

Although Karly went into the room earlier, it looks like a different woman is in the chair. Lauren is watching the footage carefully and points to the screen. "That must be a wig attached to the cap. The hair is unnaturally straight. She's slightly slumped forward and not moving. Looks like she's been drugged."

"I need printouts of him from every angle possible." The security tech nods and starts printing off what we need. Then we scroll through the different cameras' footage and watch the abductor evade the security at the front entrance. He pretends to adjust the wheelchair, keeping his head down, until security is faced with testing another person entering the hospital. Then he quickly exits through the sliding doors on the side of the foyer opposite to the entrance.

He's blocked from view due to an obstruction as he loads her into a vehicle in the garage. The video in the parking garage is a bit grainy, and a flickering light makes distracting shadows, making it difficult to see exactly what he's doing.

"Bingo," I say as the vehicle pulls out. We have to rewind the video several times to get the license plate, due to the erratic lighting. However, we are eventually able to figure out the letters and digits. *Please let it be this easy.* But as I have the plates checked, I find it's as I dreaded. Fake plates.

Clay

Afternoon. Thurs., Oct. 14, 2021

Throughout the day, I'm noticing more security guards are being stationed at the hospital, and am curious. *Has something happened at the hospital, or is it related to Karly's disappearance?*

I think about the officer leading the investigation, and wonder if he's uncovered anything yet. Hopefully the information I gave the RCMP will start them off in the right direction. *I should have been more careful.* That thought only adds to the stress I feel about the whole situation. *Maybe I can find out where they are in their investigation.*

I think about the steps I need to take after my shift. *I will be with her again soon.* Right now the longing I have for her threatens to consume me and it takes all my willpower to focus. I yearn to hold her in my arms again, to feel her right next to my body. I need her. *Karly, I'm coming for you.*

Officer Duane Saunders

Afternoon. Thurs., Oct. 14, 2021

"Do you recognize him?" I'm in a discussion with Dr. Romara, the intensivist in the ICU, and a member of the administration has joined us. "We're looking at someone around 6 feet tall, give or take an inch or two. It's difficult to tell his exact height since he's hunched over the wheelchair, keeping his head low in all the footage. Also, because his shirt bags out as he leans over, it's difficult to pinpoint his weight."

Dr. Romara is familiar with the staff from her day-to-day interactions with them. "There are several orderlies, doctors, and other hospital employees I can think of offhand that fit the parameters. They would look similar in a mask and head covering, while faced away from the camera. Someone in the Personnel Department should be able to give you a more comprehensive list of possibilities if you're looking beyond the ICU."

"I'd like to follow up with each of the staff members here at the hospital, rather than down at the station. I wouldn't want to put pressure on the perpetrator if he's an employee, or he might try to cover his tracks, putting Dr. Karly Jileski in harm's way. And since time is of the essence in this type of case, interviewing here could save us a lot of that. It would also make things much more convenient for the staff and hospital, since all it would take is a break without any travel time."

The administrator nods in agreement. I continue on. "I'll need each employee to sign a witness statement. As we sift through the witnesses, we'll at least be able to start eliminating names from the list of 'persons of interest', even if we can't identify him initially."

The administrator clears his throat. "Personnel would be best to talk to so things flow smoothly. We will arrange for an office for you. Scheduling interviews may be erratic, due to the nature of working in a hospital, but personnel can help you set up the general interviews in accordance with staff shifts."

Dr. Romara looks at me, sincerely. "I really hope you find her, and soon. Dr. Jileski has been an important part of our team and has done tremendous work under pressure. She is highly regarded by others and shows compassion in everything she does. Please contact me anytime if you need assistance in the investigation. We want Karly back." I reassure Dr. Romara we will do everything we can to find her and bring her home safely. I shake both their hands after the meeting and walk down to the ground floor.

I walk over to Personnel, and as I'm talking with them, the administration arranges a social worker's office for me where I can easily conduct staff interviews. Personnel gives me some initial information to help us sift through the potential "persons of interest" and prioritize them, then starts arranging a schedule for us for general interviews.

The woman with short curly hair and glasses from the Personnel Department hands me a printout after faxing a copy to the station. "The on-call rooms aren't in an isolated area, but rather in a section that connects with others. Whoever this guy is, he would go unnoticed since it's a general area. Cleaning staff is in and out constantly due to the concerns about COVID, which has added to the traffic." I take the information with me as I leave. There are a few things that need to be done before the interviews begin.

I drive away from the hospital, while Lauren sends out a missing person APB. I phone the RCMP detachment through my bluetooth. One of my colleagues starts running the male names from the fax provided by Personnel, to see if anyone stands out. "Run a careful check on Dr. Clay Aldridge's background first." Although he originally indicated Karly was missing, we've had cases before where the person reporting turns out to be the perpetrator.

I leave a message for Karly's therapist at the hospital, in case she has some insight into the case. Then I call Karly's father and ask to meet with him. Lauren and I head over to his home right away. We knock on the door to the trailer in the driveway.

Karly's father is a middle-aged man with hair that is starting to grey. There is a warmness to his blue eyes, as he welcomes us to his temporary home. "Thank you Doctor Jileski. I'm Officer Duane Saunders. We talked on the phone earlier today."

"Officer Lauren Friezen. Nice to meet you, Sir." They shake hands.

Doctor Jileski explains that his wife is unaware of the situation, as she is currently recovering from COVID inside the main house. He invites us to sit down with him inside the confined space. "Right now I don't want to break the news to her, or her anxiety over Karly's disappearance may restrict her ability to breathe even more." I can see his face is strained as he's talking, and that he is showing fatigue below his eyes. It's apparent that stress has taken a toll on him lately, hitting him from both sides, professionally and personally. It is regretful that a family, raw from experiencing so much difficulty, also has to deal with a missing daughter.

I describe what was on the security recordings to Karly's father. His face pales, his breath catches, and his eyes dart wildly, trying to read mine. I can tell he's trying to gauge if this unbelievable situation could possibly be a joke. It's the first reaction most parents have in a situation when bad news is delivered—it's denial. After determining that what I've said is real, his head falls into his hands, and he subtly rocks forward and backwards on the built-in upholstered bench.

"Dr. Jileski, I want you to know that the case has been escalated from 'Missing Person' to 'abduction'."

"Oh, God. I was hoping this was just a misunderstanding and that she'd be found with friends." Karly's father looks pale and drawn as he clasps his hands together.

"Is there any insight you can give us, Dr. Jileski?"

His facial expression becomes intense. "From what you've described to me, you're looking at someone with direct knowledge of her schedule and the hospital system." Dr. Jileski has easily put the pieces together despite his frame of mind.

"Yes, I agree, and we've launched the investigation in that direction. Right now the situation seems to indicate staff involvement, due to what we saw in the camera footage. The man who abducted her was cognizant of her schedule and placement at that precise time, and her abduction was very specific. Karly was clearly the target. However, he may be part of a larger group. We don't want to rule anything out yet."

Karly's father gathers himself together and faces me, his facial expression transitioning from a reflection of despair to a serious businesslike demeanor. I'm sure he's had to go into this "mode" numerous times in his career, to keep others calm. Now he's using it to stay focused on the discussion.

"Dr. Jileski, is there anyone who might want to harm you or your family? To use Karly to get to you?"

"No one I can think of." He shakes his head, looking like it's a completely foreign concept.

"Okay. If you think of anyone related to your professional practice or personal life, please don't hesitate to contact us."

Dr. Jileski is still shaking his head, looking at the floor. "When should we be expecting a ransom demand?" We can tell that the doctor is still in disbelief, thinking about things he never thought would remotely touch his life: ransom and revenge, and being robbed of his daughter.

"Usually ransom demands come in quickly. Is your home phone number publicly known?"

The doctor looks up. "Actually we're unlisted. However, my office number is public. I have it forwarded to my cell phone when I'm away."

"Hmm. Are you okay with an officer setting up some equipment, in case you receive a call on either phone? He's a tech, and would be able to trace and record your incoming phone calls, alerting us of anything related to Karly's disappearance."

"Absolutely. I would just ask anything to do with my patients is erased immediately, due to confidentiality."

"Understood. He'll also go through Karly's tech devices. We'll have them sent over to him. Can you tell us the details of her current life? What are your impressions of her colleagues and acquaintances?"

"We've been meeting as a family on Zoom, but haven't gone into much detail about her personal relationships. She has discussed her resident supervisor, Dr. Alex Jamar, and a few of her colleagues. I can quickly obtain general professional information so you have background on those she's been in contact with. Please, let me at least do that to help with your investigation."

"It would be very helpful if you could, Dr. Jileski. Time is of the essence, and any information you can fax over will save us from having to dig it up ourselves. Also, do you know anyone who owns a black SUV?"

"Yes, ours is here in the garage, and Karly mentioned her friend and colleague Dr. Clay Aldridge owns one. He's been driving her to and from work since they've been on common shifts." He pauses. "It's a pretty general description of a vehicle, don't you think?"

"Right now it's all we have to work with. Hopefully that will change in the future as more evidence comes in." I think about the graininess of the footage and the unstable lighting in the parking garage.

Karly's father gives me the contact information of Karly's best friend, Violet Lenavere. I'm hoping Karly may have confided in her and that it will give us insight into the investigation. If this was a personal abduction, rather than a kidnapping for ransom, then Karly's closest confidantes may be crucial sources of information.

"Could you give me a list of all of Karly's bank accounts and credit cards you're aware of? I'll also have the credit bureau flag any cards and new applications." I know the chances of locating her this way would be slim, since her purse was left at the hospital, but she may have been forced to take her cards or take out another card in her name if the motive was monetary. No stone left unturned.

"Would you mind letting one of the officers into Karly's apartment so we can check for a ransom note or any other evidence? That's on the off-chance the abductor used Karly's key to get into her apartment." I make a written note to have the security footage at her apartment building checked and to pick up Karly's tech devices.

"I'll get the keys." Dr. Jileski goes to the telephone desk in the hallway and opens the drawer. He hands me a fob and a set of keys. "This one's for the apartment, and this is for her storage locker on the same floor," he gestures with his fingers.

"Thank you. I'll be in touch." I arise, and Lauren follows. We both shake Karly's father's hand, then walk out the trailer door.

Karly
Evening. Thurs., Oct. 14, 2021

I've become increasingly paranoid throughout the day, especially since I haven't seen a single nurse or doctor since my first puking incident. *At least I don't think I have.* The room swirls as I stand up again. *Then why do I vaguely remember someone taking my blood pressure and vitals?*

Time passes in a strange way, as if it's slowing down then speeding up. I pace back and forth in my room so many times that I'll start leaving holes in the floor before long. My head starts spinning again and I sit down on the bed to compose myself. As I sit there, I can't tell whether two minutes or two hours have passed.

I take a look at the two books on the small dresser beside my bed. *So odd, since books are kept out of COVID wards to avoid potential transmission.* I take a closer look, and see they're brand new. *That's strange, too. Unless family or friends dropped them off for me?* I sit up straight, feeling hopeful as I perk up at the idea. *They know I'm here. They just can't visit since I'm contagious.* The thought comforts me.

The books are two of my favorite classics, and I pull one out to read to settle the confusion in my mind. Reading always relaxes me. *Someone who knows me well must have dropped these off for me.* I feel reassured that family or friends have been by, even if they couldn't visit for safety's sake.

I need to focus my mind, and stop thinking about my current condition. Between anxiety over having COVID and the symptoms I have, I need some type of mental break. *Yeah, or I'll really have a break—like a psychotic break.* I roll my eyes. Yes, I'm now being sarcastic with myself. I shake my head and the room spins even more. But something feels off about me being here. It must just be paranoia, making me feel that something's not right.

I sigh, as I lie down on my bed with the book for the day or evening, or whatever time it is. However, my eyes are unable to track even one paragraph. I'm being inundated with random, neutral images non-stop. The buzzing in my ears is persistent, until my mind finally tunes out all sensory stimuli.

Officer Duane Saunders
Morning. Fri., Oct. 15, 2021 (Day 3)

The next morning at the station I delegate tasks to the rest of the unit. Because we're in a time crunch whenever there is an abduction, numerous things need to be done simultaneously. I have people looking at all angles to get a better comprehensive picture. They're looking into the family's history and financials, to see if they may have been targeted that way, as well as at the people who have contact with Karly herself.

There are people in the lab, trying to clean up the video to get a close-up of the guy who abducted Karly. They've identified all employees on the video who are potential witnesses. They're also looking at the footage for identifying marks on his vehicle, and have checked the parking garage for tire tracks or any other evidence that could have been left behind.

Fortunately, the guy was wearing latex gloves, which can actually leave fingerprints, so we swept for those yesterday. It was frustrating because the constant disinfecting by the cleaning staff meant most prints had been wiped clean. So the forensic team focused on any surfaces the abductor may have touched in the room that may have been missed. Prints found on the head of the metal bed frame were set aside for comparison.

I read the research report on hospital staff. Clay Aldridge looks squeaky clean, as do most of the other staff members. There are a few red flags that go up, and it might be beneficial to investigate one guy who works in the hospital laundry who has a sealed record.

I write down a bunch of questions:

Kidnapping for ransom or abduction for another motive?

Target is her or those close to her?

Why abduct her from the hospital instead of from her home?

I sit back and sigh, and wipe my eyes with my fists. I rub my hands over my face, then take a slow breath in and out. I call over to the officer who's screening witnesses at the hospital and give him the list of those who came in close proximity to the abductor and Karly. Yesterday he downloaded a copy of the video footage onto his tablet. So far we've found the footage has been invaluable. Firstly, it has eliminated anyone in the same video frame as the perpetrator as a "person of interest", since it gives them an alibi. Secondly, it's helped us to pinpoint priority witnesses, those who were in closest proximity to the suspect. Thirdly, it's been providing something to jog the witnesses' memory.

My desk phone rings and I pick up. "Saunders here."

"We've got something at the digital lab." I ask Officer Friezen to join me and we head over to the adjoining building briskly, hoping something useful has come up with the digital enhancement of the footage. We're not disappointed.

"Take a look at this set of frames." The digital tech zooms in on a tiny section of the film. "Here's what this tiny part looks like, blown up and enhanced." He pulls up a still shot of the video, focusing on the ID badge of the perpetrator pushing the wheelchair to the on-call room.

"Hmm." I see the name as plain as day and am surprised. "I'll need a printout of that please." I stare at the name on the badge. *Dr. Clay Aldridge.*

CHAPTER TEN

Clay

Noon. Fri., Oct. 15, 2021

I try to put my feelings of anxiety to work by channeling that energy into hyperfocusing on my patients. It's taking all of my concentration to stay on point today, because I can't get my mind off Karly. I feel nervous and tense, a bundle of emotions all at once that if set alight will explode. I need to keep myself under wraps. I take a deep breath. *Stay calm. They're going to do some digging. That's a routine part of their job.*

I sign off on the lab results of my current patient. I phone the patient's daughter, marked as "next of kin", to keep her updated on her mother's status. Unfortunately a cytokine storm, triggered by an immune response to COVID, has caused some kidney damage. On the flip side, her condition has been diagnosed early enough that we can prevent things from getting worse.

I put down the phone, and take a quick look at my next patient's details on my tablet. *I can't let myself be distracted. I have to focus.* But then I'm being paged. I pick up the phone and click on Line 3. "Dr. Aldridge here."

"Dr. Clay Aldridge?"

"Yes."

"This is Officer Duane Saunders. We spoke earlier today."

My breath hitches, and my nerves start to get to me. "Yes, do you have news?"

"Could you meet with us near the social workers' rooms? There are some things we need to discuss."

Officer Duane Saunders

Afternoon. Fri., Oct. 15, 2021

Young Dr. Aldridge is sitting in front of Lauren and I in one of the social workers' offices. The witness interviews continue in the office next to ours. Just because the clues point in one direction doesn't mean we stop gathering information or evidence. Even if it doesn't bring about new leads in the case, additional crucial evidence and eyewitness accounts can potentially help put someone away and keep them there. I try to disarm Clay, to speak with him in a non-threatening, friendly way. If I can keep him off of the defensive, I should be able to get some important answers from him.

The first time we go through the footage, Clay is shaken, as he watches Karly's abduction. For several minutes, he has difficulty composing himself, and I watch as tears build up in his eyes. He looks like he's genuinely in anguish. When he's more settled emotionally, I show him what the lab found—I show him the blown up stills.

Clay is looking closely at the tablet, squinting. "It's not me, although he looks somewhat like me. Someone must have used a similar name badge." He looks at me in confusion. "Why would I take Karly then report her missing to you?"

"It's been known to happen before. A crime is committed, then the reporter of that crime is found to be the perpetrator. Some people just like to immerse themselves in the investigation." I look at Clay pointedly. He passes the tablet back to me, eyes lingering on the still-shot.

"Is there anyone who can verify what time you left home to come to work?"

"No, I live alone." Then his eyes brighten. "My apartment building has security cameras. You can verify the time from the cameras."

"Okay, let's just say you're being honest with me, Clay. What reason would anyone have to wear your specific ID tag, instead of, say, using a bogus picture ID or someone else's? Do you have any enemies?"

"Not that I can think of. I've always been friendly with people around me. Maybe someone intentionally wore it to derail the investigation from the beginning?" Then he suddenly looks like he's recalled something.

"What is it?"

"I just remembered. Karly mentioned to me she was receiving disturbing emails from someone a while back. She originally thought they were from me, but they gradually became more alarming and she asked me about them. She also received a written note she thought was from me shortly after the first email; it had the exact same message as that specific email. It was in her hospital mail. It bothered me because that made it sound like it wasn't just a person randomly emailing people. They knew where she worked and physically dropped something off for her."

"Do you know where that note is now?"

"She said she held onto it. All I know is that it said 'You're Beautiful'. That was right after she received an email with a link to a video of the song with the same name."

"Hmm. It's significant if she had a stalker."

"She also received a phone call in the middle of the night a while back. She doesn't remember much about it since she was so exhausted, but there should be a record of that with the phone company?"

I get on the phone with the officer who had possession of Karly's keys and asked him to search her apartment for the note. I then put in a call to the station regarding Karly's possessions. A few minutes later, the items taken from Karly's locker are being examined at the station. The note is found in a white envelope, buried in the bottom of her tote bag, and both letter and envelope are sent to the lab to be checked for prints.

I call back the officer who was checking Karly's apartment, and instead have him go check the security footage at Clay's building for the morning Karly went missing. Clay's presence will be easily verifiable, and I want to have all our bases covered. One fact at a time will help this investigation develop in the right direction.

"Thanks for your help, Clay. We'll verify your alibi through the security cameras, and will continue investigating the various directions the case could go in the meantime. If I need you again, I know where to find you."

"Please, just find *her*." His eyes, still rimmed with red, plead with me. I hold the door open for the young doctor as he leaves the room.

Anonymous

Afternoon. Fri., Oct. 15, 2021

Hmmm. Her paranoia hasn't been letting up. I had been watching the monitor app on my phone while Karly paced the floor yesterday. Today that same emotion seems to have been stirring up inside her, and she became increasingly agitated this morning until she tired herself out.

Maybe I should switch her medication? But I have to be careful as I manage her meds, since there are withdrawal effects from some of the drugs in the cocktail I've put together for her. Besides, I've been waiting until all the medications kick in. Then I'll approach her when she's conscious and move to the next step. I sigh. *I'll have to review the list and contraindications, then see what else I can come up with.*

Karly is down for a nap, so I go clear her dishes from lunch and replace her water. I look over as she's sleeping, with an adorable expression on her face. I walk over, lean down, and kiss her forehead, smoothing her hair as she sleeps soundly.

I hear her say, "Crickets," with her beautiful mouth, and I have to laugh. I can tell she's dreaming. I stroke her cheek, then regretfully have to leave the room to get some work done. *I wish I didn't have to.* I have to keep reminding myself that soon enough I'll have her all to myself, and there won't be any barriers between us. *Soon she'll give herself over to me and will beg to be mine. Fully and completely mine.*

Officer Duane Saunders
Afternoon. Fri., Oct. 15, 2021

I think to myself. If *Clay Aldridge is being truthful, how is he tied up in all this? Is he the one being targeted?* I write Clay's name in the middle of a blank page from my notebook and circle it. I surround his name with facts: *ID Badge used (as seen on footage), similar build to perpetrator, owns a black SUV, has romantic relationship with victim (according to Clay), awareness of victim's schedule and hospital routines, emails and note that victim originally assumed were from Clay.*

I receive a call from one of the investigative officers. Clay's alibi has not cleared. There is no building surveillance footage since the cameras are newly installed and are not operational yet. Hospital security confirms that Clay arrived in good time for his shift that day. However, the timeline still doesn't eliminate him. He had enough time to abduct Karly, leave the hospital parkade to take her somewhere local, and make it back to work when he did.

But if he's innocent, I wonder if implicating Clay could be a means to slow the investigation down, or if it could have been done to personally target him because of a vendetta. This could be the answer to my question about why the victim wasn't abducted from home. It would have been much easier to do that, rather than risk alerting security or leaving witnesses. *Why wouldn't Clay Aldridge just abduct her from her apartment?*

I won't get hung up on Clay as a suspect without verifying it through facts and other evidence. That conundrum has happened too many times in the past, and valuable time was lost at the beginning of those investigations. Instead, we'll objectively pursue multiple lines of investigation.

Officer Friezen and I are still in the second social workers' office, making notes and phone calls. "Hang on a minute, I've just realized something. Mind if we head back to Personnel?" I can tell from her voice and mannerisms Lauren's come up with something interesting. It isn't a rare occurrence when Lauren sees things from a different angle. She's very observant and tends to think "outside the box". We head back up to Personnel.

When we get there, she inquires at the desk. "This name tag. What do these letters and numbers mean here: CAMD, etc.?" She has taken the blown up photo of Dr. Aldridge's badge out of her folder, and is pointing to a group of tiny letters and numbers on the badge.

"Oh, that's the MINC. Medical Identification Number for Canada. Each physician is assigned a number that never changes." The receptionist uses her pen to point to the photo of the badge. "Every ID starts out with CAMD, and is followed by eight numbers."

"How can we verify what a physician's number is?"

"We have them on file. Just give me a minute. It's for Dr. Clay Aldridge?" She glances back at the badge name in the photo while stepping to the locked filing cabinet.

Back at the receptionist desk, she opens a file folder labeled "MINC", and looks up Clay's number. "Ah, see here." She points to a number on the first page beside 'Aldridge, Clay'. "You're checking to see if the number is authentic?"

Officer Friezen nods. "Yes, it may help speed up our investigation if we could do a comparison."

"Alright, let's take a look." The receptionist makes a comparison. "It says CAMD... No, the number isn't legitimate. It's not Dr. Aldridge's ID number." The receptionist sounds surprised. "This badge is fake. Hmmm. Apart from the number, the badge looks identical to the original."

"Okay thank you. Could we get a copy of this comparison document for our records?"

"Yes, I'll get you a copy. It's just the one ID number you're interested in? I'll black out the rest. Just give me a minute."

I wait with Officer Friezen, as she leans with her back against the receptionist counter. *Good girl.* I'm proud of Lauren for following her instincts and the evidence. *Unless Dr. Aldridge had an elaborate plan and purposely forged the additional name badge with the differing ID number, he is innocent. He would need to have had absolute confidence we'd notice the numbers in a blown-up photo from hospital footage, footage that is not guaranteed to pick up digits that small. So that theory doesn't ring true.* The receptionist returns after a couple of minutes with a mostly blacked out document.

"Is there something we should be concerned about?" The receptionist looks worried. "Our security checks the badges upon entry to the hospital, but doesn't check the numbers. We normally don't even check names. Because of COVID, we need to screen everyone coming in, since we're only allowing patients and staff in—no visitors. Should we be checking ID numbers now?"

"I don't think that's really necessary at this point. We're investigating an isolated case, where clearly a name badge has been forged." I'm trying to reassure the receptionist, but not sure I'm succeeding. "Good day." I nod to her as we leave the area.

I'm glad the evidence points to Clay Aldridge's innocence, since we now know the name badge is a forgery. I really like the young doctor and am glad that he's been cleared. Clay looked like he was in anguish when I showed him the clips, so I'm glad the question of his innocence won't linger on. He doesn't need to deal with additional pressure from law enforcement and the stress of having the media on his back. *He has enough to deal with right now—the demands of his job and coping with his girlfriend being missing.*

Clay

Afternoon. Fri., Oct. 15, 2021

I'm definitely going out of my mind. That saying: "I feel like pulling my hair out" finally makes sense to me. I feel so fearful and jumpy. I've never been so worried about anything in my life.

I search for a client file in a desk drawer where I set it earlier. I bring my head up after finding the file, and I suddenly startle as I realize someone is beside me. It's the nursing student, Samantha. She walks around the side of the desk. She draws her hand down my arm, seemingly trying to comfort me.

"Hi Clay. How are you managing?"

"To be honest, I'm having a rough time of it." I open the file, lay it on the desk, and make a few notations before I forget.

"You've been working non-stop. Would you like to talk about things? I'm about to take my break." Samantha looks up at me through her thick lashes. *That might entice other men, but I'm worried sick about the situation with Karly.* I feel a bit of impatience with Sam.

"Actually, I'm planning on working through any breaks today. I need to keep going and keep my mind focused." I put a sticky note on one of the pages with a few words in point form, to remind me of some pertinent items to include in my notes. I look up. "Is there something you need?"

"Oh, no." Sam starts to blush. She hesitates before speaking. "I was just seeing if you needed someone to talk to." I can see she's embarrassed, and feel a bit bad for her.

"Thanks for the sentiment, Sam. I'll be okay. I just hope Karly is okay." As Sam walks away, I see her glance backwards with a sly, predatory gleam in her eye. My lips are in a grim expression as I stay focused. *I don't know what I'd do if I lost her. We only just found each other.*

Officer Duane Saunders
Afternoon. Fri., Oct. 15, 2021

Back at headquarters that afternoon, in a briefing room where the Major Crimes Unit is about to gather, I copy the targets onto the smartboard. The elements surrounding Dr. Clay Aldridge are either meant to frame him or to stall the investigation by throwing in a red herring. I copy down details about the family history and the possibility of a ransom demand. The motive of ransom is becoming more and more unlikely as time passes by without any demands being made.

I add Karly's name to the board with some basic facts. I circle the names: "Dr. Clay Aldridge" - stall investigation or frame? "Family" - ransom or revenge? and "Dr. Karly Jileski" - victim stalked? They seem to be the most probable principal targets. Since no ransom demand has come in as of yet, we'll be primarily focusing on the two doctors as targets.

I start the meeting, and we catch up on the progress of the case. We learn that the prints from the metal bed frame in the on-call room are a match to prints found on the note Karly received in the hospital mail. This points to an abduction, rather than a kidnapping for ransom. The prints will provide enough for comparison of "persons of interest". However, there were no hits linked to offenders in the national database when the ridge characteristics were entered.

Analysis of Karly's tech devices hasn't shown much lead-wise. The questionable emails she received were connected to a generic untraceable account. At least we now know the content of the emails, as it gives us insight into the mindset of the abductor. Because of the note Karly received, quoting the first song title, we know the emails are connected to the case. That link to the abduction is verified because prints on the note match those taken from the on-call room.

An investigation into Karly's phone records show the call in the night originated from a Skype account which has since been deleted. The Skype account was charged a small fee so it could dial actual phone numbers, not just connect to other accounts. However, the payment was made with a prepaid credit card, so it looks like a dead end.

Interviews were conducted with potential witnesses and persons of interest, and we've finally made a substantial dent in the list. Doing the interviews at the hospital itself has saved us valuable time. A couple of the witnesses mentioned that they smelled a "chemical scent" as the man pushed the wheelchair by them. Alibis of those on the personnel list who have similar physical characteristics to the abductor are currently being verified.

We learn that Dr. Alex Jamar, Karly's supervisor, is on a two-week leave of absence, "attending medical conferences in Europe". However, our team has discovered that Dr. Jamar has yet to show up at the first conference. In fact, there's no indication he's left the country. It bears more looking into, so the team is on it. The team is also investigating Jacob Lefresno, the employee in the laundry department with a sealed record. Our legal division will petition the court to find out if the original charges made are relevant to the current urgent situation. Karly's credit cards and accounts have been flagged, and airports and border crossings put on the alert. So far nothing has come up with the APB—there have been no sightings of her.

I update the team with a profile of the abductor. I pull up the hospital footage on the smartboard. "This guy knows what he's doing, and doesn't intend to get caught. We can see how premeditated his actions are, between the abduction itself, being unidentifiable on the cameras, and disguising his license plates. He's an organized abductor and somehow knows the victim. He has intimate knowledge of her workplace and schedule. He even knew which on-call room she was in. He is likely affiliated with the hospital, working alone. But it's clear this abduction was specific."

"So we're most likely looking at a stalker at this point, since the prints have now been linked?" The crime unit member pauses in his note-taking.

"Yes. At this point there's been no ransom demand. Although her family is fairly wealthy, they aren't so well off as to be a natural target. The emails tied to the case, connected to prints via the note she received as well as the bedframe prints, do point to a stalker. I'm thinking personal vendetta against the young lady, with one person involved in the abduction, and that somehow Dr. Clay

Aldridge is caught in the middle." I point to his name on the smartboard.

Over the next ten minutes, I delegate assignments to the members of the team, and Officer Friezen prints off updated hard copies of the info we've gone over during the meeting. The team heads to their assignments immediately. Time is of the essence.

Karly
Afternoon. Fri., Oct. 15, 2021

I take a long shower in the adjoining private bathroom. It feels good to have the hot water run over my body. I grab the white towel hanging on the rack, wrap it around me, and leave the bathroom. That's when I realize housekeeping has been in to change my bedding and to lay out a new hospital gown for me. Someone's also placed a clean glass of water and a tray of food on the rolling table. Maybe they prefer to enter my room when there's more physical distance from me. It makes sense under the circumstances.

"Hello?" According to my chart, I have COVID, but surely I should have seen a nurse or doctor in full PPE by now. Shouldn't I have? Then I vaguely remember someone taking my blood pressure and checking my pulse more than once. *Maybe I've just been so out of it.*

I walk to my door, and try the handle. It's locked. I start to feel uneasy. I put my ear to the door, thinking I'll hear regular hospital noise behind the door, but I don't. Okay, something's not right here. Even if I'm in a private room, there should be some noise.

I go and hit the nurse call button. The speaker on the wall crackles to life, and oddly enough, I can hear hospital background noise. A male nurse's scratchy voice speaks in monotone through the intercom. "Is there something you need?"

"No, not really. I just have some questions if someone doesn't mind answering them when they have a free minute."

"Sure, we'll send someone down later on after you've had a chance to eat your dinner."

"Thank you."

The speaker crackles again then the background noise disappears. I sit down to eat my dinner. Soon I become so fatigued that I need to lie down. *It's got to be an effect of COVID.* But I force myself to get up to find out more information before I do. I stumble over to my hospital chart and read the most recent notes:

AAOx2. Neurological symptoms persist. Paranoia increasing.

Awake, alert, and oriented x2? That means I was unaware of the time or situation. Even now I'm feeling disoriented. I don't remember being assessed by the neuropsychiatrist. *Think!* I tell myself. *Remember!* But there's nothing to grasp onto in my mind. I don't remember any hospital staff coming in and out, but they must have because there are notes on my chart, they've left water, they've left food, and they seemed to be administering medication, although I have no recollection.

What is wrong with me? Is COVID affecting my memory? Normally I would be having a panic attack by now under the circumstances. However, I know from my chart I've been prescribed Xanax, which is why I'm not having a meltdown. Instead, I sit down on my hospital bed in a haze of confusion. A few minutes later I lay down and am out like a light.

CHAPTER ELEVEN

Karly

Morning. Sat. Oct. 16, 2021 (Day4)

I feel like I'm stuck in an alternate reality—I'm trapped there. *Maybe it's the Xanax making me feel like this?* So, I sit on my hospital bed, and try to walk myself through a mindfulness exercise to help me gain more control over my thinking. An exercise to help me differentiate between facts, and thoughts and feelings.

I mentally list facts I know to be true, beyond a shadow of a doubt, and my thoughts and feelings connected to those facts. *Facts: My name is Karly. I'm 24 years old. I have a mother, father, older brother, and younger sister.* Feelings: My family feels far away from me emotionally right now. *Facts: I have a friend named Violet, and a friend named Clay.* Thoughts and feelings: Everything seems to be hazy around Clay, and I feel I don't know my friends very well.

I do remember some basic facts, but so many of my thoughts are just plain messed up. *Are they giving me anything else?* I go to check my chart, and don't see any other medications besides Natural Source Gravol, which is just basically ginger to ease nausea. I'm beginning to suspect that either my neurological issues are seriously affecting me, or that additional drugs are being administered in my water or while I'm asleep. *Am I just being paranoid? It mentioned paranoia on my chart.* I'm so exhausted from trying to think and reason things out that my head starts nodding, and I'm not sure if I can stay awake any longer.

Afternoon. Sat. Oct. 16, 2021

My eyes refocus, and I'm staring at the ceiling. Something's not right. Call it a sixth sense, call it hyperalertness, call it subconscious observation, call it anything you like. *Something. Is. Not. Right.* I sit up and press the call button for the nurse, and a scratchy male voice comes on again, with noise in the background. "Yes?"

"I'd like to talk to my family, please."

"I'll have a doctor come and talk with you shortly." He clicks off.

Aaaarggghh!!! I feel so frustrated. *What the heck is going on here? I can tell by now I'm not in a normal hospital. *Where am I?*

I walk across the room, still feeling a bit tipsy-like, and try the door handle. It's locked *of course.* I sigh, and pull the rolling table over to the one chair in the room to eat my lunch. *Even the food isn't "hospital food". It's too nice to be hospital food.* I feel myself chuckle ironically. *Plus, there's definitely too much sodium in this food for it to be hospital food.* I gulp my water down thirstily, then go back and sit on my bed.

Evening. Sat. Oct. 16, 2021

I suddenly jolt awake, thinking someone must be in my room with me. I can hear the door to my room starting to swing shut slowly, and hear footsteps walking away in the hallway, then up some stairs. The hallway is completely dark which seems odd to me, but my room is dimly lit by a nitelight.

I scoot out of bed, grab a plastic bookmark from the book on the top of the small dresser, and slide across the floor in my socks, nearly falling over in the process. I jam the plastic between the door frame and the mechanism of the door so it doesn't fully click shut. I put my ear to the door and I hear a door shut down the hall or up the stairs—I'm not sure which. After that, I eat my dinner nervously, then read a book until I feel I'm ready to do this thing.

I decide to test my theory about receiving drugs not reported on my chart. The least it will do is show that paranoia is affecting me, and I'll have to face it. The most it can do is give me answers.

The most likely culprit is my water, since they've put excess sodium in my food, enough to make anyone thirsty. I pretend to drink the water I've been given, but instead walk into the bathroom and spit it out in the sink. I fill my glass up from the tap and drink the water to help offset the sodium-laced dinner I've just eaten. There are no cameras in the bathroom, thankfully. A random thought flies through my head. *That would be sooo weird...and creepy...if there were.*

I quietly walk to the door of my room, and pull on the handle. Thanks to my quick thinking earlier, the plastic wedge makes it possible for me to open the door with ease. The door quietly swings open. Silence permeates the air.

I walk out into the hallway and am stunned. I'm not prepared for what I see. I'm not in a hospital at all. *Am I in some type of private clinic or care home?* The place is huge. There are raised ceilings, and glass windows that cover two of the walls, floor to ceiling, two stories high. It is difficult to see outside because it's so dark, so I press my nose against the cool glass, and I can see that gardens and hedges surround the large dwelling where I have been staying. It looks like I'm at a manor or on an estate with full grounds.

I find a door to the outside, and only hope there's no alarm connected. Then I'm outside, boxed in by hedges, trying to find a way out, so I can get away from this strange place. I finally find an opening in the hedge, and I run through it. My bare feet slide on the damp grass, and I nearly lose my footing. I grab onto the hedge to stabilize myself. If anyone saw me now, trying to escape in a hospital gown that revealed my tush, I'm sure they would think I'm certifiable.

Having my back exposed causes a chill to go through me. I've been running for a while now, wondering when I'll get to the end of this hedge maze. I think I finally see an exit, the yellow glow given off by a lantern, and I speed up.

Just as I'm about to barrel through the exit, a large man in black with a ski mask blocks my way, my bare feet slide on the wet grass, and I plow right into him. I reverse course, and I feel a pull around my neck as he tries to grab me. My necklace snaps. Before I can scramble to get away, nearly falling as I turn around with my hand touching the ground, he grabs me around my waist from behind. My legs are kicking and I'm struggling to get free of him. He stuffs something into my mouth to stop me from screaming, and pins me down, face first, on the ground.

"Stay down." He has his mouth to my ear, and although he sounds forceful he keeps his voice at a whisper. I can feel him zip-tie my hands and ankles.

I struggle for a bit, trying to spit the gag out of my mouth, when I suddenly feel something drawn tight around my face, keeping the gag in place. He ties it at the back, and there's no way I'll be able to get the gag out now. I stop struggling, and lie there, straining to turn my head and get a look at him, even though his face is covered. I stare up defiantly at the blue eyes reflecting the lantern's glow.

I gasp audibly, the noise muffled by my gag. "Clay?" In the dark, I'm sure I'm looking into Clay's eyes. *Are we at his parents' place? But why? Why would he do something like this? It doesn't make any sense!*

Instead of answering me, I get a short lecture. "I mean to keep you safe, Karly. It's not safe for you to be wandering alone at night." He is still barely audible, and there's no way I can place his voice.

Suddenly, I wince as I feel a punch to my upper left arm and I think he's hit me. But then realize he hasn't touched me—he's given me an injection. I start struggling again, but it's no use. Everything swirls in my eyes again, and then I'm unaware of my bearings. I feel something warm and soft being placed around me to cover my chilled body. The last thing I remember is feeling weightless, rising into the air, while hearing the clanging shut of a cast-iron gate.

Anonymous
Night. Sat., Oct. 16, 2021

I can't believe she managed to get out. She's so damn spirited. I smile as I shake my head. If I'm going to make this work, I need to confine her first, then gradually release the constraints as she becomes more compliant. She's just too feisty on this low level of medication.

I walk to the sideboard for a glass, and pour myself a scotch. I turn and face the middle of the room as I reflect on the last few days. I've obviously made some major mistakes, and need to go back to square one to make this work.

I sigh as I think of her. *It didn't have to be this way. Things could have gone very differently.* Now things have to be done the hard way. No matter how hard I've tried to get her out of my head, everything comes back to her. *Karly.* If I owned the world and was without her, I'd remain empty. I know that far too well—it hits too close to home.

I've been able to keep my temper under control. Hell, I *want* to keep my temper under control, even with all the frustration and anger she's been the cause of all these years. What she did to me... She deserved it dished right back. But after seeing her up close, looking so vulnerable, if only she could be like that all the time I think I could truly love her, steadily without pause.

After seeing her in the on-call room, I decided I was going to win her over in my own way, in spite of our failed past. *Does she even remember what happened all those years ago, or has she forgotten?* But I can't bear another rejection, so the outcome *has* to be 100% in my favor. Some "persuasion" by using extreme methods may be necessary, but I'm willing to use them, to get what I want. And I want *her*. I nod as I pour myself another drink. It's time to create a different reality for her.

Karly
Evening. Sun., Oct. 17, 2021 (Day 5)

I sit in a chair at the dinner table in a gorgeous dress the color of a sunset, in a daze. I face straight ahead and hear someone having a one-sided conversation. I'm vaguely aware there's an IV needle in the back of my left hand. It faintly feels like someone keeps bruising me, but I know it's the angle of the taped-down needle that's causing the discomfort.

I listen to a familiar male voice as he tries to converse with me while eating dinner. My own dinner of steak, potatoes, and asparagus is untouched in front of me. It seems that someone has cut up part of my steak for me since I'm unable to do it myself.

The man looks over at me as he converses. "Ah, Karly. I see you're a bit more aware now. I'm still tweaking your new medications so we can find the perfect balance." The man seems familiar, and he slides his chair over so he's closer to me. He gently caresses my cheek with his left hand.

He turns back to his dinner and becomes stern with displeasure. "I don't want you doing anything unsafe like that again." He glances over at me, lips drawn in a thin line, as he cuts his steak somewhat forcefully.

I feel hypersensitive to emotions in this state, and having his displeasure directed at me leaves me feeling as though it's the end of the world. He peers over at me again and must have noticed the tear making its way down my face.

His expression changes to an affectionate one. "Aw, Love. Don't cry." He strokes my tear away with his thumb and leans over to kiss my cheek. His lips linger there then brush over my lips. Then he brings his forehead against mine while cradling my face in his left hand. "Here, let me feed you." He smiles tenderly at me as he assists me. "Don't worry, it won't always be this way. You're just very ill right now, Sweetheart, and I want to keep you safe here with me until you're feeling better." It takes some effort to chew my food, and my reflexes are terribly slow. In fact, it's an effort to do anything, even to think.

"You are so beautiful tonight, Dear. You look so vulnerable. I just want to...scoop you up and hold you close to me." My body warms. He smiles at me as he feeds me another small mouthful. "Maybe I'll do that later. Maybe we can get you out of that locked room and into a regular room, now that you're on intravenous meds. Let's see how you do first."

He uses a napkin to wipe the tiny bit of mashed potatoes off my lower left lip. Although he places the napkin back on the table, he moves his right hand to my bottom lip to stroke it with his thumb. "I can't resist you. You know I've never been able to resist you." He stares into my eyes with gentleness. "Tonight, we're going to create some special memories together, memories of the life we would have had. We're going to be taking a *lot* of beautiful pictures of you and me." He gestures to the camera on the tripod in the adjoining room. "It should make you very happy, Karly."

I stare back at him, feeling tears in the corners of my eyes. I sit there, thinking only about how much I want to please him and win his approval. I sit there in my chair looking like an empty, soulless doll.

Night. Sun., Oct. 17, 2021

Hours into the evening, I'm completely exhausted. Several different outfits, different rooms in the house, and camera shots later, I'm having difficulty keeping my eyes open. I've been allowed to nap as each scene has been set up, but I need a deep sleep. In my mind, everything's all muddled together.

"Don't worry, Karly, you'll sleep well tonight." He chuckles as he sets up one last photo scene. In this one I'm wearing a gorgeous emerald green, taffeta gown with golden heels. My earrings and necklace are made of gold, diamonds, and emeralds. We stand there, looking into a mirror behind the camera, placed there so we can avoid a lot of retakes.

I can't remember what the occasion is supposed to be. I suppose if I was more coherent of thought, I would think what we were doing was terribly strange, "making memories". *Memories of what again? And why?* I'm too exhausted to think about the answers, and focus on smiling for the camera so we can finish and I can take another nap.

"All right—that's a wrap!" He pulls me into him and gives me a big hug. My body is up against his crisp white dress shirt, paired with navy pants. *He smells so good.* His one hand reaches behind my head to cradle it, while his other hand strokes me on the cheek. He moves his lips against my cheek, and it feels like there is a butterfly tickling me.

I start to giggle. "That tickles." I hear him laugh. This time he moves his lips so I can tell he's planting tiny kisses all over my cheek. It's ticklish in a different type of way, and I start to get fluttery feelings inside my tummy, as if the butterflies have moved there.

I think I'm starting to sway a bit, and he scoops me up. "Time for bed, Sleepyhead." He carries me to my new room, and sits me down on the bed, lifting up my skirts, unzipping me, and gently helping me out of my dress. While he hangs my dress in the closet, I half lay down on the bed in my white slip, my eyes closed, my feet still on the floor. I hear him laugh as he turns around. "Karly, you're so funny." He walks up to me, gently puts my legs on the bed and takes off my heels.

I feel myself being scooted over to the side of the bed, and then feel the bed go down slightly. I open one eye and peer out. I see him lying on the bed in front of me, looking at me. "Karly." He sounds so tender and I smile. "Come here, Sweetheart." He pulls me to him on the bed, and holds me in his arms, stroking my back. I feel him gently caressing my face with his lips, then I feel nothing at all, as I settle to sleep.

Clay
Afternoon. Mon., Oct. 18, 2021 (Day 6)

I'm pacing again. Karly's now been "missing" for six days. Things don't look good. *There must be something I can do.* I decide to call Officer Saunders to see how the investigation is going, and if he needs any more information.

"Officer Saunders? Clay Aldridge here. I wanted to ask how the investigation is going, and if there's anything I can do to help."

"Hello, Clay. Thanks for calling. Since you're on the phone, would you mind if I asked you a few questions for the investigation?"

"Sure, I was hoping I could help in some way."

"Is there anyone who knows Karly that might have an issue with you?"

I'm surprised at the question. "Why do you ask?"

"Well, we have reason to believe that you were drawn into this and targeted for one of two reasons. One, in order to stall our investigation, or two, because someone has issues with you and wants you to become the primary 'suspect' of the investigation."

"Well, to be bluntly honest, setting all modesty aside, a lot of guys see me as 'competition'. So in the context you seem to be suggesting, if someone really liked Karly, they might see me as a threat that needs to be eliminated. It's happened before with Karly and I—"

Officer Saunders cuts me off abruptly and forcefully. "When? What was the situation, and who was involved?"

Karly
Evening. Mon., Oct. 18, 2021

"I think you already know the answer to that." He throws his napkin down. "Karly, Karly." He shakes his head and gives a disingenuous laugh. His mouth hardens. "You've always attracted too much male attention, and this last few months it's become out of hand. I felt I needed to intervene now, since you've been letting in *Clay Aldridge, of all people*." He scoffs at the notion, then mumbles to himself. "I warned him years ago to stay away from you."

I think of all those times in the hospital, when I thought Clay was being "cold". It wasn't Clay at all. *They both have the same blue eyes, and I never clued in.* With masks on and with the same build, they looked nearly identical. I now regret pulling away from Clay because of my assumption.

He clears his throat and shifts his body so he's looking directly at me with his piercing blue eyes. "Remember what I told you years ago: 'You belong to me'. Right?" His expression hardens as he snaps at me.

I shiver. My heart tries to reject that notion, that I could possibly belong to another person like a piece of property. But my mind is cloudy and my resistance low. In order for it to make sense, connecting my past convictions with my present predicament, my mind bends the meaning of the phrase to: "You belong *with* me."

"Yes, you're right." I falter in my speech as I show meek acceptance.

"Karly, don't get weak on me. I want to see that fire and spunk. Look into my eyes, answer me again, and say it as a statement." His piercing eyes hold me.

"Yes, I belong to you," I say, with as much enthusiasm as I can muster in my condition.

He smiles at me. "Good girl. That's a good start, Sweetheart." He rubs my cheek with his hand, reinforcing my response with affection. "My Darling, Karly." I can't stop my eyes from closing, as I reciprocate and rub his hand with my cheek. *Why do I have such a desire to please him?*

"Right now it may feel difficult to be enthusiastic, but as we continue to lower your levels of medication, you'll feel more normal again, and that fire will come back. But you need to be able to think 'clearly' while you're on a lower dose."

The idea of my fire coming back to me should make me feel so happy, but right now it's difficult to even think without the clouds threatening to move in and take over what's left of my fragile soul. A vague thought slides through my mind for a second then is gone, that to "think clearly" means "think like he wants me to".

"When will my medth be adjuthted again?" I'm slurring my words a bit again.

His smile becomes more affectionate, and he moves his chair closer, cradling my cheeks with his hands. "You're so adorable when you lisp like that." He kisses me gently on the top of my head, then looks into my eyes, still holding onto my cheeks, softly.

He begins stroking my left cheek with his thumb, and his thumb keeps straying to the corner of my mouth, trying to part my lips.

I'm perfectly compliant, and my lips part, as he strokes the inside of my bottom lip with his thumb. I look up at him through my eyelashes. "I want to see that fire and passion come back, but directed towards the *right* target."

You mean "right for you". I struggle to keep my perceptions intact. With every persuasion from him, I try to balance it with a more correct version. It's just so difficult to do with all this medication pumped into me.

"I think we could try adjusting them as you get better. Part of that means: No. Escape. Attempts." He taps me fondly on the nose with each punctuated word. "Okay?"

I nod. "And you'll change my dosage then?" It's so difficult to grasp a logical train of thought, but I have to keep trying to think clearly. Lowering my meds should help.

"Yes, if you're a good girl. But it's not all that easy. If you're still ill and unable to think properly, then I can't drop your dosage, unfortunately." He looks at me as if he really feels regret.

I feel like I should be fighting my captor, but I can't, doped up like this. I'm learning that arguing makes my situation worse, and I don't feel I could make a good case for anything right now with my words and disconnected thoughts anyway. I need to play along with him, or I may never regain my freedom. But what if I lose my true self in the process?

He reaches over the table and holds my hand, rubbing his thumb against the back of mine. "Sweet Karly. Convince me. Convince me I should lower your dosage. It's up to you, Dear."

I don't know what to say, or how to react. So I simply say, "Please?"

He smiles at me. "That's a good start. Now show me how devoted you are to me and to our relationship. Convince me of your devotion." His eyes glitter darkly as he speaks. He lifts my hand to his lips and plants a soft kiss there.

I desperately want my dosage lowered. Even though it's difficult for me to think straight, I know it's vitally important. So I take his hand in mine. I bring his hand to my face, and rub my cheek against it. I drag my lips across the palm of his hand, planting small kisses as I do so. When I get to his fingertips, he drags them lightly over my lower lip and then he brushes my cheek with his finger. He leans in and softly kisses my lips.

"That's it, Baby." He cradles my cheeks and kisses me again on the lips, then trails kisses across my cheek. He pulls me to him, onto his lap, and I know I can't pull away—I have to convince him to lower my meds. "Who do you belong to?"

"I belong to you." I rub my cheek against his cheek affectionately and I can feel him smiling. He brushes his lips against my cheek until he finds my mouth, then caresses my lips with his.

"You are so beautiful, Karly," he murmurs as he brushes his lips against mine. "I need to taste you." He gently touches his tongue to my lips, first on my top lip, then my bottom lip. He sucks on my bottom lip, and my mouth opens for him. His lips come down on mine, and his tongue gently strokes mine. Then he softly kisses me on the lips several times, and pulls me to his chest.

He leans his chin on my head, then kisses the top of my head. "Okay Karly, you've convinced me." I feel relieved and my body relaxes into his, as his arms encircle me.

Officer Duane Saunders
Morning. Tues., Oct. 19, 2021 (Day 7)

"Dr. Jileski, we've been going through the personnel list at the hospital, trying to pinpoint if anyone may have had a reason to target Karly, and we are following up with interviews." My thoughts are that we're slowly reaching a dead end in the interview segment of the investigation. "We'd like to extend our investigation back further in time. Could you give me her supervisor's name from when she was in medical school? We'd like to follow up with any previous associates."

"I don't know her supervisor's name offhand, but can get that info to you asap."

"Also, did Karly have any relationships that went beyond platonic? Or was there anyone that was interested in her, that she 'spurned' for lack of a better word?"

"Karly didn't date anyone while in med school, since she was so incredibly busy. But before that, early in her pre-med, she dated a young man named Geoff Mason. I didn't like the way he treated Karly, and was relieved when she decided to break up with him." This matches the information Clay gave me.

"Do you know of his whereabouts these days or any other info that could help us?"

"He was a young businessman. Last thing I heard, he moved out West a few years ago and opened up a medical supply company."

"Okay thanks, Dr. Jileski. Feel free to text or email me the supervisor's contact info when you have it." Dr. Jileski sees us out, and we return to our cruiser and drive to the precinct. "Lauren, could you phone Karly's friend, Violet, to get additional info on relationships Karly may have had but not shared with her parents? I'm going to try to dig up info on this past boyfriend of Karly's and see if he could even remotely be connected with the current situation."

"I'm on it!" Lauren starts looking through her binder of notes for Violet's phone number.

I have difficulty digging up information on Geoff Mason. He seems to have fallen off the grid three years ago, but there's no record of his death. Geoff specialized in pharmacology at U of T a few years before Karly attended. After completing his degree, he started a local medical supply company. Vital Signs Medical Supply had grown to include four distribution centers across the country, in Vancouver, Winnipeg, Mississauga, and Montreal by the beginning of the pandemic. During that time, the company name changed to Davenport Medical Supply. Over the last year, growth has been astronomical, as medical supplies are in such high demand.

Three years ago, the company CEO changed from Geoffrey Mason to Geoffrey Davenport, the renowned millionaire. This seems oddly suspicious. I can find no actual statement online, saying there was a name change. Upon digging deeper, I see that Davenport is Geoff Mason's mother's maiden name.

Geoffrey Davenport! When I realize who this Geoff is, I'm stunned. He dropped off the planet as an unknown. I text his photo without his name to verify with Dr. Jileski that this was actually the man who dated his daughter. I read along how he has now emerged as one of Canada's most eligible bachelors, with a net worth of... My eyes go wide at his net worth. *Holy hell!* I keep clicking, reading more information about Geoffrey Davenport.

I browse through the photos of him online, most of them of him in business suits, some at events in a tux. *Very good looking young guy. Born 1991. Tall, dark brown hair and blue eyes. He does have some resemblance to Clay.* I skim over some of the business articles with names like "Davenport's Dividends". I see one called "Hot-blooded Hunk" linked to a gossip rag and glance over it, finding several others like it. *Looks like he has a bit of a temper.*

I receive a text back from Dr. Jileski, confirming he is indeed the one who dated Karly. From reading further online, I soon find out his main residence is unlisted, but located in Mississauga.

I walk next door to dig through municipal records, since I need a break to stretch my legs, anyway. I'm just going to get information for the case, and for a bit of exercise. *Those are the only reasons why I'm going instead of phoning.* I try to convince myself. All my denial flies out of my head when I see Sharon at the administration desk. I feel my face flush slightly.

"Good morning, Officer Saunders." Sharon's smile brightens her entire face. "What can I do for you today?" Sharon is a slender woman with layered blonde hair that curves below her jaw, and a real beauty in my eyes. I find I'm humming to myself.

"Good morning, Sharon." My voice is mild, not reflecting the urgency I feel on this current case. "I need to find a homeowner's address."

"Sure, let me help you with that." She clicks her mouse a few times. "Name?"

"Geoffrey Davenport."

Sharon lowers her voice. "I know a lot of young ladies would love to get their hands on this information." She gives me a conspiratorial wink as she goes through the records at her fingertips. "Ah, here we are. Would you like a printout?"

"Yes, please."

"No problem." I can hear the printer warming up at the other end of the office.

"Say, Sharon." I feel a bit bashful as she looks up at me from her computer. "Would you like to go for coffee sometime?"

Her face breaks into a smile again. "Why I'd love to, Officer Saunders. I'm so glad you asked. Just one minute." She briskly walks over to get the printout. I can't help my eyes from trailing after her, watching her long legs as her heels tap on the flooring.

She walks back and hands me the printout. I accept it and add it to my file folder. "Thank you. Swap numbers?"

"Sure." We trade phones and I enter my contact info in hers.

"Have a great day, Sharon."

"You too, Officer." I walk back to the station, feeling good about my exchange with Sharon. Now to get back to work on this case.

Back at the office, I look up Geoff's address on Google Maps street view. If we're going to approach him, it would be best to take him by surprise. But it's as I suspected. There is no driving straight up to the door and talking to the man, since his property is gated. Not only that, but it's surrounded by privacy hedges, which means it's not easy to get a casual glimpse through one of the windows while passing by.

I play out various scenarios in my mind, and having him come into the office or going by and announcing ourselves on the gate intercom just gives him an advantage. If he is somehow connected to the case, it gives him notice we are looking at him as a person of interest. I put my elbows on my desk and rub my face with my hands. We need to find a strategy quickly that will either eliminate him as a person of interest, or implicate him if he's involved.

CHAPTER TWELVE

Anonymous

Morning. Tues., Oct. 19, 2021

I'd prefer that Karly not be too dosed up on medication, as she isn't as responsive to me when she is, and I'm sure it isn't pleasant for her either. But I can't have her trying to escape or causing issues either. I have to admit to myself, the more compliant and submissive she is without medication, the more attractive I find her to be. *Adoration instead of fear. I made a good choice.*

In the early morning I quietly enter her room, adjust her IV drip, and slide into bed beside her, where she's lying on her back, fast asleep. I cuddle up to her as she sleeps soundly. I keep my voice to a whisper. "My angel." I kiss her on top of her head. I lay in bed with her, holding her closely to my body.

I stay awake, feeling her body up against mine, wrestling with myself to quell my desire, until she finally starts to stir. When her eyes finally drift open, I can see the recognition register as she sees me, and panic arising within her.

"Shhh." I try to comfort her, but she struggles against me. I grip her solidly and keep her immobilized. "Karly, I'm just holding you, nothing else. We're both fully clothed in pajamas. Calm down, Love." She stops struggling, and it sounds like she's gasping for air. I can feel her pounding heart start to slow. "Shhhh." My hand softly strokes her back.

"Who do you belong to?"

I can tell she's reluctant to speak.

"Karly? Convince me of your devotion. Who do you belong to?" My voice is more stern as I ask her the second time, and I stop stroking her back.

Her eyes look up through their lashes at me as her lower lip trembles slightly, and she looks vulnerable once more. "I belong to you."

"Good girl." I smile at her, kissing the top of her head, and continuing to stroke her back. "Now ask me if I'll allow you to belong to me."

Karly looks at me, anxious and confused. Then she tries to put together a sentence. "Please...can I belong to you?"

"Yes you may, but only if you're a good girl." To my delight, she looks relieved when I say yes. When she pleads to be mine, she stirs pleasant physical sensations within me to the point where I find it difficult not to touch her. *Damnit!* But I try to restrain myself so I don't scare her away. It's such a delicate dance.

After a while of lying in silence, her eyes watching me the entire time, I touch her cheek with my hand, rubbing my thumb against the corner and bottom of her lip. She automatically responds by parting her lips slightly as her eyes lower. *Good. She's responding to my touch, even while on a lesser dosage.*

"You ready for some breakfast soon?"

Her eyes flutter open again, and she quietly nods.

"Alright, Dear. Let's get up. Careful not to pull your IV. I don't want you to bruise."

We both slide out of her bed, and walk down the hallway to the left to get to the kitchen. I make waffles, eggs, and bacon for breakfast, while Karly sits quietly at the kitchen table. I regret not being able to open the blinds for her so she can see the autumn colors, but I don't want to take any chances. *But maybe...maybe late morning I could take her out* there. I smile to myself at the idea. I set the table, and then serve breakfast.

"Thank you."

"You're welcome, Karly." I smile at her. "How do you feel today?"

"I can grasp onto thoughts a bit better than yesterday."

"And what are your thoughts?" I'm curious to hear what she'll say.

"Well," she hesitates. "I still feel confused. Confused about why I'm here?" Her inflection raised at the end of her statement, making it sound more like a question.

"What would you like to know, Dear?" Then I pause, reflecting, and the corner of my mouth quirks. "Hmm...you can ask questions, but with each question, there's a price." I smile at the new game I've just thought up.

"What do you mean, a price?" The confused look on her face makes her look even more adorable.

"Quid pro quo. For example, you ask me a question, and to get an answer from me, you have to hold my hand."

She looks at me quizzically, and a bit unsure.

"Go ahead, try it. For the first answer, you hold my hand while we sit at the table." I tried to make it as non-threatening as possible to start. I can still tell she's unsure, but the terms are pretty straight-forward.

"Why am I really here?" She slowly stretches her small hand out to me, placing it in mine. I can see that her large eyes are fully trusting me to give her a truthful answer.

I sigh. "Because I suddenly became a believer in second chances." She looks even more confused than before. I'm not about to tell her the original reason for which I'd put my plan in motion. No reason to spook her even more. "Any more questions?" I draw circles on the back of her hand with my thumb.

She blurts out the next question. "When will you let me go?"

"Hmmm. For this one, I'm afraid you'll have to sit on my lap. If you dare to." My eyes glitter darkly. I put out the challenge to her, not knowing which way her defiance will run.

She quickly shakes her head, looking wary. *Ah well. It could have gone either way.* After a minute, she nods her head. *She wants answers badly.* She slides onto my lap, facing away from me, and I sharply inhale. I wrap my arm around her, and she stiffens. I whisper in her ear. "Relax, Baby. I don't bite." I take her hand in mine again.

"You can go once you're well again and able to make good decisions." She turns her head sideways to look at me with confusion, and I crane my neck, curious to see her expression. It seems her questions just bring on more questions. *Or maybe it's my answers that are causing her to ask more questions.* I chuckle to myself. *This game could go on all day.* The corner of my mouth turns up. I'm really enjoying this.

She speaks a bit hesitantly, as if trying to grasp what I'm referring to. "What do you mean by 'good decisions'?" She's searching my eyes, as much as possible considering the angle she's at. But I indulge her by moving my head forward, so she can see me better.

I throw the ball back in her court. "What will you do for the answer, Love? I'll let you pick the terms this time. Just a warning though, the price you pay out determines the depth of the answer you'll get."

She considers for a moment. "I'll turn so I'm sitting sideways in your lap instead of away from you."

I smile to myself. *Baby steps.* "I agree to your terms."

She turns sideways in my lap, so her head is to my left, and I cradle her. Now I can look into her eyes, see her face. It feels so intimate, her looking up at me with those innocent eyes. I stroke her hair back with my right hand as she continues to look at me. *So*

trusting. Feelings of warmth flow through me. *This is the way I want her to look at me every day. Like she trusts me fully and completely.* I take her hand in mine again.

"So." I clear my throat. "What do I mean by 'good decisions'? You've been ill, and not making the best choices, Karly. When you're able to make decisions that are best for your life, Sweetheart, then I can let you go." *One of your good decisions being that you'd choose to never leave me.*

She looks at me skeptically, as she tries to read me. I can tell she's having difficulty thinking clearly. So I smile down at her, and that seems to put her a bit more at ease.

"I'll tell you what. Let's change up the game a bit. You tell me what you're willing to give me, and this time I'll pick an answer that's worth that price."

"Give you? I don't understand." Her brow furrows.

"Just like we have been doing. Except you choose the price before I choose the answer to something I know you're wondering about." I smile warmly at her.

She looks straight at my eyes, disarming me. *No wonder I fell for her. I was just such an ass at the time. I'm going to make things work with her, no matter what it takes, no matter what the means.*

"I'll give you a hug."

I chuckle to myself and reiterate, "*Baby steps*", to myself. "Just a hug, hmm? Well, small concessions bring small answers." I feel pensive for a minute. Then I think about trust. "Okay, I have my answer for you, but you have to keep your arms around me." I tilt her slightly, drawing her closer to me to make it easier for her to hug me. She puts her arms around me.

"I don't want to hurt you. I just want to take care of you." I can feel her body relax in my arms, and I gently rock her. After a few minutes, her eyes start to close, and she drifts off to sleep. I kiss her forehead, softly.

Karly
Morning. Tues., Oct. 19, 2021

I feel like I'm floating outside my body, looking down on myself as I sleep, as the world rotates. In my mind's eye, I'm lying on my side, spinning, as though I'm on a clock. Two men stand on opposite sides of the room, stationary, at the 9 and 3 o'clock positions.

One of the men is Clay. *Clay? Who is Clay?* He feels far off in the distance, like someone I used to know, someone from another lifetime ago. He calls out to me, and I feel sadness overwhelm me. As my world of time spins, the picture zooms out and Clay becomes a far-off memory.

The other is a man I can't place, although I should know him, if only I could jog my memory enough. He is from the past as well as from the present, but it's the present that really matters. The past has been wiped away, again as a far-off memory, and as my clock settles, my world of time zooms in on him. He holds out his hand, and I get up off my side, and walk towards him. He smiles at me, and my heart soars.

I hurry to reach him, because I'm terrified he will leave me behind, but as long as he smiles at me, I feel on the top of the world. I look up at him with adoration in my eyes, and he takes my hand with a questioning look. *He wants me to leave everything else behind and go with him.*

He points forward, off the edge of the clock, and in front of us I notice there is a sea of white. We walk towards that sea, and step into it, hearing a crunching sound as I do. I realize the white is a field of eggshells, and with each step I take, I feel more and more apprehension. With each footstep I take, his face darkens, to the point where he is glowering at me.

Tears start streaming down my cheeks, and I want to turn back, but he forces me to stop and look downwards. I then realize the crunching sound is no longer that of eggshells, but that of a field of skulls that stretches beyond where I can see.

He smiles at me and my heart lifts, then he glowers at me and my heart plummets. He repeats this painful dance, as we exist in the middle of nowhere for an endless amount of time. I know now that he has somehow captured my emotions, has wrenched them from me, and now controls the way I feel. I'm completely dependent on him to regulate my emotions.

All I can think of is how much I need him; that need is an all-consuming fire. *It's like my very survival depends on him.* And as I look at the surrounding field of skulls, I realize it's true. My very survival does depend on him.

I startle awake, and tears start streaming down my cheeks. I'm encompassed in his arms, and he looks down and sees my tears. He brushes my tears aside with his thumb, and then reaches for a napkin. I can see the concern on his face. "Shhh, Karly. What is it, Sweetheart?"

"I...I don't know." In my state of mind I can't begin to process my emotions and put them into words.

"It's just a bad dream. It's okay. You're safe here with me." He continues to dab my cheeks and kisses me softly on the forehead. These tears aren't freeing to me. If anything, my anxiety has been heightened. I feel on edge. He sits me up on his lap and pulls me to him, so my head rests up against his neck. "Shhhh." He rocks me and holds me tightly as he comforts me, but my body is still tense. The emotions I experienced in my dream feel like deja vu, a pattern from somewhere long ago in the recesses of my mind, reflected in my unconscious in the present.

"Karly, relax. Let your body relax. Breathe in and out, slowly." He speaks to me gently. Although my body tries to pull otherwise, I force my muscles in my neck and back to let go of the tension. "Now tell me what's wrong."

"I'm afraid that you'll get mad at me."

"Mad at you for telling me what's wrong?"

"No, mad at me if I say or do something wrong in the future without knowing it will upset you."

He pulls me closely to him and takes a deep breath as he tries to reassure me. "Karly, I'll try to be as patient with you as possible, and I'll always forgive you when you do make mistakes, as long as you acknowledge them." It sets my mind at ease, and I relax somewhat. He continues on. "However, you need to learn to acknowledge your mistakes. Sometimes you don't recognize them as mistakes, but I can help you with that. But only if you ask me to."

I've always been fine with owning legitimate mistakes. But I can't help feeling an underlying sense of unease, like something isn't quite right with what he's saying. I wish I could think more clearly and that my mind wasn't in such a haze.

"Well, Karly? Would you like to ask me for help?" His eyes look doubtful, as if he knows I won't ask.

I want to please him so I nod. "Please help me see my mistakes?"

He smiles back at me and I feel pure joy. "Of course, Karly. I'd be happy to help you to see your mistakes."

Anonymous

Morning. Tues., Oct. 19, 2021

"You're doing so well, that I was thinking we could sit outside on the patio for a bit today. Would you like to sit outside with me, Karly?" She nods, and I watch as her face starts to light up. I realize it's the first time she will have been outside in days. Well, apart from her little escapade the other night. The patio I'm referring to is around back, completely out of view to the outside world, since it's blocked by the privacy hedges.

I look at her sharply. "Would you like to sit outside with me?" I demand verbal acknowledgement from her.

Her face clouds over for a second, then she responds with a smile. "Yes, I would really enjoy that."

"How much would you enjoy sitting with me?"

She looks up at me with an open expression. "I'd enjoy it very much."

I disconnect her IV carefully. "Good girl. Go put on something for the day." She obediently goes to her room.

After I've made myself presentable, I stop by her room to collect her. She has on a beautiful purple dress with floral appliques with a pair of strappy black heels and a black velvet wrap. I feel pleased that the clothes I ordered last week suit her so well. I enjoyed selecting a closet of clothes for her, each design of my personal preference. I can see she's applied some lip gloss, and her blonde hair is loose and shining around her shoulders, gentle curls cascading down her beautiful neck.

"You look beautiful, Karly. I feel like a lucky man." She blushes, then looks adoringly up at me. *Now* that's *the look I want to see from her. Every. Single. Damn. Day.* I hold out my arm for her, and walk her downstairs, then out the glass doors to the patio. The day is perfectly cool and crisp, my favorite time of year. I watch and smile as she audibly gasps, seeing my Japanese garden for the first time in daylight. The last time she'd run through it was when it was cloaked in darkness.

I make sure she's settled in a comfortable beige padded lounge chair, acting as the perfect gentleman and host. Then I step inside the cabana bar to make us drinks—keeping an eye on her of course. Thankfully, she isn't making a move to run, or we'd be back at square one *again*. I can see she is enthralled by her colorful surroundings, and I don't think leaving has even crossed her mind.

I make us both mojitos sans alcohol, knowing that she loves cocktails. I skip the alcohol, not wanting to intensify the drowsy effects Karly already feels from her medication, as I want her to stay responsive to me. Besides, it's too early in the day for alcohol anyway.

I walk behind her with our drinks, placing them on the table beside her. I cover her shoulders with her wrap, planting a gentle kiss on the top of her head. I pull out an extension on a sectional piece right beside where she is lounging, so we are lounging beside each other. I move closer to her and put my arm around her to get my drink. She doesn't seem to notice, so I leave my arm draped around her and gently rub her back. *The more she gets used to me being close to her, the easier this will all be.* Karly still looks as if she's in awe of this small paradise in my backyard. I can tell she's taking it all in. *Having her here makes this haven perfect.*

"So what do you think?" I watch her carefully for her response.

"It's beautiful back here. So peaceful and serene." She closes her eyes and inhales.

"I like having you here." She glances up at me with a shy smile, and I can see her skin flush.

I nuzzle her head on the side, and plant a kiss there. I inhale her scent, and drag my lips down to her earlobe, where I softly kiss her. I want to nip and suck on her earlobe, but restrain myself.

A few minutes later, I give in to my desire to play with her earlobe, and nip and suck on it. I hear her audibly gasp, and she pulls away. *Ah, I was worried about that.* But it will be alright. She's now used to gentle touches from me, but that was a new sensation for her. *It's all about baby steps.* After all, I really am in no hurry. *It's just a matter of time before she fully gives herself over to me.*

Around lunchtime, I check the fridge and cupboards in the outdoor kitchen and pull out some finger food for us to eat. I carry over plates and napkins for us. Karly says an appreciative thank you, as I lay out the lunch preparations. I coat a baby carrot with ranch flavored dip, and a whole grain cracker with smoked salmon cream cheese. I breathe the cool air in deeply, and can't remember the last time I've felt so peaceful.

I pick up a red grape, and put my arm around Karly, pressing it to the corner of her mouth. At first she doesn't realize what I'm doing and resists. But I playfully try to target her mouth, and she actually laughs when I finally squeeze the grape through her gorgeous lips. It's so good to see her become playful around me.

After that initial grape, I constantly try to feed her grapes and other finger food. At first she is reluctant to open her mouth, and I give her a pointed, stern look. She looks like she's going to burst into tears. "Karly, I'm not mad at you, but you need to be obedient and let me look after you. I'm doing it because I care about you and want you to be happy and healthy. Remember, you asked me to help you with your mistakes? Now open up, Sweetheart."

After that, each time I press food to her lips, she readily opens and takes it. She no longer closes her lips when I sweep my finger along the inner part of her lower lip. When it's time to administer her medication, she doesn't resist.

After lunch, I stroke her cheek tenderly with my hand, and she closes her eyes and leans into my palm. "How was lunch, Karly?"

She looks up at me appreciatively, through her fluttering eyelashes. "Really beautiful and peaceful. Thank you for bringing me outside. I hope we can go outside more often."

Although, I'm more than happy to bring her out to the back patio, I just need to make sure that it isn't a ploy of hers, to make it easier for her to get away from me. She seems genuinely sincere, but caution is what has helped me to be successful in my business dealings in the past. I'm assuming that caution will make up for a variety of deficits in our relationship. *If I'd been more cautious before, I wouldn't have had to go this long without her in my life.*

During the afternoon, Karly falls asleep, and I cover her with a blanket from the blanket box I keep outside. I light a fire in the outdoor fireplace, and the flickering light causes the shimmering outdoor ornaments to glow. Although she's not awake to enjoy it now, I know she will, once she wakes up. I pull out some marinated pork chops, and start cooking on the grill as she sleeps. After a while she starts stirring, I turn the heat down to low to keep the food warm, and I join her on the lounger.

"Sleep well, Darling?" I bend down and kiss her on the cheek.

"Yes, thank you." She then notices the dancing lights all around her and her sleepy eyes open wide. "Oh! I didn't think it could get more beautiful out here!"

"This could all be yours and mine to share, you know?"

She looks at me confusedly. "Aren't we sharing it now?"

I decide to drop the subject for now. It's a delicate conversation I shouldn't have brought up yet anyway. *She's not ready for it.*

"Hungry?" I ask her. The food smells great, and my mouth is watering.

"Mhmm."

"I'll get dinner plated then." I finish getting dinner ready, and we eat outside by firelight.

"This has been a really beautiful day. Thank you for this." I see those adoring eyes looking up at me again, and feel I'm getting closer to my objectives.

"You're welcome, Karly. I'm so glad you enjoyed it. I know I really enjoyed spending it with you." I bend down and kiss her lightly on the forehead, then on the nose, then gently brush my lips over her cheek. I whisper to her, "Ask me if you can belong to me."

"Please, can I belong to you?" Her large eyes reflect the glimmers of the outdoor ornaments.

"Only if you give me a kiss, Dear." She leans over and kisses my cheek. "You can say it now."

"I belong to you." Her face bursts into a beautiful smile.

Later in the evening, I offer her my hand to steady her as she rises, then my arm to walk her inside. I flick a switch and the outdoor lighting turns on. The view from the inner room is spectacular. Hundreds of tiny white outdoor lights shine around my Japanese garden, and with the lights turned down low inside, we can see the view without the reflection of indoor lights and other obstacles on the windows.

I have Karly rest on a settee, and I lay down behind her. I am happy to see Karly's reflection in the window. Her dress has a bluish hue in the window's reflection, making it look more navy than purple. Most importantly, I can see her facial expressions, and gauge her reactions and sincerity. She still looks as gorgeous now as she did this morning.

I put my arm around her waist, and Karly leans back into me. Her eyes flutter and her facial expression shows contentment in the reflection, rather than disdain. I start nuzzling the back of her hair, placing a kiss here and there, and she sighs, her body relaxing. *She feels so soft in my arms. I don't want this moment to end. Ever.*

I gently turn her onto her back, and kiss her softly on several parts of her face, while she looks up at me. I brush my lips on the side of her neck, her ears, and under her chin. I tentatively touch my lips ever so slightly to her collarbone, hoping she won't stiffen at my touch. She doesn't.

This spurs me on, and I reach over to take her hand in mine, gently brushing my arm against her thigh, as if it was unintentional. She stiffens slightly, still looking up at me, as if trying to focus. I massage her hand in both of mine, and keep brushing against her thigh and stomach, as if it's unintentional, and she finally relaxes.

I distract her with soft kisses on her face, while my hand reaches to stroke her cheek. My arm "inadvertently" brushes against her breast, and she gasps. I take the opportunity to brush my thumb against her bottom lip, and whisper to her. "Pretend my thumb is a grape." Her lips obediently close around my thumb, and it's my turn to gasp. I'm having difficulty keeping my desire at bay, but I continue with the "accidental" touches, while she lays there, looking up at me, wide-eyed.

"Baby, put my hand where you want it most." Karly just continues to stare up at me, but she's starting to look like she's waking up from a dream.

"Wait." Karly suddenly sits up, looking confused, but more aware than earlier.

That's when I realize her medication is passed due. *Damnit! I'm such an idiot.*

"You're right, Karly, it's getting late. I was just about to escort you up to your room for the night. Thank you for such a pleasant day in the garden with me." She nods, looking at me strangely.

I reluctantly walk her upstairs and see her to her room for the night. She looks at me doubtfully as she eyes the medication in my hand, so I make absolutely sure she takes it and swallows it. Thankfully she does, or I'd be forced to give her a shot. I then kiss her hand goodnight, and leave her room.

Karly

Night. Tues., Oct. 19, 2021

I'm lying in bed in a nightie, medication swirling through my system, and there's just one word that sums up everything I'm thinking and feeling right now. That word is: Confusion. I'm so confused I don't know which end is up, and I'm an emotional mess because of it.

Today in the garden was the most amazing day I've had in what feels like forever. I know there is no reliable frame of reference for me because time is so uneven, and each day that passes feels like a lifetime. It may be that I did enjoy my life before—I just can't remember much, and glimpses I do remember are distorted. Perhaps if my sense of time wasn't so messed up, I would at least be able to sort fractions of memories into a logical order.

I know today in the garden was very real. I felt a closeness I haven't experienced in a long time, or at least it feels that way in my world of warped time. I need and desire the closeness I felt today. I feel so much attachment to *him*, but I have an impression, just a feeling, I was attached to someone else? It's all hazy and I can't remember. Maybe my impression is a result of one of the dreams?

I remember from a dream that *he* and Clay stood on the edges of a clock, with me spinning wildly in the middle like clock hands.

194

Is Clay a real person or just a figment of my imagination? Does he just represent an abstract concept from my unconscious mind? Maybe Clay represents the past and *he* represents the future? My whole reality feels strangely warped.

What do I do? Do I accept what could be perceived as "overtures" from *him?* I feel my inhibitions may have been lessened, and I may be prone to acting on impulse. Today I felt like giving in to desires I never realized I even had. I was lying there downstairs beside *him*, but something was holding me back. There was some type of awareness that was trying to press through into conscious thought.

Who am I really? That is the million dollar question right now. I can't remember who I am and have a deteriorating sense of self. I don't mean just remembering in a cognitive way, but in a deep-down gut-feeling kind of way. Like the core of who I am. Morals, values, beliefs, ethics. Character. It's character that determines how I will act or react. I feel like my character has been dismantled like a cardboard puzzle, and the pieces that are being put back together form a different picture than the original. It's not the original "me".

But then whose idea of "me" is emerging? I've been dreaming about butterflies and the transformation they make in their cocoons. Have I somehow gone into a state of stasis, and am emerging as a different person? I feel like I have lost my identity. Or maybe I didn't have one in the first place? I can't remember. Everything gets so hazy and it becomes difficult to think. I have lapses in memory, and it's like the tracks of whole trains of thoughts have been nixed.

Maybe if my sense of discernment and sense of judgment were intact, I would be able to tell what's true and what's not true. One delicate cognitive system rests dependent on another, and if there is a flaw somewhere or a fracture, then everything comes tumbling down.

Maybe going back to a mindful exercise will help. Fact: I have a family *Feeling: They are no longer with me.* Fact: I'm here with *him*. *Feeling: He desires me.* Fact: My mind is a mess. *Feeling: I need a tangible point of reference before I go crazy.* My mind keeps going, making no sense that I can rely on. After a while, my mind relents and I go to sleep.

Anonymous
Night. Tues., Oct. 19, 2021

I stay up, working on my phone, while keeping an eye on Karly's door, then quietly sneak inside her room to make sure she's asleep. She's out cold, and once more I stroke her cheek and give her a kiss on the forehead. *God, I'm so in love with this woman.* I just need to guarantee that she will always be compliant and always will be mine.

Although I don't want her to feel as if she's being confined if she wakes up earlier than myself, I won't take any chances. I set the security system in lockdown mode so she's unable to leave the house. I'm about to head to my room, but I just can't seem to force myself to. I pace hesitantly in the hallway, finger and thumb pinching the bridge of my nose, then finally make a decision. I head back to my room to change, and brush my teeth in the adjoining bathroom.

Once I'm ready for bed, I quietly walk back down the hall, carefully open Karly's door, and slip into bed with her. My arms automatically go around her, and I pull her to my chest, spooning her. I bury my face in her hair, inhaling her sweet scent. Feeling her against my body like this is pure heaven. She sighs in her sleep. It's at that moment I realize I can never let her go.

CHAPTER THIRTEEN

Officer Duane Saunders

Morning. Wed. Oct. 20, 2021 (Day 8)

The Major Crimes Unit receives an update from the officers who are interviewing the witnesses. "The perpetrator seems to be of average weight and was thought to have medium to dark brown hair, tucked under his cap. The only staff member we weren't able to contact was Dr. Alex Jamar, who was still on leave, but unaccounted for. A few other staff members were interviewed by phone."

We are now digging deeper into Karly's history, looking at the time when she was in med school in her Toronto placement, and even before. However, most of our focus is on Geoffrey Davenport. We brainstorm for a way to investigate him discreetly. The best we've come up with is to obtain his fingerprints and connect them with the prints from the on-call room and the note Karly received from him. But still, it may end up as a waste of time and a dead end. We need to allocate our resources more effectively. "What are his ties to the hospital?"

Another team member who was looking into Geoff's company and business dealings responds. "He owns a medical supply chain. I can check to see if Trillium is one of their clients."

"That would give him access to all three hospitals if they are. Keep looking into it. The more connections, the better understanding we have of what transpired, and the stronger case we can build."

The reminder that he owned a medical supply company only strengthened my suspicion that Geoff is involved. It would explain how he would have obtained Karly's schedule and kept an eye on her. It would mean that he had knowledge of how the hospital operates and could potentially provide him access to all areas of the hospital for supply reasons. *Geoffrey Davenport is definitely on the top of the list for persons of interest.*

Clay

Afternoon. Wed., Oct. 20, 2021

I can't just sit around and do nothing. Every moment when I'm not working is consumed with thoughts of Karly, hoping and praying that she is alright. I stand up, but fall into my habit of pacing again. I pull out my phone and text Justin.

Me: "Hey. Could you do me a favor?"

Justin: "Anything, bro. How you holding up?"

Me: "Not so well. I just can't sit around and do nothing."

Justin: "What do you need?"

Me: "Could you have Shirley track down info on someone for me?"

Justin: "Sure. Text me what you have."

I text my brother the name. *To think that Geoff Mason might be involved. It's probably just a loose end the officers want to eliminate. Ever since the officer and I discussed Geoff, I've wondered if there's a chance he could be involved. I can't just do nothing. I have to do something, at least to feel like I'm helping.*

I try watching TV for the next few hours, but find myself fidgeting, not paying attention. Finally, I start pacing again. Justin's best friend, Shirley, is studying Cyber Securities. I hear a ping on my phone, and dash over to grab it. I see Justin's text.

Justin: "Wow. New name: Geoffrey Davenport. Address: 2415 Doulton Dr."

Me: "Thanks, man."

I check Google Maps. *Only 15 minutes drive.* I grab my coat, shoes, and a flashlight out of the kitchen drawer. I put on a mask and gloves, lock my apartment, then call for the elevator. In the parkade below the building, I jump into my SUV, and start driving towards my destination.

My heart is pounding. I know there's really nothing I can do, but I'm still curious to see where Geoff is now living. Although our interactions were brief, they were intense and left a bad taste in my mouth. The farther away from Karly he is, the better.

I remember he owned a medical supply company. *He must have done well for himself, especially due to COVID and the demand for supplies.* I remember what Karly told me about the way he emotionally abused her, and my mouth sets itself in a grim line. *She didn't deserve that kind of treatment; she should be treated as the beautiful woman she is.*

I slowly drive down Doulton Drive, taking in all the expansive properties. Some of the houses are so far back from the road they can't even be seen. People like their privacy here.

I come to 2415, and continue down the road slowly. I don't want to stop or it might look suspicious. The house, *or mansion I should say,* is set back from the road, with hedges providing privacy, and what I assume is an alarmed gate. I drive around the area to get a sense of how the lots are situated, and am not able to see a way to drive and get a glimpse of the back of the property. I will have to check it out on foot later.

Am I really going to do this? I have no idea if he's even involved. Perhaps I'm motivated in part by the way Geoff treated Karly years ago, and right now he provides a target for my anger and frustration over the current situation. I decide to cool off, and drive to a nearby Tim Hortons to grab something to eat. I buy a maple strudel and an apple-cinnamon fog tea, which helps me to relax.

When I'm ready, I drive to a local public school and park in the parking lot. I get out of my SUV, then walk over to Doulton Drive. *Does this make me a stalker?* It's kind of a silly notion considering the circumstances. *No, I'm just looking for answers.*

As I walk, I pull up Google Maps on my phone to try to get an idea of where the property lines intersect. I wanted to check out the manor from another angle, possibly from the back. I can see that the part of Doulton Drive I'm looking at is a semicircle, the straight line being Blythe Rd. and the curve being Doulton. It looks like the best approach between the properties is from the Northeast. *Here goes nothing.*

Evening. Wed., Oct. 20, 2021

By the time I arrive back at Doulton Drive with my flashlight, it's dark out. Lanterns light the street, giving off a yellowish glow, and the moonlight creates a shimmering stream as the clouds roll by. I find my point of entry and walk a few feet in, only to find there is a narrow sunken brick path, hidden from the road by another hedge.

I follow the pathway, lit by a few lanterns, checking my phone GPS as I'm walking. I stop when I get to the right property, and can see the mansion rising above the hedges in the back of the property. There is a small, yet high black iron gate covering an opening in the hedges. *There's no way to see inside the house.* The way is completely blocked.

I stand there for a minute, contemplating what I should do. The clouds roll away from the moon, and the area brightens up. I can see something glinting in the moonlight behind the gate. I crouch down to get a closer look, and I gasp. *It can't be!* On the wet grass, illuminated by the moonlight, is the sterling silver locket I had given to Karly only last week. I pull out my phone and snap photos from all angles. However, I don't reach onto the property to touch it or move it. I leave it as is. I need to get back to the road unnoticed and send this info to Officer Saunders.

Karly
Evening. Wed., Oct. 20, 2021

I feel like I'm in a dream, or maybe a drug-induced fugue.

I'm sitting at a table in a beautiful dress with Geoff, and he's leaning towards me. His hand gently touches my cheek, and he looks at me with a tenderness that makes my heart want to melt. "Karly, I can give you *anything* your heart desires. I want to give you the world." Then everything swirls around me.

Geoff sits on the couch with me as we cuddle up and watch a movie on the big screen with popcorn. He feeds me popcorn, then kisses me on the forehead. Everything swirls again.

Geoff and I sit at bar stools in a kitchen. "I'll always look after you and protect you from the people who tried to take you away from me." I feel confused, but I know he'll make everything right. My whole world swirls again.

I wake up, head swimming as usual, and stumble out of my bed. I'm so confused that I need a point of reference. I look over at the small couch by the table with magazines, the large built-in bookcases, and wish there was a window. All the furniture is beautiful and made of cherry wood. I wobble over to the tall dresser, and see photos in frames on top. My heart stops as I stare at the pictures of Geoff and I. My mind is completely confused, and I would be panicking by now, if not for the drugs in my system.

Take a deep breath. I breathe evenly and mindfully. I have so many mixed up memories, but strangely, I remember each one of the events in the photos. I open the frame back of the picture of Geoff and I dressed up formally. There is writing on the photo back:

Karly and I at our five year anniversary together.

I feel like my heart has stopped. *But have we really been together that long?* I feel panicky. *I can't remember what's real and what's not. Which memories are from a dream and which are from reality?* My head is in my hands. *I feel like I can't trust my own mind.* I have memories of the event, of the anniversary we celebrated when we had been together for five years. I remember Geoff was so sweet and endearing, even though I wasn't feeling well. I shake my head out, thinking I can chase away the cobwebs.

I walk back up to the dresser and I check the backs of the other photos. They have dates on them as well. And I have actual memories of all of the events, of being with Geoff. I just don't understand it.

Officer Duane Saunders
Evening. Wed., Oct. 20, 2021

That evening I have a date with the lovely Sharon, and I take her to a place called Studio 89, a non-profit coffee bar that provides a free venue for community groups. We enjoy our Nutella lattes while we listen to local musicians, then chat and get to know each other better.

A couple of hours into our animated conversation, I receive a text from Clay Aldridge. Attached is a photo of a piece of jewellery on green grass, taken from the other side of a black iron cast gate.

Clay: "This is Karly's! I'm sure of it."

Me: "Don't move it or touch it. Where are you?" I punch the letters in on my phone.

Clay: "Doulton Drive. Between 2415 and 2425."

Geoffrey Davenport's address. What is he doing there? I text him back.

Me: "I'll be right there. Stay out of sight." This is great news, finally a solid lead in the case.

I apologize to Sharon, and ask if she'd mind if we reschedule. She is very gracious, and agrees to another date. *Thanks to Dr. Aldridge, I now have a second date with Sharon.* I walk her to her car, we share a friendly hug, then I head over to Doulton Drive.

I have a forensic team meet us on Doulton. Using unmarked cars only makes us slightly less out of place in the neighborhood. We are still the only cars actually parked on a street where cars are always parked on estate grounds. Clay quietly leads us down the slim path, until we arrive at the black gate seen in the photo he had sent me. He crouches down and points. "There."

The forensic team gets to work, snapping photos, taking measurements, and finally carefully removing the broken necklace from its resting place. They continue taking photos of the indentation in the grass, to circumvent the argument that Clay himself dropped the necklace there to incriminate Geoff. If we could prove the necklace had been sitting there for, say, a period of days, then we should be in the clear when presenting evidence in court. If this ever goes to court.

I'd rather not think of the chances of successfully laying criminal charges and having them stick in a situation like this. Historically, these cases aren't very successful in court, when you weigh the victim's emotional pain of going to trial against the perpetrator's sentence. But first things first. Let's find the girl and bring her home safely.

We head back to our cars, armed with the bagged necklace, digital photos of the inside and outside of the locket, and other notes. Photos are sent from my tablet with my "Information to

Obtain" form and warrant draft to the judge, to show we have cut and dry evidence to reasonably search the grounds and any buildings.

I have Clay sit with me for a few minutes to talk in my vehicle. I can see he's shaking, and it seems to be from a combination of anger and worry. "You did well, Clay. This has given us the biggest lead yet. We now have a clear direction to take the investigation. We weren't completely sure until now."

Clay nods his head, but I can tell he is still stricken. He looks pale. "All I can think of is that the necklace is broken. Someone must have ripped it off her."

"If they had, I don't think they'd have left it lying around as evidence for someone to find."

"True." Clay looks doubtful. I'm trying to set his mind at ease, but I can see force had to be involved for Karly's necklace to be broken like that. We both know it. And both of us know she could have been hurt in the altercation. Clay goes with the forensic team to be dropped off at his car, and Lauren and I wait for an approved search warrant to pop up on my tablet.

Geoff

Evening. Wed., Oct. 20, 2021

Damnit! How the hell…? I glance at the monitor as I walk by, and can see police at my back gate, in the dark, looking closely at something on the grass and taking photos. They must be good, if they've tracked Karly this far. *I wonder how they managed it. I covered my tracks so well.* I wonder to myself what they've found out back.

I walk around my home at a good clip, collecting anything that might look suspicious, cause further alarm, and further cause for a more detailed search. In situations such as this, there's an urgency, so there is more leniency getting a search warrant pushed through with a judge. But I still know they're going to do everything strictly "by the book", since they know I have the means to sue the everliving pants off the RCMP.

I walk over to the guest room where Karly is staying, and look at her sweet face as she sleeps. I need to move her, but she looks so peaceful. I walk over to the bed, scoop her up in my arms, and head to the stairs leading to my basement. I carefully carry Karly downstairs, and open an almond colored panel next to one of the inset bookcases. It blends perfectly into the wall, and no one will suspect it leads to an inner room.

The air is musty, as I scooch into the dark space, and I turn on the light by pulling on the chain in the middle of the room. This is the room I was originally going to keep Karly in, before I had a change of heart towards her. Rather than conditioning her with fear, as was my original intent, I shifted to trying to win her adoration. Well, the game was rigged so I wouldn't lose, but look at her now. Sure I've had to use medication to make her compliant from the beginning, but now having her look at me with those adoring eyes, instead of fear-filled ones—it makes the transition all worth it.

"I'm not letting you go, Baby." I kiss her on the top of her head as she sleeps, while I lay her on the small bed in the corner of the room. "You won't be in here long. Just until things blow over." Anxiety grips my heart and squeezes. I want to lie down with her and be close to her, but I have too much to do. I figure I have minutes before the paperwork for the warrant is presented outside my gates. Technology now allows an affidavit to be submitted and a warrant to be approved of in mere minutes.

I grab what I need from the hospital suite next door, and give Karly an injection while she's sleeping. She stirs, but I lull her back to sleep. *Damn. I need to move faster.* I replace the almond panelling, layered with heat-reflective mylar foil, same as the walls and ceiling, and it's impossible to tell there's another room behind the bookcases.

I walk upstairs and call my lawyer, asking him to be at the gate as soon as possible, in order to stall the warrant. I clear the kitchen and Karly's bedroom of anything that might reveal her presence, and hide it behind another secret panel. After everything is clear, I head down to the hospital suite, remove Karly's "chart", and any other evidence that someone had been staying there. Since I own a hospital supply chain, there's nothing out of the ordinary with having equipment in my home, and a private hospital room "just in case" I contract COVID. I walk over to the downstairs bar, pour myself a scotch, then head up to the main floor.

Officer Duane Saunders
Night. Wed., Oct. 20, 2021

By the time Geoffrey Davenport's lawyer has read through the search warrant and lets us through the gates, it's late at night.

"Mr. Davenport." I hold out my hand to greet him at the door. He shakes my hand, and I note that he's holding onto a glass, presumably of scotch. I keep my expression neutral. "I'm Officer Duane Saunders and this is Officer Lauren Freizen."

"Officers, what can I do for you?" He has a clearly bored expression on his face mixed with displeasure.

"We are looking for a young lady who is missing. Karly Jileski." I ready myself to gauge his reaction.

"Karly!" Geoff acts somewhat genuinely surprised. "I haven't seen her for, what, four or five years now? You say she's missing?" His lawyer whispers something in Geoff's ear and Geoff nods.

"She's been missing for a week."

Geoff's lawyer nudges him. Geoff raises his index finger to me. "Give us a moment." The two of them walk off and have a brief discussion facing away from us, then return. "She's been missing for a week? So why are you here and not out looking for her then?" Geoff's lip is drawn up in a thin line.

"We found something near your property line that belongs to her."

"My lawyer just mentioned it was some type of jewelry? What makes you think it's hers?"

If I didn't know better, I would say Geoff is enjoying this. "Her photo is inside the locket."

Geoff really does seem genuinely surprised this time. He sounds as if he's contemplating to himself. "So there's no way it could belong to someone else." Geoff then snaps at us and sternly looks at Lauren and I. "What were you doing by my property line?"

"We received a report from a concerned citizen and the locket was in plain view."

"That sounds awfully suspicious." Geoff doesn't bother to hide the disdain in his voice. "Someone *randomly* trespassing and finding a piece of jewelry on *my* property that belongs to a missing woman. If anything, I would suggest someone is trying to frame me." Geoff's lawyer nods at the sentiment.

I'm not interested in playing games, and request that he lets us through the door. "The court order gives us permission to search the house, the grounds, and any other buildings on site."

"Let me walk with you." It's obvious Geoff's lawyer is going to stick with us like glue, making sure the letter of the law is followed. He also looks at Geoff slyly, and I wonder why they are being so laissez-faire about it. Maybe they believe the search warrant will be thrown out if the case ever goes to court because of the issue with the property line. Well, I have a few tricks up my sleeve, too. But right now my focus is on finding Karly and returning her home safely.

We walk through the expansive house. There is a lavishly finished basement which is above ground at the back of the manor. There also seems to be room for an attic, just from looking at the structure of the house, and I plan to inquire about that possibility before the end of the search.

Lauren keeps up casual conversation, asking questions about the architecture of the house, while I make it obvious that I'm putting my full focus on the search. At the same time, I know Lauren's putting on a ruse. She's the epitome of multitasking and is as observant as a hawk. We work well this way, as usually people become wary of me, while Lauren disarms them.

I see Mr. Davenport put down his scotch glass, and I decide to make a move, hoping Lauren will catch on. "What's this?" I ask sternly, as I march into the adjoining room. Geoff and his lawyer look at each other and quickly follow me to see what it is I've zoomed in on. At the same time, I know Lauren is pulling out her phone to snap enlarged photos of the scotch glass.

I march up to the first door I see since it's the first thing I can think of, and pull on the handle. I'm actually stunned when I open the door to a hospital suite. "What's this for?" My tone is suspicious, and I'm hoping it's enough to keep them preoccupied while Lauren finishes her task.

"That's in case I get COVID." Geoff smirks at me with his arms crossed in front of him, legs spread slightly. A stance of confidence. Or maybe arrogance? He suddenly realizes Lauren isn't with us, and abruptly turns his head back towards where he last saw her. He starts walking back over to her.

"I see." I mumble something about eccentric millionaires, and close the door to the hospital suite. Since I don't know much about medical supplies, I don't see the point in me going through the room. Someone knowledgeable will check through tomorrow, since the search warrant will still be good.

Lauren is busy looking closely at the inset bookshelves, and I can see that Geoff is becoming irate. I wonder if it's because of our general intrusion, or if he suspects Lauren has snapped photos of his fingerprints. *Or could it be for another reason?*

We continue to go through the house during the night, and Geoff finally turns in to bed, after calling an additional lawyer in to "babysit" the two of us. He obviously doesn't trust us. Or he's hiding something. If he's not involved in Karly's disappearance, I don't know how to explain her locket on his property. There's no way in hell it's a coincidence.

Morning. Thurs., Oct. 21, 2021 (Day 9)

During the day, the team searches the grounds. Unfortunately, it seems to be a dead end, as well as the searches of the other buildings on the property. Heat imaging done over the entire house shows up nothing, and we've found no evidence that Karly has been inside Geoff's mansion at all.

I think the best plan is to put a tail on him. He must be keeping her somewhere else. We'll have to check the list of properties he owns. He's definitely involved in her disappearance, I'm sure of it. I just don't have any idea where he's keeping her.

After a full day of nothing, I talk with Geoff as he sees us out. I ask him to please contact us if he does happen to hear from Karly, as her family is desperate to find her. For a second I see an expression of shame and possibly regret flicker over his face. Then his face becomes impassive again, and he nods at us and closes the door. His lawyers see us to the gate.

"Well, that was a whole lot of nothing." I walk beside Lauren on our way to our vehicle.

Lauren has a small smile on her face. "Well, we'll hopefully know about those fingerprints soon enough, the ones I took photos of from his glass. I forwarded them to the lab right away for comparison."

I'm feeling disappointed that even the heat imaging came up negative. I thought for sure we'd find Karly and deliver her back to her family. I feel discouraged at the thought of not being able to reassure them. It's difficult to think about it, but she may have already met with foul play.

"I know what you're thinking, and it's not the case." Lauren won't allow me to slip into a depressed stupor. "We keep going, look at the case with fresh eyes, and try to get a different perspective on things." I nod and sigh. She's right. We aren't about to give up on this young lady. Just looking through her file, even the last few months employed at the hospital, it's obvious Karly isn't the type to give up. She would hang on until her last breath.

CHAPTER FOURTEEN

Karly

Morning. Thurs. Oct. 21, 2021

I wake up in a pitch black room, and can't hear anything except the buzzing in my ears that sounds like an electrical current. "Hello?" It's as if the room is insulated. I have a vague memory. I've been in a music studio before, and I know what it's like to sing with insulated walls surrounding me. My voice just dissipates and disappears. That's how it sounds in here, and since I can't hear a thing from outside, I'm assuming it's been insulated both ways.

I feel afraid. I don't know why I'm here in the dark, instead of in my own bedroom, the one with the beautiful cherry wood furniture. I start to panic. *Where is Geoff? Doesn't he care about me anymore? I really need to go to the bathroom.* All kinds of thoughts are flying through my head in random order, and I feel irrationally emotional, hypersensitive.

I set my feet on the floor, and try to examine the room in the dark by touch. The room feels bare, apart from the bed. There is no light switch. I swing my hands around up in the air, in case there's a string for a light. I doubt it, but maybe I'm in some type of cellar?

After a minute, my hand hits something that swings back and forth. I pull on it, and suddenly the room is illuminated. I close my eyes, and see the flashes of white behind my eyelids. Although the light isn't very bright, after stumbling around in pitch black it looks like the sun.

I examine my surroundings, and after looking under the bed, I find some water bottles, hand sanitizer, a bucket, and a roll of toilet paper. As I reach to get the items, my arm brushes on an indentation in the floor. Over the top of the indentation, it feels like there's a handle. I push the handle and it slides the indented panel backwards, under the floor.

I feel around the small alcove and find a box. I pull it out from under the bed, open it, and take a look inside. I see some items, a blanket, a hat with fake hair, and scrubs. Attached to the scrubs is a pager, which I remove and put in my pajama pocket. I pull out the blanket, in case I get cold in the tiny room. I put the rest of the useless items back under the floor and close the panel.

I use the bucket and my bladder feels relieved. Then I clean up with the other items from under the bed.

A tear rolls down my cheek. Did I do something to upset Geoff? Why did he put me in here? Doesn't he know that I just want his approval, that I've always just wanted his approval? I vaguely remember that he always tried to make me feel like I wasn't good enough. But lately, he seemed to be happy with me, and that I wasn't disappointing him.

"Hello?" My voice is a hoarse whisper. I lay back down on the bed, wondering when I can see Geoff again. What if he never wants to see me again? The thought causes me to start sobbing, soul-wrenching sobs. "Please, I need you, Geoff." I feel absolutely devastated.

My mind is a confused mess of mush again, but I try to go through my mindfulness exercise again. *Fact: My name is Karly and I'm 24 years old. I have a mother, father, older brother, and younger sister.* Feeling: I feel isolated from my family. I don't think they want to see me anymore. *Fact: Geoff is the love of my life and I just want him to approve of me.* Feeling: I feel somehow that I'm living inside a strange dream. I feel like I'm not good enough so I keep trying harder. *Fact: I'm in a small, bare room by myself.* Feeling: I feel like I've done something to displease Geoff. I'm being punished. I desperately want his forgiveness. *Fact: I think I'm getting my facts and*

feelings mixed up, and is this even real? Feeling: I feel like a child emotionally. I can no longer regulate my emotions properly.

I don't feel like myself. I feel like I'm some other person. Like I left my innermost self behind somewhere in a cage, and just continued on a journey without it. *Who am I?* I drink from one of the water bottles, trying to formulate coherent thoughts that will help me understand my situation better. But all I can think of is not disappointing Geoff. I must have done something terrible for him to put me in here, away from him. I lean into my hands, and continue to sob.

Geoff
Evening. Thurs. Oct. 21, 2021

As soon as the search warrant is up, everyone leaves, including my lawyers. Once I'm locked up in my fortress again, I run downstairs so quickly I almost trip over my own two darn feet. I have to get to Karly. I remove the almond wood panel and see she has been able to turn the light on. She sits there on the bed, tears streaming down her cheeks. I run to her and hold her.

"I'm so so-rry." She can barely speak, she's sobbing so hard. *Is she having a panic attack?*

"No, Baby Girl, it's not your fault." I pick her up and cradle her on my lap, rocking her like a child. *She's so vulnerable and helpless.*

"I thought you were...were upset with me." Tears are still streaming from her eyes. I can feel the front of her white shirt is soaked through. I try to keep my eyes averted so I don't see her chest. "Please, I need you, Geoff."

My heart soars, hearing that from her without any prompting from me. "No, hun, I'm not upset with you. Let's get you upstairs and into a nice, warm bath." I carry her carefully up the stairs and lay her on her bed in her room. She curls up in the fetal position on her side. I draw a bath for her in the ensuite.

When it's ready I scoop her up off the bed and help her out of her pajamas in the bathroom while my hands involuntarily linger, brushing over her skin. Her skin feels like silk, and I can't stop myself from staring at her. I'm fascinated by her curves. She didn't have them when we dated years ago, but instead she was very slender back then.

She starts to step into the bath and I assist her. She crouches down and leans back against the tub with a little sigh, closing her eyes, while the soap residue swirls around her on the top of the water, covering her body so I'm unable to see much. I walk over to the light switch and turn down the dimmer. I hope the low lighting will help her to relax. I sit opposite her on the floor and watch her, more aware of things I haven't noticed about her before, like the cute way she scrunches up her nose sometimes.

To be honest, I usually get so caught up in myself, I don't pay attention to others. I think of Karly and our relationship in the past, and think about the hard truth. *And when I do pay attention it's usually to strike out in anger.* But maybe I could change. Possibly. When I was with Karly years ago, I was so insecure that I felt I had to put her down so she felt worthless, or she'd end up leaving me. *But she ended up leaving me anyway.* I sigh to myself. *I'm not going to let that happen this time. I'll do anything to keep her with me. She is my life.* I feel resolute.

I slide over to the other end of the bath, kneel on the floor, and cradle Karly's head in one of my hands, while gently wetting her hair down with water from a container. She nuzzles into my hand, looking up at me with adoring eyes. *There's nothing like being adored, instead of feared. I never realized the rush it gives until now.* I lather up her hair, then rinse it again, eventually working in conditioner. Then I rinse her hair again.

I clear my throat. "Karly, would you like me to wash your back for you?" She nods at me, and turns her back towards me. I take the sponge and soap and move my hand in circular motions around her back. She gently sighs.

Should I risk it? Should I? "Hmm. The rest of you needs washing, too, Karly." I try to smile at her. "Would you like me to help you with the rest of your bath?" Karly looks at me with those big, darling eyes. *I can see that she completely trusts me now.* I feel a sense of triumph, and can anticipate what her answer is going to be. Karly nods.

"You need to use your words, Dear. What is it you would like?"

"Please help me to wash?"

"Good girl. Of course I'll help you." I pick up the sponge and start soaping it up. I gently lather up her entire body, taking note of her expressions when I move over specific parts of her body. I watch as certain types of strokes with the soapy sponge across parts of her body make her shiver, and hear her little gasps as her eyes close. *Damn this sponge, being in the way.* But I need to condition her to these new physical sensations gradually without alarming her. I know she's inexperienced and pure from years ago, and that Clay is too much of a gentleman and obviously hasn't put his hands on her…

I wash her body three times, unnecessary of course, but I don't want to stop watching what type of movement triggers each physiological reaction from her. *And maybe I can stimulate her desire to the point where she submits herself with wanton abandon to me.* The idea excites me immensely. Then I suddenly realize I've been at it too long. Karly is non-stop shivering—the water has gone cold.

Reluctantly I turn the shower on, the warm water rinsing her off, the only upside being that I can get a good look at her while she stands there. A *really* good look at her. My desire arises, stronger than it ever has before. *How am I going to keep my hands off her tonight?*

When she's done her bath I help her out, trying to avert my eyes, not very successfully. I wrap her in a warm, thick towel. I try to think of something to prolong the experience, then I realize there's a bottle of moisturizing lotion on the counter. I grab the bottle. "Hold out your arm, Karly." She obeys me readily and I squirt the lotion in my hand, and gently rub her arm, shoulders, neck, and then her other arm.

She holds the towel to her front, and I face her, rubbing moisturizer into her back, all the way down to her ass. I cup her cheeks in my hands rubbing in circles with my fingers, and it's all I can do to not slide my fingers between her legs. Inwardly I groan. I move my hands downwards and moisturize her legs back then front, then start again at her shoulders. "I need to do your front now, Karly." By this time, my heart is pounding with excitement and I'm struggling with self-control.

She looks into my eyes for a moment, then nods, biting her lower lip. She shifts her towel so it now covers her back half and drapes over her sides. I start to work the moisturizer down the top of her chest, eyeing her beautiful rounded breasts. Just as I begin moving from her underarms to the upper part of her breasts, she draws her towel around her again, and instead holds out her palm.

I squirt some moisturizer into her palm, and she lets her towel drop, revealing her entire body to me, mere inches away. I inhale sharply. She rubs the moisturizer into her breasts while I stand there, slack-jawed and staring. I try to tear my eyes away but I can't. She finally finishes massaging the lotion into her skin. She holds out her hand again and absentmindedly I squirt more moisturizer into her hand. After she finishes rubbing moisturizer into her stomach, she moisturizes her inner thighs, and then between her legs. I swallow audibly.

"Done." It takes me a moment to realize what she means, a moment to refocus myself. *I think I could convince her to let me massage her entire body next time. Wait, maybe she'd let me touch her now?*

"Karly, do you, um...think you could direct my hand next time to show me the best way to rub moisturizer all over your body?" She looks up at me for a moment. Then she nods. "Do you think you could show me now?"

She looks at me strangely. "But we're already finished." She picks up her towel and encompasses herself with it again. I can't stop myself and I grab her arm before she leaves the bathroom. She startles, and when her head snaps back to look at me, I can see she's scared.

But when I see her reaction, I want to defuse it, so I smile down at her and hold her hand. "You missed a spot."

"Oh!" She seems surprised, but trusts me, dropping her towel on the floor again.

I put moisturizing lotion on my hand, and show her she missed her hips. "Show me how to massage it in, Baby." I stand behind her and hold out my hand to her. "Convince me of your devotion by showing me." She takes my hand, and places my hand on her hip, moving it in circles.

The back of her bare body is pressed right into me, and my hand is on her hip, massaging her. I take the bottle and put lotion on the other hand as well, and I use both hands simultaneously, making small circles from her outer hip bones, as far inward as I dare.

I pause for a moment, ripping off my shirt, so my bare chest is against her bare back. "Just keeping you warm, Sweetheart." She leans into me slightly and I'm kissing her neck and behind her ear. I put more moisturizer on my fingers, then I go back to massaging her with tiny circular movements, until I can't control myself anymore.

Hands over her hips, I pull her hard against me, and my hands move further inwards. I hear Karly gasp. *This is it.* I continue to rub in tiny circles. "C'mon Baby, you're going to love this, stay with me." I become very aware of her ass pulled tightly up against me. She gasps again, and I continue with my fingers, and move inwards until my fingers are at the point where they're about to touch each other.

Suddenly, she grasps my hands firmly and holds them. I can feel her panting for breath, but she's not letting my hands move, and I won't fight her. I need her to keep trusting me.

"What is it, Karly?" I realize I'm panting as well.

"I think you got all the missed spots."

How can she have this much willpower, under this amount of medication, when experiencing pleasure like this? I'm at a loss, so I turn her around to face me. "Okay. I think it's time for a hug then."

She smiles up at me, and I pull her body up against mine. I can feel every curve and contour against my front, as I pull her in close. I cup her naked bottom, and pick her up to carry her, and she looks at me with surprise. "Come on, let's go to your room for your clothes." Her expression relaxes and she slowly smiles up at me.

Carrying her to her room like this does nothing to lessen my desire for her. It just heightens it. I press into her naked front, feeling her naked breasts against my bare chest. My groin strains against her, feeling her pressed up against me through my clothes. *If only there wasn't this barrier between us. These pants.* Desperately, I try to think of a way I can rationalize to her that being naked together would be a good thing.

I gently lay her down on the bed, leaning on my elbows and caging her between my arms. "Karly," I moan, kissing her softly on her face. "Convince me of your devotion, Baby." Those are words that now trigger her to be compliant. I move over to the corner of her lip, and she responds. I lick her lower lip and she parts her mouth.

I kiss her on her lips, and although she doesn't respond at first, I deepen the kiss. My restraint is at its breaking point. I'm not going to be able to hold back much longer. But she needs to be the one to invite me to do those things to her I only dream about. My kissing becomes more passionate. *Take me, Karly. Oh hell, take me.*

But instead I feel her tense up and put her hands against my chest, pushing me firmly away from her. *Damnit!* Her face is full of anxiety, and her eyes are sliding back and forth between mine, trying to read me through her drug-induced haze. "It's okay, Karly. I was just giving you a special kiss and hug. Like friends do." She regards me doubtfully. I kiss her on the cheek. "C'mon." I reluctantly, very reluctantly, stand up and offer her my hand, which she takes.

"Let's get your clothes ready for this evening. I got you some pretty dresses." She smiles up at me in delight. *I love seeing that expression on her face, knowing I'm the one to cause it.* I smile down at her, and stroke her underneath her chin with my fingers.

This time instead of choosing her dress for her, I tell her which dress I would love to see her in, but let her make the final decision. She chooses the one I had suggested. I smile at her, and her eyes look up at me, glowing. I zip her into her dress, and scoop her up while she squeals and laughs, carrying her to the kitchen. I kiss her on the nose before setting her down in a chair.

I open the freezer. "Hmm. Pasta night tonight I guess. Well, we could have spaghetti with carbonara sauce, tortellini in butter garlic sauce, or linguini in a cream sauce. I'd personally prefer tortellini in butter garlic sauce. What about you?"

Karly answers without missing a beat. "Tortellini in butter garlic sauce, please."

My smile grows wider. "Tortellini it is." I walk over and give her a kiss on the top of her head, brushing her cheek with my hand. "Good girl."

I enjoy a nice dinner with my Karly. Yes, *my* Karly. It was good to recover from the last couple of days when we were interrupted and my home was invaded. I knew it would happen at some point, that the police would come snooping. I just didn't think they'd have a search warrant or that it would happen so quickly.

"So Karly, I'm thinking you're doing so well, we can wean you off your meds now. Would you like that?" I slide my chair over and stroke her cheek, so she knows I'm pleased with her. Her smile is open and innocent, and she nods her head.

"You might feel a bit confused, coming off those meds, but just remember I'll help you. That's because you belong to me—if you want to…"

She cuts me off, urgently. "Please, let me belong to you?"

I can feel her urgency now when she pleads. I feel something akin to euphoria, and my face reflects how pleased I am with her. "Good girl, very good girl. Yes, you can belong to me. You can say it now."

"I belong to you." She smiles gratefully.

"Convince me of your devotion." I stroke her face and kiss her on both cheeks, and her forehead. I brush her lips with mine, and when I start to kiss her mouth and try to part her lips, she doesn't pull away. I cradle her face in my hands, and kiss her more deeply. I can finally feel her start to respond, a natural physical response since her inhibitions have been dimmed by her medication.

My hands start to roam slowly and softly over her body as I moan into her mouth, and it takes every ounce of willpower I have to keep the caresses gentle. But I finally can't control myself any longer, and my hand strokes her inner thigh through her dress, bunching up the material between her legs.

I gently move my hand over the bunched up material, but Karly breaks the kiss and pulls back instinctively with a look of confusion on her face. I give her a pained smile. *I'll just have to give it some more time and be patient with her.* I'm afraid she'll start to cry, so I cradle her face in my hands and talk to her. "I know you're not ready right now, Sweetheart, and it's okay. It will come in time." She tentatively nods at me, as if she's confused. So I tuck her hair behind her ear, and boop her on the nose so she laughs.

After I clean up the dinner dishes, we get ready for bed. I feel exhausted from the lack of sleep last night. Karly's about to crawl into her bed, when instead I scoop her up and take her to my room and place her on my bed. She looks at me uncomfortably.

"I just thought we could watch a movie together in my room, Love." She visibly relaxes and smiles.

"So what would you like to watch? A comedy, action, or horror? I'd prefer horror."

"I'd like to watch a horror."

"Actually," I look at her slyly, "I've changed my mind and want to watch an action movie."

"Oh, I'd rather watch an action movie. I'd like that better." Her adoring eyes look up at me. I look back down at her, smiling, and stroking her cheek. *Oh, I'm liking this much better.*

Officer Duane Saunders
Morning. Fri., Oct. 22, 2021 (Day 10)

The Major Crimes Unit brings together all the updates for the debriefing on Friday morning. Interviews with hospital staff are pretty much finished now. Some news has come in on the fingerprints. The prints Lauren photographed from Geoffrey

Davenport's glass have come up as a match with the other two locations, the bed frame in the on-call room and the note sent to Karly through the hospital mail. It looks like he messed up and assumed that all gloves eliminate fingerprints, which is not the case. This just confirms what we already have suspected for a while, that Geoff is the abductor and we're on the right track.

A tail has been assigned to Geoff, in case he's been keeping Karly at a different location. I think it's safe to say she isn't at the house, since we did a heat imaging scan. Although it's true there are some things that can block a scan, like foil, normally those things aren't used in practicality. Then again, there is nothing normal about Geoffrey Davenport or this case, for that matter.

The Major Crimes Unit moves onto looking at Geoff's properties now, places he could possibly be keeping Karly. If he's leaving her for hours or days at a time elsewhere, there's a real concern she could become dehydrated and very ill. The list of properties is immense, so I hope our team is able to tail him and find her that way. Otherwise, we'll systematically go through the list and go through the process of elimination, until we have a short-list to concentrate on.

We also discuss the risk factors involved in all of this. How likely is Geoff to panic and dispose of Karly? In our discussion, we're in agreement that 24-hour surveillance on him should prevent him from doing anything stupid. *Hang in there, Karly. We're looking for you.*

Clay
Morning. Fri., Oct. 22, 2021

I felt so sure we were going to find Karly by yesterday, that the let-down is unfathomable. I'm glad my family is staying in touch on Zoom, although I don't feel like talking about the case. It's just good to know they're there for me and to feel their support. Mom and Dad have cut their trip short, and are travelling home as soon as they can.

Officer Saunders is keeping me more in the loop now, along with Karly's family and Vi, which I appreciate. He's asked me not to go and do anything else independently, and to notify him if I have any theories so he and the team can follow up on legitimate ideas. I know he's not just looking out for me, protecting me from personal liability. He's also looking at the integrity of the entire case, if eventually charges are to be brought, once we get Karly back. To conclude a different outcome is unspeakable. *We will bring you home, Karly. I promise.* This morning I start a 24-hour on-call shift, so I prepare to leave. I just hope there is good news about the case today.

Karly
Morning. Fri., Oct. 22, 2021

I wake up in Geoff's bed, his body tight up against mine, spooning me. I feel uncomfortable in such close proximity to him. I carefully try to slide out from underneath his arm, but he catches me and pulls me back into him as I squirm.

"Karly." There's a low-rumbling laugh vibrating in his chest. "Come back here, you." Although we're both in pajamas, I still feel uncomfortable, lying in the same bed with him. "It's okay, there's nothing to worry about. We both fell asleep during the movie last night. It's just like you having a slumber party with your friends in the old days, remember?" I relax a bit when he explains it that way. "Let's just chat a bit before breakfast."

I turn around to face him and nod my head, my eyes looking directly at his. He reaches out his hand to my face and strokes my cheek. "God, Karly, you're just so...beautiful." I smile at Geoff and again feel that urge to please him. "Here, let me hold you for a bit, you look cold." He gestures to me to move forward towards him.

Although I don't feel cold, after a minute I nod my head and move into his arms. It seemed as though he was holding his breath, waiting. He holds me up against him, stroking my hair off my face and caressing my cheeks. While cradling my cheek, his thumb toys with my bottom lip, stroking it so my lip drops open. He brings his face closer to mine, and I feel panicky, like I'm about to tense up, but then he's just rubbing his cheek against mine. My heart begins to calm down again.

"So you're starting on an even lower dosage of medication today. At this rate, you'll be off it in no time. Karly, you're getting better, and that makes me happy. Last night during your bath, in the bedroom, and in the kitchen, well, it showed me how well you are doing." Geoff smiles at me, looking genuinely happy. Although I can't remember what I was ill with in the first place, I smile back, my heart soaring that he's pleased with me.

I try to remember back to my bath, bedroom, and the kitchen last night, and feel pleasurable physical sensations shoot through me, along with an overwhelming sense of guilt. The weight of the guilt dwarfs the physical sensations, but my body still yearns to feel those physical sensations again. The conflict starts to suffocate me.

Geoff continues to drag his cheek over mine, and then I feel his lips brushing my cheek as well. I start to become both alarmed and wanting at the same time. He just kisses me gently on my cheek and keeps caressing me. He moves his lips closer to my mouth, kisses the bottom of my lip gently, then moves back to my cheek after I tense up. He repeats this a few times and I stop tensing up. "Convince me of your devotion, Karly." He puts his lips on mine and my lips stay open as he draws me into a deep kiss.

I'm plagued with guilt while my body betrays me and floods me with pleasurable physical sensations. I can feel his hands slowly and gently roaming over parts of my body as he pulls my body closer to his, and I gasp as he gently brushes his hands over certain areas.

He reaches his hand up my pajama shirt, and strokes the side of my breast. His other hand goes down beyond my waist, up the leg of my pajama shorts, and gently touches the inside of my thigh. The physical sensations are so heightened now that he's touching me directly on my skin, and I don't know what's happening to me.

Geoff's hand starts to massage my breast while his other hand strokes the inside of my thighs, one at a time. It's all so overwhelming, confusing, and I feel so guilt-ridden that I feel tears streaming down my face. Everything intensifies and his hand slides as if his fingers are about to grasp my nipple, while his other hand slides up my thigh and is about to move between my legs. But before he can do anything else, I slowly pull away from him.

"What is it…" Then he sees my tears, and I can see the shame on his face. He covers it quickly, and suddenly acts tender with me. But I don't buy it, and I pull even further away.

I sit up, looking away from him. "We should get breakfast."

He nods at me, seeming reluctant. "Sure, let's get up for the day." He gets out of bed, and pulls a warm hoodie on. "Here's one for you." He passes me one of his hoodies and I put it over my head. It's so big on me that it nearly goes down to my knees. Geoff chuckles when he sees me wearing his clothes, but I can still see the flash of shame on his face.

We walk to the kitchen, and Geoff whips up a batch of pancakes, eggs, and bacon. My tummy starts to growl. As we eat at the kitchen table, Geoff puts his hand over mine. "Karly, look into my eyes." I obey him and look directly into his eyes. "I'm…sorry about earlier, I…got carried away." I can hear him mutter to himself. "You're just

225

too damn irresistible." I keep staring at him unflinchingly. "I don't want you to worry. Okay? Do you trust me not to hurt you? I want to protect you."

My first instinct is to want to please him. I nod. "Yes, I trust you." I feel relief as I place my trust in him. I know he'll protect me and keep me safe.

Afternoon. Fri., Oct. 22, 2021

Later during the day, I ask Geoff a question. "Those pictures in my room. I remember those events, but I'm confused. We've been together for years?" The time frame in my head feels all smushed together. As if all of the events happened over the course of a day instead of years.

"Well we've been together for over five years now, Karly. You might not remember everything correctly because you've been ill, but yes, those events did happen."

"But—"

He cuts me off with a warning tone. "Karly. That's enough." He throws his napkin down on the table and looks at me harshly.

I feel the tears well up in my eyes and my lower lip trembles. I'm asking because I don't understand, not because I want to argue with him. "Something in my mind is broken, and I can't figure things out. Maybe you could help me figure what's real and what's not real?"

His eyes change then from stern to sympathetic and affectionate. His thumb caresses my cheek while his hand strokes my hair, and my lip is automatically drawn to his thumb like a reflex. He smiles at me, and whenever he smiles like that at me, I feel everything is going to be alright.

He kisses me softly on the lips. "It's okay, Baby. I'll help you figure out what's real and what's not. You're going to be better before you know it."

CHAPTER FIFTEEN

Officer Duane Saunders

Afternoon. Fri., Oct. 22, 2021

I rub my eyes, and try to refocus on the computer screen, as I go through the list of Geoff's personal properties as well as his company's properties. The list is too darn long, and the properties are not small. For now, I decide to stick to the properties located within a two-hour drive of Mississauga. *Heck, I might as well add in a two-hour jet ride as well, since he owns his own private jet.* No, too many flights might draw attention. He's got to know that. I'll stick with driving distance to start with and radiate outward as we increase the perimeter.

It is nearly lunch time, and the team is hard at work sifting through properties and their layouts so we can get a better idea of where Karly could possibly be located. The guys doing surveillance said there hasn't been a peep from the manor, and Geoff is still inside. They speculate he is running his businesses remotely from home like many other people, to avoid risking contracting COVID.

At 2:00 pm, I receive an excited call from Clay. *Good, maybe he's thought of something. He's a smart kid and completely invested in Karly's well-being.* I smile, hoping he has more to contribute to the case.

"I'm on-call right now, like Karly was the morning of her abduction. She was wearing a pager, one assigned to her by the hospital."

I feel a bit disappointed as I respond to him. "Pagers aren't trackable in general, Clay."

His voice keeps at the same level of intensity and excitement. "The one the hospital assigned her is a two-way pager, so it transmits as well as receives. Although she normally always phoned in out of habit when she was paged, she could have responded through the keys on the pager and transmitted a return message. Plus, the batteries on pagers last forever. They're not like cell phones which have to be recharged. So it's likely it's still turned on and transmitting."

My mood is on an uptick as Clay shares the information and his idea. If we can track her pager, it might give us an indication of which property she is at, and also provide more evidence for court. "Good work, Clay. Do you have her pager number?"

"I don't, but the hospital will have it."

I think of my call to the hospital's Records Department I'd made to track Karly's pages previously, to trace her steps on the morning she went missing. "I know exactly where to call for it."

After following up with Records and then with the paging company, the location of Karly's pager was to be found, as suspected, at 2415 Doulton Drive. I shake my head and wonder how it was possible we could have missed her at his main residence. Unless he had just kept her belongings there after he... No, I wasn't going to let my thoughts head there. Surely, there is some type of attachment with her, his former girlfriend, to keep him from committing a grave crime like murder. But then, in many cases warped attachment was the reason why one person harmed another.

I run my mind over the search we did. Lauren sits at her desk beside mine, pouring over property plans. "Hey Lauren."

"Yeah?" She sounds absentminded. "One sec." She rubs her eyes and turns towards me. "What's up?"

"Remember when you shot photos of the prints on the glass?"

"Mmhmm."

"Did you notice how Geoff looked when you were examining the inlaid bookcases?"

"Yeah, he seemed kind of freaked out as he stormed over to see what I was doing."

"The reason we stopped looking at the house was because the heat search came up negative. But there are ways to fool it, and with the amount of time he had to plan all his moves, months or even years ahead of time, he would have had plenty of time to set up a room immune to it."

"Are you saying we should get a search warrant now based on the pager?"

"Not yet. It would alert him and we'd be right back in the same position as before. This is all based on speculation, of course, but maybe to avoid alerting him we could do the same heat scan, since no warrant is needed for it. We can have the guys doing surveillance scan the residence occasionally, just to make sure. In case she's inside and he's just moving her around."

Lauren nods. "On it. I'll send some guys over with the equipment."

"The other idea is we can leave a pager message for Karly. She can communicate through the two-way pager itself if she can't get to a phone. I'm assuming she would have already called 911 if she had access to a phone."

Lauren picks up her phone and starts to get the ball rolling. "I'll have a tech guy meet with you, to show you how to transmit an actual message, not just how to send your phone number."

After the tech guy arrives, I dial the pager number, and leave my own for Karly to text a message to. I hope she'll get the message and respond.

Karly

Afternoon. Fri., Oct. 22, 2021

I wake up from a nap in my room to a beeping sound. My pager. My pager has gone off. I scramble to find it because I know deep down that beeping always means something urgent. I find it in my pocket in one of the PJ sets, the one with pants I'd laid at the bottom of my bed on a blanket box.

Normally, I would find a phone and call the number on the pager, but there's no phone I can use. So instead I use the alphanumeric system. *What do I say?*

"Karly here." I type the letters and send it as a text to the number that was paged to me.

A few minutes later I get a message. "RUOK?"

"Yes. Who RU?"

"911."

I take a deep breath, and I'm not sure what to do. Geoff wouldn't approve of me talking to the police, but I know I need to get to a hospital because something is desperately wrong with me. My mind is broken.

"Help me pls."

Officer Duane Saunders

Afternoon. Fri., Oct. 22, 2021

I put the word out right away to the team that Karly is indeed inside Geoff's manor. The relief is short-lived as we still have a job ahead of us, one that could turn very dangerous very quickly. The surveillance team sees two people on a heat imagery scan, one in a small room, and the other at the other end of the manor. Surveillance sits tight for now, as we plan our next move.

We decide to call in the RCMP's Emergency Response Team, since we're not willing to take any chances. We don't know what Geoff's frame of mind will be. We meet with the ERT at their mobile HQ out of view of the manor cameras. The operation itself is simple. The team will draw out the subject with a ruse and the ERT will neutralize him, safely giving us the opening to get to the victim.

Geoff
Afternoon. Fri., Oct. 22, 2021

What the hell are those people doing outside my gate? I roll my eyes and shake my head as I look at my security monitor. I see a bunch of guys and a couple of girls hanging around a car right in front of my property. *Damn university students.*

I close my eyes and massage my temples. I'm convinced the numbers from the spreadsheet are now burned on my cortex. I try to get back to work, but the group seems to be getting rowdy. They crank up the car stereo. Then someone starts setting off firecrackers.

What are we, 15 years old? I get up, fists clenched as tightly as my jaw. *I don't need this. I'm still trying to get by on lack of sleep after that darn search warrant.*

I walk to the other end of the house to peek in on Karly. She seems to be fast asleep. I smile and stroke her hair. She subconsciously nuzzles my hand, and I consider staying with her— until I hear more fire crackers from outside.

Back at the front door, as I slip on a pair of loafers I hear more noise and raucous laughter. *Those idiots!* I fling open my front door and stalk up to the gate, yelling at them to get away from my property. "Hey! Go hang out somewhere else before I call the police!" I don't feel in any danger telling the group off, since there's a cast iron gate between us.

They continue laughing with one another, as one of the guys directs their attention my way. "What was that, Buddy?"

"I said—"

"Down on the ground!"

What the hell? There were officers behind me *in my driveway. How did they...?* Then I see the hole they'd cut in my hedge barrier.

Karly

Afternoon. Fri., Oct. 22, 2021

I'm lying on my bed, facing the wall, listening to a woman call my voice gently. "Karly. Karly, you awake?" I freeze, and lie perfectly still, not knowing what's happening. "Karly, I need to take your vitals. Can you let me know you can hear me?"

I roll over to face her and another male paramedic standing further back. I also see a female police officer by the door. My eyes open wide, and I hold out my arm to the first woman. She walks me through everything, step-by-step then covers me with a blanket, which I pull tightly around me. "Karly, can you walk?"

I nod. "Yes." My voice comes out like a croak.

"Okay, let's get you out of here. There's an ambulance waiting outside for you, so we can get you checked out at the hospital." I solemnly nod, and take her hand, like a child might take a parent's. We walk out of my bedroom, through the foyer, and out the front door.

I stop before going any further. "I need to come back right away, after they fix me. I don't want to leave Geoff."

The female police officer comes closer to me and smiles. "Hi Karly, I'm Lauren. Let's get you to the hospital first before making any decisions. You can tell me about everything on the way." I still just stand there.

"How about we make it a girls-only thing." She glances at the male paramedic and he steps back, nodding. "Just you, me, and this other nice lady here? Would you be okay with that, Karly?" I nod my head. I let them assist me into an ambulance, which is parked right beside the front door, and the other two ladies get in with me. I'm offered water, then need to lie down. They strap me in, and we travel to the hospital.

Clay
Evening. Fri., Oct. 22, 2021

I wait with Karly's family and Vi, hoping to see her soon. All of us have tears of relief in our eyes, and Karly's mom and sister are shedding them openly. A doctor walks into the room where we are waiting. "Dr. and Mrs. Jileski." The doctor shakes their hands, then nods to the rest of the family and myself.

"Doctor." It's odd for both myself, and I assume for Karly's dad as well, to be on this side of the conversation. We're usually the ones discussing our patients with their families.

"As you may guess, Karly's been through quite an ordeal. We've been running standard tests, blood tests, toxicology screen, etc. She's lucid, but there are a lot of things she's saying that don't add up."

We glance at each other worriedly, wondering what this exactly means. Dr. Jileski speaks directly. "What exactly are you saying?"

"Karly has experienced psychological trauma. It seems like brainwashing and drugs are involved, and we suspect she may have been molested. We'll know more once the tests are back."

"Oh my God." Mrs. Jileski is gripping her chest in anguish while Katie clings to her. Mitch looks angry as hell.

I turn and face the wall, my body shaking and lower lip trembling. My arms are folded against the wall while my head bows and leans forward on them. I can feel tears coursing down my cheeks. *She must have gone through hell.* I want to weep for her pain. I feel so guilty. *I should have done more to protect her and keep her safe.*

"It's going to take her some time to adjust, and we don't want her to feel overwhelmed. So I wouldn't advise regular visits at this point."

"Of course, Doctor," Karly's Dad chokes out. "We understand."

"For now, I'd suggest that we start with Mrs. Jileski. Karly's responding well to a female presence." I glance over and nod, with a sinking feeling. I have a fire in the pit of my stomach, stoking my fears and anxiety. The agony is overwhelming. I need to calm myself. Karly is back and is physically safe. *One step at a time.*

Officer Duane Saunders
Evening. Fri., Oct. 22, 2021

Geoff and his lawyer sit in front of Lauren and I in one of our discussion rooms. I knew from the beginning that cases like this usually came down to one person's word against another, which is one reason why I was so meticulous while gathering evidence. However, in this case, Karly hasn't voiced much yet about her ordeal, and may never be able to do so.

"As you very well know, the search warrant you executed turned up nothing, except to show that Karly was clearly not in the vicinity at that time. Your surveillance team sat there in plain view after that, and Mr. Davenport didn't leave his residence once, until Karly was found on his property.

"Mr. Davenport asserts that Karly snuck onto the property last night, clearly on drugs. He was concerned for her well-being. He merely offered her food, shelter for the night, and some comfort. They watched a movie last night, and she rested today. He was going to notify you later today that she had come by so you'd know she was okay."

I didn't believe one word of it, of course, but there was no proof otherwise. The burden of proof would be on us when it came to providing evidence; it wasn't up to Geoff or his lawyer to provide camera evidence of her sneaking onto the property in order to clear him. Because of nothing showing up when we executed the search warrant, the argument that she wasn't there before last night would stand up in court. *Unless she testifies or directs us to a "smoking gun".*

Geoff had vehemently denied there had been anything "sexual" between the two of them, and would have assumed she would be getting a Sexual Assault Forensic Exam done at the hospital, so I believed him to some extent that "specific acts" hadn't occurred in the previous 72 hours. However, Lauren indicated to me there had been a lot of manipulation involved. Things may have been done to Karly that wouldn't show up in the results but would still be classified as sexual assault.

Without Karly's testimony, there was a big nada when it came to the case. Nothing to prosecute at this time. Everything could be explained away, including the reason behind the fingerprints and finding her locket on the property. And the defense team could even counter, saying Clay's ID badge was worn by the abductor, and that Clay was the one who found the locket, which meant that clearly he was involved. No, there were too many holes to lay any charges at this time.

But the important thing, the *most* important thing, was that Karly was safe and sound physically. At least we knew she was safely in the hospital and would soon be with her family. *This story had a happy ending, from the perspective of someone who's seen many horrific endings. Not the most ideal ending, but at least a hopeful one.* I feel relief, knowing that a young lady will have her tomorrows.

After Geoff and his lawyer left, I made sure the evidence for the case was clearly labeled and documented, in case there was ever a time in the future when Karly would be able to testify. In Canada, there is no statute of limitations, because abduction, kidnapping, sexual assault, and everything related to that are indictable offences.

Karly

Afternoon. Fri. Nov. 12, 2021

I'm sitting in my therapist's office, both of us wearing masks, and socially distanced. It's a relief to finally be able to see my therapist face-to-face. The previous weeks have been beyond difficult. *Geoff sure did a number on my mind.*

After the drugs left my system, I went through an intense program to help me regain who I am, my true identity. A lot of the program was parallel to treatment for victims of cults, to help them gain psychological independence from the controlling, brainwashing organization. Only in my case, it was to break free from the aftereffects of a manipulative, controlling relationship.

During therapy, I learned about the process of what's called "grooming", which is what I experienced. "Grooming is the slow, methodical, and intentional process of manipulating a person to a point where they can be victimized." I have that definition in my phone, in case I ever doubt my perception of what I really experienced. It's a reminder I pull up and read whenever I hear in my self-talk: *What he did wasn't that bad. He was just demonstrating romantic feelings in a twisted way.* Or when I ask myself the question: *Was I falling in love with him?* That definition reminds me of what his end-game was.

It's hard to believe that in such a short time, my goals had changed from finding independence and what makes me feel fulfilled, to wanting desperately to please someone and win their approval. But it was the drugs that had made me easily compliant and so prone to suggestion. That, in combination with Geoff's attempt to isolate me and "gaslight" me, had made it impossible for me to tell the difference between what was true and what beliefs were being forced upon me.

My earlier experience years before had made me vulnerable to Geoff's manipulation, so I was very impressionable. As a result I was unstable, due to the emotional whiplash which I had been conditioned to, as he used his on-again-off-again approval to manipulate me.

However, with all those "memories" of events he had simulated to make me believe we'd been together for a long period of time, like the "five year anniversary", there was a "tell". With each of those memories, I now realize there was a "queasiness" connected with them. That abdominal queasiness was a result of the drugs I was on during the camera shoots and charades, and it now helps me to tell the false memories from true memories. Whenever I have a memory of an event with Geoff I'm unsure of, if I recall feeling nauseated, the chances are it wasn't a true memory, but a contrived one.

I've been living with my parents since I don't have the courage yet to live by myself. I'm glad my apartment itself doesn't hold any negative memories for me, but having people around makes me feel safe.

Next week my therapist would like Clay to attend a session with me. This will be a big step for me, since I haven't seen him since before my nightmarish experience. I felt so ashamed about what I went through that I didn't feel I could ever face him again. But every day I'm getting stronger, putting one foot in front of the other.

Clay

Afternoon. Thurs. Nov. 25, 2021

Tomorrow is the day. After going six weeks since the last time I saw Karly, tomorrow will be the first day seeing her since she switched to 24-hour on-call shifts. That feels like a lifetime ago.

During our intimate Thanksgiving dinner in October, I told her how thankful I was to have her in my life. Now I'm just thankful she's alive and recovering well. *Sometimes it still hurts so badly, knowing what she's gone through.* I've received regular updates from her family, and I've heard she's taken so many positive steps in her rehab, but I am a doctor, and realistic. Because of that I feel afraid.

Although the patient rehabilitation I've been part of has been primarily physical, there's always a secondary psychological component involved. The outcome of rehab is heavily dependent on how well the patient deals with the psychological trauma of the event. Karly's rehab is primarily psychological. She's dealing with obstacles that none of us can see, apart from the way they manifest themselves in her life.

It's easy to know how to treat someone's physical wound, because the damage can be seen, is measurable, and we can observe what stages of healing it's in. Friends of that person know which activities to avoid that might exacerbate the wound, and what will help ease the pain and contribute to healing. However it's different with invisible psychological wounds and trauma, and what helps versus what makes things worse can be difficult to discern. *Will my presence be helpful or harmful to her?*

I know Karly won't be the same person she was before her kidnapping, and she may have undergone a personality change. Her father has talked to me about how she has become timid and fearful, and prone to anger, easily upset. I've been told she knows who I am, although some of her memories are still somewhat confused and distorted, and that she's making progress every day. However, I am afraid that when I see Karly, she won't really "know" me, that we will no longer have the same "connection" we had.

For the first few weeks after her trauma, Karly adamantly refused to see me. I was completely devastated. However, as therapy progressed, her father explained her refusal was due to the personal shame she felt, not because of any anger towards me. It reminded me to keep things in perspective. *It's all about her, not about me.* My focus is on *her*, on her recovery, and what is best for her life, considering what she's been through. Right now, my needs are secondary.

To me, it didn't matter how long it would take, I had planned to support Karly in her recovery, whether it meant I was part of her life, or not. However, last week, her therapist notified me that Karly was willing to have me attend a session with her, in her journey towards healing. After I got off the phone, I realized my face was damp. I'd been stirred deeply emotionally. I can't put into words, the relief I felt.

I was asked to meet with Dr. Mazik the day before to prepare me for my first time seeing Karly. Today is that day. I'm determined to do whatever it takes to help Karly. *Whatever it takes.*

Dr. Mazik greets me as I enter her office. "Dr. Aldridge, I'm Dr. Mazik. I'm so glad you could make it."

"Please, just call me Clay." I smile through my mask, grateful for this doctor who is helping Karly find her way back home.

"Karly's father has let me know he's been keeping you up-to-date about her therapy. She waived confidentiality for her family, and now she's done the same for you, since you will be attending sessions together. It's taken her a lot of courage to be able to trust again, so this has been a positive step for her."

I nod, thankful that Karly has made it this far.

"So just to update you, Karly's a victim of 'perspecticide', similar to what's commonly known as 'gaslighting'. She was controlled and manipulated to the point where she lost her grasp on reality and lost her sense of self. As you know, she was in an inpatient program at Trafalgar Addiction Treatment Centre for both detox and recovery from psychological trauma.

"She did very well in the program, and they were able to build on the strong analytical foundation she had already laid down years earlier. I'm thankful she already had these tools, as they've helped her to recover with less complications than usual."

I nod. "So what can I do that will help with her recovery?"

"Although I know this must be very difficult for you, patience is the number one thing she needs right now. Patience and acceptance. She needs to go at her own pace, and right now she feels tentative about taking steps. She feels a great deal of shame, blaming herself for what transpired. Because of that, she needs understanding and reassurance, reinforcement that she isn't to blame, no matter what she did or what she experienced.

"Often victims of molestation feel tremendous guilt, because as the abuse occurs, there are physiological responses such as arousal and sensations of pleasure. Karly feels she has betrayed you because of physiological arousal during her experience, even though she wasn't to blame in any way."

"I could never blame her for what happened to her. She had no control over it." I feel compassion welling up inside me, and I hurt for her.

"She also feels she's betrayed you because her actions felt 'intentional' due to the drugs and manipulation. This is again because of the perspecticide. Part of her believed she was in a relationship with the perpetrator, and of her own choice. Because of that she has feelings of worthlessness and self-doubt. She feels she's not good enough for you.

"It's one reason why some victims stay with or go back to their abusers. The shame drives them to the point where they are convinced they will never be good enough for anyone else. Some victims are triggered at a later time and return to the abuser because they believe they deserve punishment and should continue to be abused. That's why unconditional love from those around her is so important for Karly's recovery. To help her deal with those feelings of shame and guilt and take steps forward in her life."

"I understand."

"Another thing. Karly is also hypersensitive to others' negative emotions. Disapproval especially, also anger, whether it's toward her or anything else."

I take a deep breath. "Right. I'll need to keep my anger towards the guy who did this in check and deal with it on my own."

"That's one reason why it would be beneficial if you also went for therapy. To help you vent and deal with that anger towards the perpetrator, so it doesn't carry into your relationship. She's so hypersensitive at this point that she feels any anger, even if directed towards another source, is directed towards her. That can also trigger her feelings of lack of self-worth, like she isn't 'good enough'.

"Certain phrases trigger her. Words and phrases like 'convince me', 'devotion', 'belonging' to someone, the idea of ownership. She was conditioned using those words, so avoid using them until they no longer carry the weight and connotations they currently do. Also, let any physical interaction go at her pace, even small touches like holding her hand. Let her do the initiating or give you permission. Certain things may trigger her physically, so be aware of that for the future."

I find the hour spent with Dr. Mazik to be incredibly helpful in my understanding of where Karly is at in her recovery, where she has come from. *She's already come so far. It's horrific that nine days of conditioning and abuse could take her years to recover from. She's such a beautiful person, and never deserved any of this.* Again I find my face damp, as I think on Karly and her journey back from the darkness she had been drowning in. *You don't have to do this alone, Karly. Please let me in.*

Geoff
Evening. Thurs. Nov. 25, 2021

It's been over a month since they took Karly away from me. I've been laying low, and no charges have been laid. Just in case, I've had a firm of lawyers on retainer, ready to jump on things.

I know Karly would never have left me if they hadn't taken her, and I'm not going to give up. *What use is all my money, if I can't be with the woman I'm in love with?* I have to plan my next steps carefully, since the last thing I need is to be slapped with an ex parte restraining order. That would complicate things.

I will get her back, no matter what. I feel emotion pouring into me, like a flood of liquid fire and ice, mingled with hope, anxiety, and despair. Obsession and desperation held in check in the past, now threaten to completely take over my soul.

Clay
Afternoon. Fri. Nov. 26, 2021

I arrive early the following day at Dr. Mazik's office, and sit in the waiting room. I know Karly is in the office already. I try to stay composed, as I wait to see her for the first time in weeks.

Dr. Mazik opens the door to her office. "Dr. Aldridge. Please come in." I put my phone away and eagerly walk to the door, slowing down as I enter the room.

There she is. *Karly. Beautiful Karly.* There has been such a change in her. *She seems so frail.* I wonder if she's been eating properly. She's sitting in one of the chairs which is socially distanced from the other two. She's wringing her hands, something I've never seen her do before, but it's a sign of her growing anxiety. It's difficult to get a read on her, due to her mask which is hiding her facial expression. I sit in the empty seat.

Dr. Mazik starts the conversation. "Clay, so glad you could join us today."

"I'm very happy to be here with you both." I glance at Karly, and she glances away from me when she sees me look at her. Before she does though, I'm able to catch a glimpse of the pain that dwells in her glassy eyes.

"Karly, Clay has been kept up-to-date with your treatment, and we met yesterday to go over some things about your condition." She looks at Dr. Mazik and nods. Karly seems withdrawn, like she's clammed up. "Clay, was there something you want to say to Karly?" Karly looks down at her hands, trying to avoid my gaze.

I feel like I need to use kid gloves, I can tell she's so fragile. "Karly, I'm going to take my mask off because you need to see my face." She glances up at me, and her eyes stay on me, while I smile gently at her. I see a tear forming in one eye. "It doesn't matter what you've done or what's been done to you, I love you, and I'm here for you, every step of the way." She keeps her eyes on me. The tear trickles down her face, soaking into her mask.

She looks down at her hands again, playing with her nails. She speaks, so I can barely hear her. "You don't know what I did. What I felt."

"Karly." She looks up at me again. "It doesn't matter to me what you did or how you reacted. What matters to me is you. That you're here, safe." She tears up again. I speak softly, "You're what's important to me. Your family and I, we all love you."

She looks down again. This time she speaks quietly, her voice cracking, "I'm so sorry." I can see more tears coming, then streaming down her face. She starts to sob, with her elbows on her knees, face in her hands. "I'm so sorry, Clay."

I just want to go to her, to comfort her, while the grief and anguish pour out of her soul. I walk over, careful not to startle her, and get on one knee to talk with her. "Karly, is it okay if i hold your hand?" After a minute her tears start to subside and she lifts her head to look at me. She cautiously nods her head. I gently take her small, delicate hand in my own. "You don't have to be sorry for anything, Sweetheart."

"But I --"

"Shhh, Karly." I speak slowly, looking her directly in the eyes. "*None* of it was your fault. You did what you needed to survive, whether you consciously knew it or not. No matter what you did or felt you had to do, or what he did to you or what you felt when he did it, *I still love you.*" She keeps looking into my eyes, and after a bit, she squeezes my hand. I can tell she's understood me. I can feel her anxiety dissipate.

"Clay." Karly's voice is broken when she says my name. She gently pulls my hand towards her. "Please hold me."

I carefully take her in my arms as if she could break apart, and hold her head to my chest, still kneeling on the floor. I rock her gently as she lets out her pain, sobbing until she has no tears left.

She rubs her eyes and looks at me. "I thought you would despise me." Her lower lip trembles.

I look her in the eyes. "Never. I'd never despise you, Karly." I pull her head back to my chest, continue to hold her and rub her back. "Karly, I love you and I always will." *I will always love you. I will always cherish you.*

Karly

Afternoon. Fri. Dec. 17, 2021

I met with Clay a few weeks ago during my therapy session, for the first time since my ordeal. Since then, we've spent a lot of time together talking things through and dealing with the pain and hurt. He has been so patient with me and so understanding, and doesn't blame me for what happened. I carry a lot of guilt, because during my confinement, Geoff was my "world". But Clay just empathizes with me, and holds me during the times when I share things I feel so ashamed about.

Clay tells me he loves me, but at times I feel so unloveable. I feel my heart wasn't faithful to Clay when I was in confinement. Instead, in my mind, if I felt if I didn't please Geoff and he was displeased with me, then it was the end of the world. Back then I felt I'd be devastated, being torn away from Geoff.

I still have to analyze those feelings when they surface, to fight them and to regulate my emotions, but I'm getting there. I've been told it can take time to work through the layers. I may need to continue battling Geoff's hold over me for a long time. That means continually wrestling to gain the upper hand in this struggle within my psyche. If I feel strong enough to testify someday, I might still have to fight his hold on me—because I'm vulnerable.

I do have an advantage though. Because I've been tracing back my emotions to their source for years now, it's like a habit. Those pre-learned skills from earlier therapy have propelled me through my recovery, more successfully than originally hoped. They are "life skills" I can use whenever I need, and boy have they helped me through these last several weeks.

Clay has told me over and over that he loves me and cherishes me. Geoff triggered so much self-doubt in me, that I still need constant assurances from Clay weeks later. But Clay never grows impatient with me. If he sees I need reassurance, he reassures me, even if he's had to repeat himself a hundred times.

Because I'm so sensitive to the idea of being "owned" or thought of as someone's "property", Clay is helping me in that area. He's careful when he speaks and leaves everything open-ended so I can make a choice. That way I don't feel he's trying to control me. I'm hoping over time I'll be able to meet him halfway. He has a protective side which sometimes comes across as possessive, so we're working on things. I want us to function interdependently, as the couple we were becoming before my ordeal.

My family has been extremely helpful, and Vi has been there for me as well. They help me to correct false statements and get back on track. If I keep correcting cognitive distortions in my self-talk, I can move towards healing.

I still haven't returned to work at the hospital, and I'm not sure when I'll be able to return. I'm really benefiting from attending a support group for emotionally abused women. I could see myself working with victims of abuse in the future, and becoming an advocate. I can draw on my experience from years ago and my recent experience, to help me be effective in that type of work. But that's something for me to think about in the future, when I'm ready to start considering my career path again.

As for the immediate future, drawing closer to the Christmas season, I'm excited about being able to spend special moments with family. But with that excitement comes a certain amount of nervousness and apprehension. I still feel skittish sometimes. This year, I'll be spending Christmas Eve with Clay's family, and we'll be with my family on Christmas Day. They're all trying to make it a "no pressure" affair for my sake. If I need to escape for a while, I can go lay down somewhere quiet. It means a lot to me, having an option that will help me avoid "triggers" that could lead to a panic attack or worse.

I know it will take time for me to heal, and I may always have sensitivities. However, it feels so comforting to have Clay, my family, and my friends supporting me. I hope that over time I can work through my challenges, and become stronger because of my experience. With their support I know I will.

ABOUT THE AUTHOR

Anjula Evans is a writer living in the Toronto area. She started writing and illustrating children's books in 2014, and started writing novels in 2019.

She enjoys time with family, writing books, and composing music.